W9-DET-733

Last - 9/8/08
VG+

The Villains

The Villains

A Haunting Tale of the Marshes

Charlotte Keppel

ST. MARTIN'S PRESS
NEW YORK

YA

CRANSTON PUBLIC LIBRARY
WILLIAM HALL LIBRARY

3/82

Copyright © 1981 by Charlotte Keppel
For information, write: St. Martin's Press,
175 Fifth Avenue, New York, N.Y. 10010
Manufactured in the United States of America

WITHDRAWN FROM
WILLIAM HALL LIBRARY

The Villains

Prologue   1734

I first saw Cudden Hall when I was eight years old. My little sister, Leonie, was too young to travel, so she stayed at home with Maman, and Papa and I travelled together, all the way from London to Suffolk. It was a wonderful adventure. I think I must have seen my aunt and uncle before, on their rare visits to London, but I did not remember either of them, and the only thing I knew of my Aunt Elizabeth was that she was a famous novelist. This did not mean very much to me but added to the excitement.

The first half of the journey was glorious, and I could not keep still or silent; I had to keep on asking Jem if we were nearly there, how long it would take, what would happen if the horses grew tired, what was this and what was that. But after a while I quietened down, much no doubt to Papa's relief, grew tired, fretful and a little bored. Maman had dressed me in all my best clothes, with the little fur tippet that was my proudest possession: everything was starched and shining and clean, and my thick hair that was so hard to curl, twisted into ringlets. I must have looked like a little doll, but as a child I was very vain: I thought I was beautiful and my Aunt Elizabeth would at once love me.

'You must not forget to curtsey,' Papa told me, eyeing me with some apprehension, for he must have seen that I was grossly over-excited. 'And remember,' he added, 'that if your aunt kisses you, you are not to fling your arms round her neck and untidy her. Ladies do not always like being hugged –'

'Maman liked being hugged.'

'Well, yes, but she's your aunt, not your mother, and she

is a great deal older.'

'Yes, Papa,' I said. I was not really listening. We were near the end of our journey. The countryside looked bleak and forbidding, not at all as I had imagined it. Cudden Hall, which I could now see in the far distance – 'It's on top of that hill,' Papa said – stood on its own, except for what seemed to be the ruins of a church below it, and there was nothing else except for a handful of cottages. It was late September, and the sea was very rough, beating against a long, shallow wall. I always thought the country would be full of little fields and woods and streams, but all I could see was flat, sandy land.

I said, 'Papa, why is the village so small?'

'You are not paying attention to me, Nanette. I was not talking about the village. Besides, I told you all about that on the way down. Have you already forgotten? Greymanswick was once a big city, but now most of it lies under the sea.'

'Why isn't Cudden Hall under the sea too?'

'Now that's a silly question isn't it? You can see how high up it is, safe on top of that hill. One day,' said Papa with a sigh, almost as if he were talking to himself, 'it may well be destroyed like everything else. It is a wicked sea here, and that wall offers little protection.' He added quickly, 'you're not to say anything about this to your aunt. You would only frighten her, besides, I'm probably quite wrong. I daresay Cudden Hall will last to the end of time.'

Jusqu'a la fin du monde. It was a song Maman used to sing. I began to hum it. I spoke French quite well: Maman insisted. Then I said a little fretfully, 'I don't think I like it here, Papa.'

'Oh you're talking nonsense, child,' said Papa. He sounded suddenly very jolly, only though I was so young I somehow knew he was not feeling jolly at all, that like me he was wishing he was back in London. He said firmly, 'It's a beautiful old house. Queen Elizabeth visited it once. You are going to enjoy your stay very much. You are lucky to be

2

invited.'

'Will there be any other children, Papa?'

'No,' said Papa with some irritation, 'I shouldn't imagine so for one moment.' He looked at me, tweaking one of the ringlets. 'You'll have to behave like a grown-up. There's Virgil, of course, but I think he must be about fifteen. I don't imagine he'll have much time for little girls like you. Boys of his age never have.'

I knew I would detest Virgil. We were approaching the drive and I was beginning to feel afraid. I said, 'What a funny name. I've never heard of anyone being called Virgil.'

'It's a family name. Your Uncle Constantine has the family name too. Virgil was a great poet. One day, when you're older, you will learn Latin and read his books.'

I suppose that at this point I became a trifle confused. It had been a long, long drive and I was both tired and hungry: besides, as Maman always made me say, I wanted urgently to make a little journey. She would have realised this at once, but Papa did not, only grew cross with me because I was fidgeting. I was now convinced that Virgil Cudden was a great poet, and this alarmed me more than ever. What with Aunt Elizabeth writing gothic romances and Virgil writing poetry in some unknown language, there was not going to be much scope for a little girl who had only just learnt to read.

I said miserably, without interest, 'I suppose Virgil is Aunt Elizabeth's son.'

'No, he is not. He is her nephew. His parents are dead, so your Uncle Constantine has adopted him.'

It seemed dreadful to have no mother or father, and this depressed me so much that I stopped my chattering. By now we were going up the drive, then the front door was flung open and my Aunt Elizabeth came out to greet us.

I was very young, of course, and rather spoilt, but I knew at once that I was not going to like her, and I could see quite plainly that she did not like me. I suppose I was prejudiced

3

from the beginning for Maman did not like her either, and made no pretence of hiding it. It really was all my aunt's fault because she had always deplored Papa's marrying a Frenchwoman, and Maman in revenge made merciless fun of her, said she had no chic, too many teeth, large feet and no feminine charm whatsoever. As for her novels, they were ter-r-rible; Once or twice – when Papa was not there – Maman imitated her in a kind of English drawl, which convulsed me with giggles. Then she would grow ashamed and say she did not mean it, but by now the harm was done and Aunt Elizabeth became in my mind a kind of comic dragon.

I had not however expected such a small, rotund dragon. She was a plump woman, under five foot in height, and everything about her was round: her head, her bust, her hips. Of course, as a child I did not see it quite like that, only thought that Maman was so slender and graceful, and this lady looked like a cottage loaf. Her face was powdered almost white, without rouge, and the only beautiful thing about her was her hair, which was a chestnut-brown, thick, glossy and curly. It went strangely with the rest of her, like a lovely flower in a garden of weeds. As for her clothes, I, accustomed to Maman's Parisian elegance, thought they were frightful, dull and dark and dowdy, taken in over-tightly at the waist so that she bulged above and below. It was very bad-mannered of me to sum her up like this, but I was always an observant child and I think I was too cold and tired to show better behaviour. I forgot all about the curtsey and simply stared at her, ignoring the little prods that Papa was giving me, and in all fairness I must say that she was no better than I, for she stared back, without so much as the glimmer of a smile.

Papa said, giving my petticoats a final little pull, 'This is Nanette, Elizabeth. She is very shy, so you must forgive her. Give your aunt a kiss, Nanette. She has been so excited at the thought of meeting you that she has quite lost her tongue.'

All this was quite untrue. I was not shy at all, and as for

4

losing my tongue, I daresay that Papa would often have been pleased for me to do so. But his remarks made me go pink, and I at last made the little curtsey that Maman had taught me, and lifted my face for the expected kiss: though she was so small she was a long way above me.

She made no move to embrace me. She said in a cold, flat voice, 'I see you have given her a French name. I should have thought a good English name would have been better.'

'That,' said Papa in the dry tone that signified he was angry, 'was what Hortense wanted.' And I think he might have said something more, and I could see that Aunt Elizabeth was growing angry too, only at this moment an old gentleman came out, supported by a heavy cane, and he and my father at once embraced, so I knew this must be my Uncle Constantine.

I suppose he was not really old at all. To a small child anyone over the age of twenty is virtually in his grave. I do not imagine my aunt was more than forty, and my uncle would only have been a few years older. But he was in all truth near his grave, for he was dying of some mortal sickness, which was the real reason for our visit. I could only see what seemed to me an old, old man, with a grey pallor to his skin, and a body so emaciated that his clothes hung upon him. When he held out his hands to me I saw that he was kind, and I ran to him as I should have done to my aunt. He at once picked me up, kissing and cuddling me so that I buried my face in his shoulder and hoped he would not go away.

My uncle remarked, tilting my face up, 'How like she is to Hortense. She is a real French little girl.'

I imagine this must have made my aunt angrier than ever, but she remained silent, and my father answered with a smile, 'They are both like their mother, only not quite so pretty.'

At this I cried out, 'I am quite so pretty!' and both gentlemen began to laugh: Aunt Elizabeth must have been

5

furious at my pertness being so encouraged.

Presently Uncle Constatine put me down, and it was at this point that I realised that if I did not make that little journey soon, there would be a shameful disaster. I did not know what to do or where to go. If my aunt had been a more homely person, I could have whispered in her ear, but I felt I could not go near her with such a predicament. I shifted from one foot to the other, feeling more and more desperate. Fortunately for me there was now talk of the log-fire in the drawing-room and glasses of wine and so on, the kind of thing that always engrosses grown-ups, so I was ignored. When they all stepped back into the hallway, I ran out into the garden and, thinking the dusk would conceal me, relieved myself on the grass. It was of course disgraceful, and what Maman would have said I shudder to think, but the alternative did not bear thinking of, and I felt much happier as I ran back to the door.

It was shut fast. I was appalled and terrified. I felt that I was abandoned. I banged repeatedly on the door, but my small fists made no impression on the four hundred year old surface. They would all be in the drawing-room, with the door shut. Papa would be talking to his brother, and my aunt, if she noticed my absence at all, would probably be glad that such a bad-mannered little girl was not there. I began to cry. In childhood everything that happens is a stop in time, and it never entered my head that in a few minutes everyone would be wondering where I was, and come running out to find me.

I only knew that I was alone and lost. It was almost dark and raining hard. I could hear the sea crashing against the wall like cannon. I was hysterical with fear, I remembered my father's words, and half expected to see the waves rising over the lawn to drag me back with them. I sobbed frantically, 'Oh please someone come and help me, please, please!'

A voice, gruff and rough as a boy's voice is when it has not long broken, said, 'What the devil are you doing here? Oh

6

stop all that noise, for God's sake. If you are locked out, it's entirely your own fault.'

And that is how I first met my cousin Virgil.

I cannot really explain this, and I was far too young to work it out, but somehow when I heard that voice with its undercurrent of amusement, I knew that not only did I detest my horrid cousin with all my heart, but also that somehow he had witnessed my disgraceful behaviour on the lawn. It was by now quite dark, except for the lamp in the hall, but at the time there had still been a little light, and I was convinced that he had looked out of the window and seen me with my petticoats raised. The humiliation of it was such that I grew dizzy and had to clutch on to the wall. I wanted to die and I wanted to kill him. I will admit that he did not refer to it, but I could hear that he was trying not to laugh, and somehow this pulled me together so that I stopped my howling and walked past him into the house, my disreputable head – the ringlets of course had all fallen out – held high.

In the hall we at last looked at each other. What a miserable little rat I must have seemed! My hair, which is dark and thick, hung over my dirty face, my petticoats were bedraggled, and the fur tippet I was so proud of, was flattened by the rain. And I saw a very tall, very dark boy, who at once epitomised for me all the other boys I had met, who pulled my hair and teased me and upset my dignity. He was of course very handsome, and I think I was aware of this, but that kind of thing is unimportant when you are eight years old, though Leonie, for all she was so young, would instantly have responded. However, the circumstances were such that his being handsome was the final insult, and I could only see him as a boy with a capital B and the enemy. With Papa so often away on business I had always lived in a feminine world, with Maman and Leonie and old Bettine who cooked for us, cleaned for us and looked after us, pretty well for nothing. It was a lovely life with no boys to tease me, and it was only much later on that I realised we

7

must always have lived on the fringe of the Fleet. I think now that there must have been many times when Maman's delightful accent and charming smiles no longer touched the hearts of the tradesmen to whom we owed so much money. But all this meant nothing to Leonie and me: we were teased, indulged and sometimes screamed at, and the one memory of that childhood that will never leave me is the fragrance of Maman's delicious (and expensive) perfume that even permeated the kitchen.

In this delightful world of scent and pretty clothes and feminine temperament, boys seldom intruded, and those I reluctantly met at friends' houses seemed to me rough, alarming animals. I once remarked to Maman when I was six that I would never have anything to do with boys. She looked at me. She made one of her monkey faces, then laughed. She said, 'I do not think so, Nanette. I think you will have a great deal to do with boys.'

I said, 'Why should I? I don't like them. Besides, I'm not nearly as pretty as Leonie.'

'No,' she said, rather to my annoyance, 'no, but you have something else.'

'What do you mean, Maman?' I was quite excited, and I picked up the mirror on her dressing-table and peered into it.

'You would not understand if I told you. But you'll have to be careful, Nan. Boys can be dangerous.'

'I don't see why they should be. I've told you, Maman, I don't like them.'

And I now said to Virgil in a loud, defiant voice, 'I don't like you.'

He made a frightful face at me, then burst out laughing. 'What a pity,' he said, 'for it is possible that later on we may have to see a great deal of each other. But, if it comforts you, cousin Nanette, I find I don't like you either.'

Naturally, I was outraged. It was all very well for me to dislike Virgil, but it was insupportable for him to dislike me. I began to cry again, out of sheer temper, but at this point Papa came running out of the drawing-room, followed by Uncle Constantine and Aunt Elizabeth.

Papa cried out, 'Where have you been, you bad, wicked girl?' and began to shake me. Then he must have observed that Uncle Constantine was fighting back his laughter and, drawing back, he took a full look at the pair of us. We certainly looked quite ridiculous: the bedraggled little girl and the big lanky boy, glowering at each other. He was compelled to laugh too, ignoring my stammered explanation, then my aunt, who did not look amused at all, said in an icy voice, 'I cannot imagine what you have been doing, Nanette, but you should instantly change your clothes, for otherwise you will catch a chill, when no doubt I will be expected to look after you.'

There was no sympathy in her voice, only irritation and distaste. I feel now I cannot really blame her. Nobody could pretend that I had made any kind of good impression, and Maman, who believed devoutly in what she called *les convenances*, would have been very cross with me: she would put up with pertness, even disobedience, but she could never endure bad manners. I had behaved abominably, and the only excuse I can offer for myself is that it had been a long day for one so young, and the atmosphere in Cudden Hall had not been comforting.

I stood there, sulky and snivelling. I wished passionately that I was back home. I knew I was in deep disgrace, and wondered mainly if I would be allowed any supper, for I was dreadfully hungry. Isolation and bread and water would be the last straw.

It was only when my aunt continued, 'John Gonomanaway will take you upstairs and help you change,' that I raised my head to stare at her. It was impossible that a man should help me undress, and never in my life had I heard such an extraordinary name. Gonomanaway! It was absurd. But I had just enough sense left not to voice this, and presently John Gonomanaway, who was always called John-Gon by the family, appeared and escorted me upstairs.

As John-Gon plays an important part in this story, I will describe him. He was then of course quite a young man, and he acted as butler, footman and general factotum, though in all truth he resembled none of them. He was big and broad and very dark, with a great black beard, and to me, as he calmly enclosed my hand in his, he seemed some fairy-tale ogre. He was a local man who came from the neighbouring village, and he spoke with so thick a burring accent that I found him hard to understand. He conducted me to my room which was on the first floor: it was very small and the window, which was open, looked over the sea. The rest of the house seemed enormous to me, and I marvelled at all the wonderful things I saw: silver and china and pictures. Our cosy little home in Bloomsbury possessed nothing so fine.

I stood by the window, and John-Gon began to unpack my little portmanteau.

I said at last in a small, timid voice, 'The sea is very rough, sir.'

I did not know if one should so address a servant, but there was something about John-Gon that forbade familiarity, and he seemed to accept this as perfectly natural.

The great dark eyes moved over me, in the flickering light of the two candles on the dressing-table. He answered calmly in that burring voice of his, 'Here in Greymanswick we'd not call this rough, young lady.' He pronounced the name 'Gremmich', which, as I was to learn, was the local way. He went on, selecting a pretty muslin that Maman had packed especially for the first evening – he handled the material with a surprising delicacy – 'The storms come later. There was a storm once, four hundred years ago, that took our city away. There was fifty churches here, young lady, and now there's only a piece of St. Saviour's on the hill below us. They say the bells ring at night, and when you hear them, you'll know how rough the sea can be.'

I said, shivering a little, 'Can the bells ring under the

sea?'

'That's what they say.'

'Have you – have you ever heard them, sir?'

He did not answer this directly. I think that under the beard he was smiling. He only said, 'You'd better listen tonight. There's St. Peter and St. Andrew and the Church of the Blessed Virgin, but if it's St. Botolph that you hear, you can pick up your petticoats, young lady, and run like hell, because that will be the end of Greymanswick and Cudden Hall too. Come. I daresay you can undress yourself. Take those wet things off you, and I'll have them dried in the kitchen. You're in a right pickle, aren't you? My lady will expect to see you properly dressed for dinner.'

I was enormously relieved to hear that blessed word 'dinner'. But my eyes were still on the window, watching the waves, white-topped in the dark, as they lashed the sea wall. Then I suddenly saw lights flickering, so small and distant that, if it had been daylight, I would never have noticed them. I obediently stepped out of my soiled dress, then I said, 'What are those lights?' And I pointed in their direction.

'That's the marshes, young lady.'

'Are there people out at this hour? It must be so cold and wet and lonely.'

I thought he smiled again. I wondered why. I could not see that I had said anything funny. But he only said, 'There's lonely people here and lonely work.'

'Can I go and see the marshes tomorrow?'

But this he did not answer, only pulled the muslin dress over my head, even doing up the buttons for me. Then to my amazement he picked up my brush and began to brush my hair, doing this with the utmost dexterity. When he began winding the ringlets round his finger, just as Bettine would have done, I could not stop myself from asking, 'Do you have a little girl of your own, sir?'

'No, young lady. I am a single man.'

'Then who taught you how to make ringlets?'

11

He said in a rough voice, 'You ask too many questions,' and after this I dared not utter another word.

When at last I came downstairs I was neat and tidy. I came a little apprehensively into the drawing-room, and they all turned to look at me. I was determined to make up for my wicked behaviour, so I curtsied and went meekly to the chair pointed out to me. And for the rest of the evening I behaved myself like a good little girl, only speaking when spoken to and taking great pains with my eating, though some of the food was hard to manage and I left a great deal on my plate.

I found the dining-room very grand, with so many candles and all the gleaming silver and pretty glass. There was more food than I had thought possible for one meal, and a different wine with every course. Uncle Constantine, who sat next to me, insisted on pouring me out some, but I did not like it very much and it made my head feel strange. My cousin Virgil sat opposite me, but I avoided his gaze as much as I could, for the memory of that shameful episode in the garden was always with me. Once, when I caught his eye, I blushed very red. But he did not speak to me, and I tried to concentrate on the general conversation, though most of it was very dull and well above my head.

Towards the end of dinner I became sleepy. Once or twice I all but dozed off and had to jerk up my head. But it was no good, it had been too long a day and too much had happened. Someone said, 'The child's half asleep,' and the words boomed out at me from what seemed an immeasurable distance. I tried to protest, but it was no good, and presently my aunt said, 'Take her upstairs, Virgil. She should have been in bed a long time ago.'

The horror of this quite woke me up, and I tried to say that I could go upstairs by myself, but nobody listened to me, so I rose from my chair and did my round of good-nights. Virgil, who must have disliked this as much as I did, waited impatiently by the door.

Papa said, 'When you're in bed, I'll come up to say good-

12

night to you,' then added, 'You've been a very good girl. Maman will be pleased with you.'

This made me almost happy again, and I followed Virgil up the stairs to my little room.

He did not speak to me. He seemed very tall: indeed, my major impression of Cudden Hall was that everyone except my aunt was enormous. His shadow, huge in the flame of the candle he was carrying, loomed against the wall. I crept softly after him as if it was important not to make a sound. It was only when he opened the bedroom door that I began to feel frightened again. It was all so strange and the sea sounded so loud: I was possessed of a panic that I might hear St. Botolph's bells ringing.

But I only said goodnight in a small, shivering voice, and he must have sensed my fear for he said suddenly, 'Are you all right, Cousin?'

'Of course I'm all right!'

There was a sudden mockery in his voice. 'Perhaps,' he said, 'you'd like me to tuck you up.'

I said with all the dignity I could muster, 'I'm not a baby.'

There was a pause. I could not see him any longer except as a shadow in the doorway. He had left the candle by my bedside. The roar of the sea was so loud that it seemed to shake the room. The cold, salty smell of it came through the window. Then he said, 'You've no need to upset yourself. It will make the flowers grow.'

Then he shut the door behind him. I heard his running down the stairs.

I was so angry and upset that I once more burst into tears. I banged the pillow with my fists. But I was too exhausted to continue; the humiliation dimmed, and the roar of the sea, that had so frightened me, became like a lullaby. I must have fallen asleep almost at once. I was half awakened by Papa's hand on my forehead; I turned instantly to him, to snuggle into his arms.

He stroked my hair, telling me to go to sleep again, but I

13

did not want to leave the shelter of his embrace. I mumbled, 'Can't we go home tomorrow? I don't like it here, Papa.'

I thought in my sleep-soaked mind that this might make him scold me again, but he simply said rather wearily, 'We are here for only four days. You must say goodbye to your Uncle Constantine, for you will never see him again.'

I did not take in the implication of this, but I heard the sadness in Papa's voice. However, I was already sinking back into sleep. I muttered drowsily, 'Aunt Elizabeth doesn't like me.'

'Well,' he said, with for the first time a hint of laughter in his voice, 'I am not sure, Nanette, if you have given her much reason to do so. I daresay you did your best, and you behaved most beautifully at dinner, I was very proud of you.' And I think he said, 'You're so very young,' but I am not quite sure, for sleep at last overwhelmed me and I did not even hear him go. The next thing I knew was the bright, clear morning light coming through the window, and a servant girl setting a lovely bowl of hot chocolate by my bedside.

It was only later that it struck me this was the first female I had seen in Cudden Hall. It was John-Gon who served at table, and it was a boy who brought the dishes up from the kitchen. Aunt Elizabeth seemed to prefer an all male household, and I thought at the time that it was a good thing Leonie and I did not live here.

If I had known – but it would of course have made no difference.

The four days seemed to pass quickly enough, and on my second day Papa and Uncle Constantine took me down to the sea wall. 'It won't last much longer,' my uncle said, then he quoted a funny sort of rhyme:

> 'Dunwich, Sowl and Greymanswick
> All go in at a lousy creek.'

I remarked, 'I didn't hear the bells,' and Papa asked me

what I thought I was talking about. Only Uncle Constantine gave me a strange look, saying, 'They have been heard. Soon they will be sounding for me.' But this meant nothing to me, and I amused myself by picking some of the flowers that grew by the wall, while Papa and my uncle talked gravely together.

After that the main things that remain in my mind are large, heavy meals of a kind I was not used to, little walks and a long talk with the girl who had brought in my chocolate. My cousin Virgil was away for the day, which was a great relief to me. As for the servant-girl, her name was Dolly Easey, she was extremely pretty and I liked her very much.

She was sixteen, she told me, she lived in a cottage by the sea, and her father was Tom Easey, the fisherman. She came in every day to Cudden Hall, mostly to do the laundry. I did not like to ask her too many questions, but she was so friendly, bringing up some little tarts from the kitchen, that I at last told her how much my aunt frightened me: perhaps it was because she was so clever and wrote novels.

'Have you read them, Dolly?' I asked.

'God love you,' she said, 'I can't read one word of anything. Can you read, Miss Nanette?'

'Oh yes,' I answered proudly, 'I can read very well, even long words. I speak French too.'

She might well have laughed at me for the conceited little show-off that I was, but she did nothing of the sort, only sighed, saying, 'I wish I could read.'

'I'll teach you, Dolly!'

Then she laughed and said, 'I'll remind you of that, Miss Nanette, when we meet again.'

When we meet again – Dolly Easey and I were indeed to meet again, but neither of us knew it, nor did we know the circumstances in which the last meeting would take place. I only knew that I had found a friend, and I asked her if I might see her cottage: she looked doubtful, saying that my lady might not like it.

'Oh please, Dolly,' I entreated, for I was so bored with Cudden Hall where there was nothing to play with, and where the only person who took any notice of me was my Uncle Constantine. The meals were too rich and the formality weighed me down: I was expected to sit still in a hard-backed chair, with my hands folded in my lap and, though I did go into the garden, I was not encouraged to run about. As for my aunt, she always went to her own rooms in what was called the west wing, from ten in the morning till four in the afternoon. I was told she was working on her latest romantic novel. I would have liked to ask her about this but dared not: besides, I unhappily remembered the fun Maman made of her writing. 'All about wicked nuns and monks,' she used to say with the utmost scorn. But I had to think that anyone who wrote a whole novel must be clever, and if my aunt had ever discussed her books with me, I should have been her friend for life.

Of course she never did. We did not set eyes on her until the clock struck four, but eyes were kept on me nonetheless, and John-Gon had a strange way of suddenly appearing the moment I grew wild or excited. I could not help longing for Maman and Leonie and old Bettine, and this made me beg Dolly again to take me to her cottage.

She was silent for a moment. She really was beautiful, with a great deal of curly black hair and large, long-lashed eyes. I thought she and Maman would get on very well. She said at last, 'Well, Miss Nanette, I oughtn't, and you knows I oughtn't, but I'll tell you what you can do. If you can get yourself out of bed by six o'clock, I'll take you down to see my pa, and then I'll bring you back in time for breakfast so that old John-Gon will never know you've been away.'

I thought this was prodigiously exciting, a real adventure. Cudden Hall was not so bad after all. When Dolly stole in next morning to wake me, I was already waiting for her, my clothes thrown on and my un-ringleted hair piled up on top of my head so that it was difficult to get my bonnet on. And a few minutes later, with a hot roll inside me that Dolly insisted on my eating, I crept down the stairs and we walked quickly towards the fishermen's cottages.

I had not yet seen Greymanswick in the early morning. It did not look inviting and I was glad to have Dolly Easey at my side, her warm, strong hand clasping my own. The sea was not so rough now, but it still sniped at the wall as if determined one day to pull it down, and the marshes where I had seen the lights that first evening, were frighteningly desolate.

'Do people live there?' I asked Dolly.

'You ask too many questions, young lady!' But she said this as if she were amused, and I could see she did not mean to scold me.

I persisted, 'Do people live there?'

'People work there, Miss Nanette. I'll tell you something –'

'Oh please!'

'Do you know what smuggling is?'

'No.'

'Then I don't know how to explain it to you. But we are not so far from Holland – you will have heard of that – and some of our menfolk go out there o'nights and bring back brandy and gin. That's smuggling. The law's against it. If they're caught, they are hanged. Oh yes, Miss Nanette. So if you see lights on the marshes, you say nowt like a good little lass, because if you don't, some poor fellow may swing for it.'

'I'll never say a word, never, never, never!'

'Good girl. And this is where I live, Miss Nanette, and my pa is waiting to see you.'

I thought the cottage was gorgeous from my very first glimpse. It was on the edge of the marshes, and the sea lapped against one side. The door was so low that even I brushed the top of my head against the lintel, and to my astonishment fishing nets were hanging down on both door and windows so that I was quite entangled. But inside it was

17

warm and welcoming and even the strong smell of fish seemed lovely to me. I do not know how many there were in the family, but there were several children there, all very shy, and Tom Easey came up to me at once and gave me a hug. After that I felt entirely at home and prattled away in a fashion that would have given my aunt the hysterics.

Tom was a smallish, stocky man, with a weatherbeaten face and his daughter's black curly hair. As I did not really understand what a smuggler was, I could hardly say that he resembled one, but I had the vague impression that he ought to look wild and desperate and dangerous, which of course he did not do at all. He at once assumed I was hungry, which I was, despite the hot roll. He set before me a vast dish of fish which seemed to me the most delicious food I had ever tasted. There was too much for me to finish, but I infinitely preferred it to my aunt's highly seasoned dishes, and by the time I had regretfully done, I was quite swollen with food and almost collapsed back in my chair.

I wished I did not have to go. The small Easeys, one of them about my own age, were becoming friendly and I wanted to play with them. I did not see a Mrs. Easey so I assumed she was in the kitchen: I was sure she must be nice and kind. The cottage was crowded with furniture and I suppose it was both dirty and untidy, but I was sick of the rich orderliness of Cudden Hall, and almost crying at the realisation that I must leave. But I could see that Dolly was becoming impatient: she even began tugging at my hand.

She hissed at me, 'Miss Nanette, you must come. There's the church clock striking eight, and you know breakfast is served on the dot of half-past.'

'I couldn't eat another crumb!'

'Well, never mind that, you've got to be there. There'll be hell to pay if my lady finds out where you've been. Oh,' cried Dolly, her voice rising, 'do get a move on –'

Her father said in his soft, deep voice, 'You'd best go, young lady. There'll only be trouble for all of us if you don't.'

I said, almost in tears, 'Can I see you again before I leave?'

He and his daughter exchanged a brief look. I could not read it but it made me uneasy. But he simply grinned at me without saying yea or nay, and Dolly was fastening my tippet and pulling my bonnet on, so I began to walk rather sulkily towards the door.

Then just before I stepped out into the cold morning wind blowing from the sea, I remembered something, and of course I had to ask what it was, if only to delay my parting by one more minute. It was very ill-bred of me and the kind of thing that would have provoked a scold from Papa, but the words popped out before I could stop them.

'Why,' I demanded, 'do you have fishing nets hanging over your door and windows?'

There was a pause. I cannot quite describe what happened but it was as if a cloud passed over the sun. In that moment Tom Easey, who had seemed so kind, looked almost as if he were my enemy, mouth pursed in a soundless whistle and eyes fixed on me in such a way that I was terrified. Then he burst out laughing, and Dolly joined in, though I had the impression that she was as frightened as I was.

'Why,' he said, clapping me jovially on the shoulder, 'what an observant little madam it is! How do you like that, Doll? I shouldn't have thought she'd even notice. You London ladies certainly use your eyes. Why do we have fishing nets over our door and windows! Who'd have believed it?'

In all this he did not of course answer my question, and Dolly seized hold of my hand, and almost ran me down the street, but not before I noticed something else: a face peering from behind the half-open kitchen door, of a dark, untidy, suspicious looking young woman who did not in any way resemble my idea of Mrs. Easey.

I wanted to ask about her too, but something restrained me. Instead I demanded breathlessly – for we were going at a vast speed – 'Why is that inn over there called the "Cuckold's Point"? It's a funny name. I don't know what a cuckold is.' Then, as Dolly, whose patience must have been tried to the utmost, did not answer, I pointed at a boat moored a few yards away. I could see the name painted on it: the *Holy Margaret*. I said, wanting to propitiate, 'That's a fine ship. Is it your father's?'

For once before I had spoken of a boat when I should have said 'ship', and I thought this was the polite thing to do.

Dolly repeated, 'Ship!' then said simply, 'Yes, that's my pa's.'

Only as we turned into the drive that led to Cudden Hall – I could hear the clock striking the half hour – I said again, 'Please, Dolly, why do you have those fishing nets?'

She answered in a snap, 'To keep the bloody Preventives out!'

'The –?'

'Interfering folks. Like you. Miss Nanette! You must stop asking questions.'

I said meekly, 'Yes, Dolly. Dolly, what are Preventives?'

'Did you hear what I said?'

'Yes, Dolly. I'm sorry, Dolly.'

'Then do as you're told –'

She broke off. We both gave a great gasp. The front door of Cudden Hall was wide open. My aunt Elizabeth stood there on the top step, a shawl round her shoulders, and behind her I could see my father, John Gonomanaway and Uncle Constantine. They were all watching us. They did not utter a word. A dreadful condemnation blew from them and I was instantly aware that I was only a child and a naughty one at that: everyone was angry with me and awful things were going to happen.

Dolly muttered, 'Oh lord!' and then, 'Oh Christ!' She whispered, 'You'd best go and get it over,' then dropped my hand and deserted me, running like a hare to the back entrance.

I do not know how I managed to walk those last few yards of the drive. My knees were giving beneath me. The tears were trickling down my cheeks. Nobody said a word as I climbed the steps.

Then my aunt spoke, in a voice so cold that it cut into me. 'You wicked girl!' she said. 'How dare you go out without permission? Where have you been?'

I was too frightened to lie. I stammered through my tears, 'I've been visiting Dolly's father.'

'You've been visiting Tom Easey! Am I hearing correctly?' cried my aunt, her voice rising. 'Tom Easey! And with that slut of his –'

She broke off, and my father, who had been trying to speak, cut across her.

He said sternly, 'You have been very naughty, Nanette. I am ashamed of you. You have no right to go out like that. No, I don't want to hear any excuses. Go straight to your room. You will not come down again until I give you leave. You will have no breakfast. Go upstairs. You are not fit to associate with us.'

I sobbed my stumbling way up the stairs. It is only fair to say that the non-breakfast threat was unimportant. I was so full of fish that I could not have eaten a crust of bread. But my father was seldom angry with me, and to have such dreadful things said to me in front of everyone was more than I could bear. Through my crying I could hear my aunt saying that I ought to be whipped. 'It's all she deserves! You've always spoilt her, Charles, I told you from the beginning, and now see what happens. A sound whipping and bread and water for the rest of her stay are what she needs to bring her to her senses –'

I slammed the door on her furious words and flung myself face down on the bed. I did not even take off my bonnet and tippet. I cried until my eyes were red, my throat sore and my strength gone: when my father took me by the shoulders and lifted me up, I simply drooped in his hold,

21

staring at him from swollen eyes, unable to produce more than a croak.

He did not look angry any more. He wore an exhausted and baffled air. He said, 'Nanette, I do not know what to do with you,' then more energetically, 'Now stop that crying. It won't do anyone any good. What got into you, child? To walk out like that – We were all frantic with worry. Didn't you think of that at all? You are only eight, after all, and this is a notoriously dangerous coast, there are bad tides, and besides – Oh, stop snivelling. Are you hungry?'

'N-n-no!'

'Your uncle wishes to send some breakfast up to you. It is more than you deserve.' He added, 'For God's sake, don't tell your aunt. She keeps on ordering me to whip you, and if she knew I was feeding you instead – What? Of course you're hungry. I've never known you anything else.'

'I couldn't eat anything, Papa.'

'Nonsense! Why not?' Then it began to dawn on him. 'Are you telling me that this fellow, Easey, gave you something to eat?'

'Yes, Papa!'

'Oh stop it,' cried my father, obviously appalled by the tears that were still rolling down my cheeks, then, 'What did he give you?'

'Fish. Oh Papa,' I sobbed, 'it was so lovely!'

Then he burst into a roar of laughter, and somehow this stopped my crying. I began to laugh too, in an hysterical fashion, and we both rocked and gasped. My aunt, if she had seen us, would have murdered the pair of us.

When our hysteria was done, I lay back in Papa's arms, so exhausted that I was half asleep. He was speaking a little sadly as if he did not really wish to scold me, and I hiccupped in a penitent manner and thought I was a very bad girl indeed, I did not deserve such a wonderful father.

Then something came into my mind so that I interrupted him. I said, 'She won't send Dolly away, will she?'

'Nanette, are you listening to a word I've been saying?'

'Yes, Papa, only –'

'Never mind Dolly. She should be ashamed of herself. No, she won't be sent away, she's too useful. Now forget about Dolly, and listen to me. We have been here two days, Nanette, and during that time you have twice scared us out of our wits. You weren't even civil to our aunt when you first met, and of course you had to make it worse by being so friendly to Uncle Constantine –'

'But I like –'

'Be quiet. Don't interrupt. You are always far too anxious to air your own views. I know you love your uncle and so do I–'

My father paused. He looked so sad that I nearly began to cry afresh, but I knew this would upset him so all I could do was to put my arms round him.

He patted me, continuing more briskly, 'I suppose you are too young to understand all this, but really, you have put me in a most difficult position. We now have two more days here. Is it too much to hope you won't get into any more mischief? I'm not asking a great deal of you. I simply want you to behave yourself, be polite to your aunt and stop asking these incessant questions. Why you had to visit that scoundrel, Easey –'

'Papa, he's not –'

'Will you be quiet! I suppose in your usual way you just wanted to see what he was like. Well, I could have told you. He is the most notorious smuggler in the district, he has a shocking reputation, and he will certainly end by being hanged. I cannot blame your aunt for being so angry. It really seems that we dare not leave you alone. I'm sure your little sister would never behave like this. Now I want you to give me your word to be good for the rest of your stay. If something excites your curiosity, you simply come to me. Do I have your promise?'

'Yes, Papa.'

'No more little excursions?'

'No, Papa.'

He gave me a look. He said, 'I wish I really trusted you. One day, if this goes on, you'll get into serious trouble. However, I suppose I have to accept your word. Now, you will blow your nose and tidy yourself up, then you will come downstairs and make your aunt a full apology.'

He must have seen the mutinous look in my face, for he gave me a shake and said in a voice I had seldom heard from him, 'That is an order, Nanette. If you don't obey me, you stay in this room until we leave. I mean that. Well? Are you coming down to apologise?'

I mumbled, 'Yes, Papa.'

I daresay my expression revealed my rebellion only too well, for my father sighed as he rose to his feet. He said, 'I sometimes think we've made a poor job of your education. We've always indulged you as much as possible, and I have never believed in severe discipline, but upon my word – Well, I'll send one of the maids up to help you change and do something about your hair.' He glanced at the wretched remains of my ringlets, blown into a tangle by the sea wind. He said explosively, 'You look terrible. For God's sake, don't let your aunt see you like that.'

I hoped the maid would turn out to be Dolly, but of course that was stupid of me. It was instead a girl I had never seen before, and I did not like her. She made my scalp sore with her combing, she put soap in my eyes and she did the buttons of my dress up wrong. Perhaps she felt it was not part of her duties to look after such a badly behaved little girl. However, when I at last came downstairs, I was clean and neat, with my hair flat to my head and my eyes red with all my weeping.

I made my apology to Aunt Elizabeth. My father and Uncle Constantine were there, but Virgil seeing what it was all about, left the room with some speed. My father looked down but, when I at last managed to raise my head, my uncle winked at me. This cheered me a little, but then I had to stand there with my hands clasped behind my back while my aunt delivered me a long lecture, all about ill-behaved children, the iniquity of disobedience and the appalling curiosity which would one day land me on the gallows. I cried, of course, but it was mostly temper, and it was all I could do not to answer her back. In the end she accepted my tears as a sign of penitence and told me curtly to go away and find myself something to do.

'If you could read,' she said in her most disagreeable fashion, 'I would give you a book, but naturally –'

'I can read, Aunt Elizabeth!'

She ignored this. 'Have you not brought a sampler with you?'

'No, Ma'am.'

'Then I will give you needle and thread and a pretty piece of material. You can make a little mat.'

There was a suppressed silence. I could see behind her my father making threatening faces at me. I had no wish to make a little mat. I had never made a little mat in my life. However, a workbasket was set beside me, and for a while I amused myself by cutting the material into odd shapes: fortunately my aunt did not see this and Papa later removed the pieces, giving me a forbidding look as he did so.

It was a very boring day, and I was glad to go to bed. My cousin Virgil must have received a full account of my misdeeds, but he hardly spoke to me, only I had to notice that he kept an eye on me, for whenever I wandered off on my own, he somehow seemed to be there too.

The next day was the last. I longed to see Dolly, and once or twice I wandered towards the kitchen stairs, but that abominable Virgil immediately appeared so I was compelled to wander back again. It was still very stormy, but I did not dare walk to the sea wall to watch the breakers crashing against it. However, I discovered there was a big library in Cudden Hall and I spent a happy afternoon there. Most of the books were too difficult for me, but I found a book full of beautiful maps, and for a few hours nobody could have grumbled about me. I could never stay still for very long, and it was growing dark so I put the book away

25

and came out into the hall. I was absurdly pleased with my own virtue. In the morning I had played cards with my uncle Constantine, and I had taken great care to eat nicely at luncheon, wiping my lips with the napkin, and remembering not to crumble my bread. I could see Papa was greatly relieved, and my aunt looked gratifyingly surprised. And to spend the afternoon reading a book – I even smiled prettily at John Gonomanaway on his way down to the kitchen, then fell to wondering what else there was for a good little girl to do.

It was a pity that John-Gon had left the door open. But I could not see any possible harm in stepping out on to the lawn. I had had no fresh air all day and, though the wind was blowing violently, the rain had almost stopped. I had no intention of going far and I would keep an eye on the door to make sure I was not shut out again.

It was a wonderful evening. I always loved storms and even in London had to be restrained from dashing out when the rain was pelting down. And this was grand, the wind howling, the sea crashing against the wall, and the black storm clouds racing across the sky. For the first time I really liked Greymanswick. It was not of course a patch on my darling, smelly, noisy old London, but it excited me, standing there with flapping petticoats and my hair streaking across my face. It must have been like this when the city drowned in the sea, and I could somehow picture people screaming and running, houses toppling down and St. Botolph's church bells ringing. In the end I made myself so afraid that I was sure I heard the bells, and I half turned to run back to the warmth and safety of Cudden Hall. Only as I swung round, pushing the damp hair out of my eyes, I saw something so interesting that I forgot both fear and resolutions.

Across the marshes, now black-dark – oh, it must be terrible there, unprotected from the wind – the lights were flashing, and I knew from the direction that this must be near Tom Easey's cottage. Then, as I stared, I saw the flash of a lantern, and in that light the *Holy Margaret* slipped down into the sea. The lantern was extinguished almost immediately but not before I saw men running after the boat. Then there was nothing, and I knew that Tom Easey and his friends must be out on the stormy sea, out to smuggle strange things from the Holland coast. It seemed an awful night to choose, and the *Holy Margaret* did not look very big, but I was so fascinated that I had to go a little nearer, to lean over the garden wall in case anything more happened.

Then I decided I must explore, and I flung one leg in a most unladylike fashion over the wall.

A voice said, 'Exploring again, Cousin? And what has attracted your attention this time?'

I was so taken aback that I nearly fell over the wall: a strong hand caught at my petticoats and pulled me back. I jerked round to be dazzled by another lantern: above it I could see the silhouette of my cousin Virgil.

I was furious. It seemed that every time I met Virgil I was at a disadvantage. I had behaved so beautifully all day, and now he had to find me disobeying Papa's orders once again, with my hair wild and my clothes in disarray. I stamped my foot at him, nearly losing my balance in the wet grass. I shouted, 'Go away. I don't like you following me. You're spying on me.'

But he ignored this. He steered me back into Cudden Hall, keeping a tight hold of my arm; once in the hall he released me and looked me up and down. He said, 'What a nuisance you are. You seem incapable of keeping out of mischief. What is it this time? Were you planning a little foray on the marshes? Perhaps Tom will enlist you as a member of his crew.' Then he exclaimed in an angry voice, 'You are boring me. I was asked to keep an eye on you, but after all I'm not a nursemaid, I'm not here to look after silly little chits who should be slapped and locked up. Thank God you're going home tomorrow.'

It was not a phrase in my vocabulary, but in my temper it appealed to me. I shouted back at him, 'Thank God I am

27

going home,' and this took him aback so that he burst into a sudden laugh. 'And don't laugh at me!' I cried out, stamping my foot again. Then I said in a small, tense voice, 'I hate you.'

'I don't love you very much myself,' said my cousin Virgil. 'I only hope that when I marry and have children, as I suppose I have to do some day, I'll not produce a brat like you. You should have beeen thrown back into the sea.'

I tilted up my head at him. It was one of Maman's gestures. It must have looked extremely silly in a bedraggled little girl of eight. 'You'll never find anyone to marry you,' I said. 'You are a horrid boy. I wouldn't marry you if you were the last boy on earth.'

He was a little startled by this. I daresay the other children he met were less outspoken. He said a little roughly – after all, he was only a schoolboy – 'I don't think you've been asked. I assure you, that's something you need not worry about.'

I realised much too late that I was behaving more abominably than ever. My temper fizzled out. I began to back away towards the staircase. He stared after me. I said in my most social fashion, 'Well, I'll leave you to your poetry.'

He repeated in a bewildered voice, 'My what?'

'Papa says you are a famous poet.'

It took him a moment to assimilate this, then he suddenly grinned. 'Oh,' he said, 'you are of course referring to the *Aeneid*. A little thing, Cousin, that I tossed off in my spare time.' He added, 'You are of course acquainted with it.'

'Of course,' I said, but I knew he was making fun of me, and my voice sank down.

He paused. I think it was at this moment that he fully took in my deplorable appearance. He said, mockery vibrating in his voice, 'Ah well, *paulo majora canamus*, as we poets say. That means of course, let us sing of rather greater things.'

'I know,' I said, with cold dignity.

'Naturally you know. How could you not?' Then with a

mixture of derision and urgency, 'What I really mean, little cousin, is that any moment now my aunt will descend from her rooms for her evening glass of wine, and I feel it would be inadvisable for her to see you looking like a gypsy brat dragged out of the sea. I suggest you run like the devil to your room and do something about your dress and hair.'

The thought of my aunt seeing me in such a state appalled me. I began to go up the stairs, when Virgil remarked, 'Unless of course you wish to make a little excursion to the grass first –'

Then I forgot that my father might be listening, that my aunt might appear on the landing, that the servants might come running to see what was happening. I screamed at him in a shrill, furious voice, 'Oh how I hate you, you're the nastiest boy I've ever met, I wish you were dead!'

And with this I tore up the stairs and, when I reached my room, slammed the door.

I was luckier than I deserved. The servants must, of course, have heard me, but within a few minutes the girl appeared who had dressed me the day before. From the looks she gave me, I could see she was longing to slap me. But she did not say one word and when at last I came downstairs I looked perfectly respectable, except for my hair which the girl had fastened into a knot on top of my head. I think Maman would have been angrier over this than anything else. She herself had pretty, naturally curly hair, and she always took infinite pains over mine, saying that it was thick and a lovely colour as she tried to tease it into waves and curls.

I felt very apprehensive when I came into the drawing-room, but obviously no one had reported my conduct, and my only bad moments were caused by John-Gon, pouring out the wine, and my cousin, Virgil, who was lounging in a corner, reading a book. John-Gon of course knew all about everything, and when he handed me the wine and water which was all I was allowed, he gave me a look that made my cheeks burn. As for my cousin he raised his head to glance

29

at me, and his mouth twitched, but he did not say a word.

We left early next morning. I am sure my aunt was as thankful as I was. She said goodbye very coldly and did not offer to embrace me. My uncle, however, kissed me with great affection, and put a golden sovereign into my hand, which made me feel very rich. But I cried for him, not the money, for I loved him and, though I did not realise I would never see him again, knew instinctively that this parting was a final one.

The carriage was waiting for us, the horses fresh and fed and watered, and Jem looked as if he had enjoyed his stay in Cudden Hall. I longed to say goodbye to Dolly, but there was no sign of her. My cousin Virgil, however, was there, leaning against the door post. He looked very tall and very dark, and I hated him with all my heart.

I made him a curtsey and said, 'Goodbye, Cousin.'

'Goodbye, Nanette,' he said. His mouth was grave but his eyes were laughing. Then he said, 'I believe we should not be enemies. As I wrote the other day – these things come to me, you know – *Arcades ambo*, which means – but of course you know.'

I remained sullenly silent, my mouth in a pout. I had had a little talk with Papa when he came to say goodnight, and I knew now that the Virgil who wrote poetry and was so famous was nothing to do with my cousin at all, except for the sharing of a name.

'In case,' said my abominable cousin, 'your memory has slipped, it means, Arcadians both – in other words, we are villains of the same stamp. Goodbye, my villain Cousin. I am thankful my days as nursemaid are over.'

I turned my back on him and stalked towards the carriage. When Cudden Hall was well out of sight, I flung myself on Papa's shoulder, crying, 'I hope I never see that horrid place again.'

He put his hands on my shoulders, holding me away from him. He said gravely, 'You haven't exactly distinguished yourself, Nanette, have you?'

I said miserably, 'No, Papa.'

'Why are you such a bad girl?'

'I don't know, Papa. I don't mean to be.'

'I gather that yesterday – oh yes. I heard all about it. I'm afraid your aunt did too, though your uncle and I did our best to keep it from her.'

I forgot my remorse. I cried out, 'Virgil told you!'

'No,' said Papa, looking surprised. 'Virgil never so much as mentioned you.' Then he said sternly, 'What is all this? John-Gon told me you had been out in the wind and rain. I see there is more to it. Well? I'm waiting, Nanette.'

After that I had no alternative but to tell him everything, and he listened in silence. He only said, 'I think it is as well that our visit was a short one.'

And he did not mention the matter again, only on our way to London I kept on thinking joyously that I would never see Cudden Hall again.

I never dreamt that ten years later Leonie and I would come to live there.

1744

It was September again when we set forth, Leonie and I. I do not know why September should always be the month for Greymanswick and Cudden Hall. We were eighteen and fifteen apiece and still in our black. We had decided it would be more seemly to retain our mourning, even though the official period was passed, partly, I suspect, because we thought it would touch our Aunt Elizabeth's heart and make her more friendly to us. This of course was perfectly ridiculous for she was the last person in the world to have any truck with such nonsense, yet in a way this harmless little piece of playacting soothed us, helped us to forget our unhappiness. We had of course no money to buy new clothes but we had nonetheless a large wardrobe which we had packed into several portmanteaux: I fancy that both of us were longing to wear bright colours again.

Even as we jogged along in Mr. Prendergast's ancient carriage, we could hardly believe we would never see our London home again. But, then, until the last of the furniture was carted out, neither of us could quite believe in the death of Maman and Papa: then realisation dawned upon us, and my little sister stood in the middle of the drawing-room, staring about her in bewildered disbelief.

Yet it was she who cheered me. There we were, with no furniture but a broken table, all our personal possessions packed: there were dusty marks on the walls where the pictures had hung, more dust on the mantelpiece and bare boards that creaked as we moved. Apart from a parcel of food that neighbours had brought us, together with a bottle of wine, there was nothing in the kitchen, indeed there was nothing anywhere but one double bed for us to sleep in, this last night. There can be little more depressing in the world than a dismantled house: in a way it is a merciful preparation for how can one be sentimental over dust and emptiness?

And then Leonie burst out laughing. I was quite shocked, but she refused to become grave again, only kicked at the dust beneath her feet, saying, 'Oh Nan, you look so gloomy. You have the air of one whose head will soon be laid on Tower Hill. Like the Jacobite rebels who are coming over –'

I exclaimed, 'You are talking nonsense. Who said any rebels were coming over? I'm glad you at least call them by their right name.'

For Leonie was an ardent supporter of the young man they called Bonnie Prince Charlie, and it was true that last month a fleet of 1,500 men set out to land in England. But I could not find this in the least romantic for the French were merely retaliating for their defeat at Dettingen, and in any case a storm scattered the fleet and the attempt was abandoned.

'Some of them managed to land,' said Leonie.

'You don't know that!' I did not realise at that moment that she was trying to take my mind off tomorrow's journey. Her adoration of this young prince always exasperated me, for I found him more tiresome than romantic, and I could not understand her dislike of poor German George: he was after all a good king, and he had won the battle. I declared fiercely, 'We'll never have a Stuart king again, I can tell you that.'

We must have looked absurd, two girls in black, standing in the middle of an empty room, positively shouting at each other. Leonie, smiling at me wickedly, said, 'I love the Stuarts. At least they're better than our fat Hanoverians with all their horrid mistresses.'

'Leonie!'

'Well, so they are. Why the first George couldn't even

33

speak English properly. He talked of "boetry" and "bainting". And you can't pretend that any of them are good-looking.'

'What have good looks to do with it? I hope you don't talk to Aunt Elizabeth like this.'

'Perhaps she's an ardent Jacobite. Perhaps she's organising some secret rebellion, hoarding arms and – and –'

I was compelled to laugh, despite my unhappiness. The thought of my aunt romanticising over anything but her own novels was ridiculous.

'Perhaps,' went on Leonie, carried away by her own imagination, 'she is responsible for the French who landed and who are to prepare the way for him.'

'What are you talking about? You don't know if anyone landed.'

'I read it in the *Gentleman's Magazine*. I wouldn't be surprised,' cried Leonie, her face lighting up – she is much prettier than I am, so very like poor Maman – 'if some of them had not landed in Suffolk. Near Cudden Hall. Oh Nan, wouldn't that be wonderful? We could look after them. We could bring them food –'

This brought me back to reality. I said wearily, 'You are being very silly, my darling. From what I remember of John-Gon, every crust in the kitchen would be counted. In any case you would hardly want to help traitors.'

There was a pause. Leonie did not answer my last remark. Then she said, 'Let's open that bottle of wine. And I am longing to see what is in the parcel. I'm starving, Nan. I know I shouldn't be, but I am. Shall I bring it all in? There's neither table nor chairs in the kitchen.'

I wanted to say she was too young to drink wine, but it really was not important and, shameful as it seemed in the circumstances, I was hungry too. So I made no protest, and presently we sat there on the floor on copies of the *Morning Courier*, drank wine out of the one chipped glass left, and ate cold roast chicken and meat pasties with our fingers. It was all very good and satisfying, yet it was strange to sit here

34

where everything had once been pretty and comfortable: as the evening shadows lengthened I felt for the first time that I would be thankful to be away.

In bed that night we both cried. Leonie huddled in my arms and sobbed, 'Oh Nan, I do so long for Papa and Maman to be back with us.'

Oh God, yes –

It all started in the most ordinary way. Papa and Maman were going to a party. Perhaps this was not so ordinary now that we had so little money, but after all, Maman was so pretty and my father could be amusing company when he chose: it was natural enough they should be invited out. I still can see Maman in a ravishing new gown that was certainly not paid for, while my father as always looked very dashing and for once without his habitual careworn expression. Leonie and I saw them off in a cloud of perfume and a frou-frou of silk. Maman promised to tell us all about it next day, and we waved from the doorway as if they were setting forth on some long, perilous journey.

And so they were. It was the last time we would ever see them. But no premonition disturbed us and, though we were resolved to stay awake until their return, we slept deeply until there was the knocking on the door, and Mary, Bettine's successor, burst hysterically into the room.

It was a highwayman who stopped them in Hyde Park, on their way back. I thought afterwards, when I could think at all, that at least they passed a happy last evening. Maman always adored parties, and I am sure she was the most sought-after lady there, for all she was nearly forty. London has always been plagued by these gentlemen of the road, but it was unusual to meet one so far from Holborn. I suppose it was late and dark and he took his chance, believing there would be no one within call. Nobody knew exactly what happened, for Jem, though thrown clear, suffered a severe concussion that affected his memory; even when he recovered he could only weep and say it was all his fault. It seemed that the highwayman fired his pistol, probably simply to alarm, and the horses bolted, flinging the carriage on to its side. Maman was killed immediately and Papa died soon afterwards.

Leonie, a long time afterwards, cried out, 'It was all so unnecessary.'

I will not go into detail over the weeks that followed; indeed, I could not. Mr. Prendergast, the family lawyer, took charge, which was just as well. He was a good man and as honest as any lawyer is like to be, but he was over fifty and really had no idea how to deal with two spoilt young girls who, as he immediately told us, had almost no money at all. And as money was the thing that most concerned him, he spoke of little else, though at that moment Leonie and I would not have cared if we had not a penny in the world. At least this interminable talk of debts and commitments and liabilities checked our crying, and it was plain enough that poor Mr. Prendergast, if he had tried to console us, would have driven us into the grave too.

He came regularly to see us at least twice a week. Our parents, we learnt, were utterly in debt: only the sale of the house and everything in it, including Maman's jewels, could clear us. It seemed that we had been living in this way for the past ten years. The pretty clothes that Maman so loved, for us as well as herself, were never paid for; the lavish food and wine that we offered our friends was all on tick, and even the carriage, now totally ruined, was borrowed. Poor Jem, who would never be able to work again, had not received his full wages for years. We found all this almost impossible to believe. We looked around us at the beautiful furniture, chosen so expertly by my father, the fine glassware, the porcelain, the priceless little knickknacks, – and none of this was ours, it must all be returned.

'Your father,' Mr. Prendergast said, adding hastily, 'your poor father was ruined.'

'But is there no family income?'

He brooded for a while on this, obviously doing abstruse mathematical calculations. He said at last, 'When all the

36

debts are paid and the house sold –'

'But you can't sell the house! We must have a roof over our heads.'

If he had been a more brutal man, he could have told us that we would be fortunate not to be taken into an orphanage, but he did not do so. He only said in a heavy exhausted voice, 'The house must be sold. It is in a good district and should raise a fair sum of money. It will not cover all the debts, but I believe the creditors can be persuaded to take a smaller amount. It would hardly benefit them to drive two young girls into the Fleet.'

'The Fleet!' whispered Leonie. She had gone so pale that I feared she would faint. I quickly put an arm round her shoulders. She added in a trembling voice, 'That's where they perform those horrid marriages.'

Mr. Prendergast said quickly, 'I have told you this will not arise. But –'

Leonie, apparently comforted, said, 'We will have to work.' She looked quite pleased at the thought. 'Nan will be a governess –'

'I will not,' I said firmly, for I had little patience with children.

'– or a companion to some dear old lady who will leave you all her money. While I –' Leonie paused dramatically. Mr. Prendergast and I gazed at her. She said at last, 'I could be a governess too. I like children. Or perhaps a servant maid. I should not mind that at all. Yes, Ma'am, no, Ma'am – I would do it rather well. And of course in the end we shall find ourselves rich husbands.'

'With no dowry?' said Mr. Prendergast. He was never a man with much sense of humour, and I could see he was shocked by this levity. It would never enter his head that Leonie was on the verge of hysteria and that this frothy talk was her way of staving off tears.

However, when she began, 'Well, we do not have to marry them –' I saw that this had gone far enough.

I said, 'Leo, be quiet. Mr. Prendergast is doing his best

37

to help us. If he feels we should look for employment, he will say so. Forgive us, Sir. You were about to inform us on the family income.'

'I have worked it out,' said Mr. Prendèrgast. He might not have a talent for coping with two unhappy young women, but I knew that in working out an income he was entirely dependable. He said, 'You should be left with twenty pounds a year. Between you.'

Leonie cried, 'Why then we have no need to worry. We shall be quite rich.'

I knew we would not be rich at all, especially as we had no roof over our heads. I knew there was more to come and I looked at Mr. Prendergast and waited.

He said at last, a hint of unease in his voice, 'I believe I have good news for you. I have waited until it was confirmed, and I can now say it is certain. I have received instructions from your father's sister-in-law, Mrs. Constantine Cudden, to bring you to Cudden Hall, where she will be pleased to offer you a home.'

He waited, I suppose, for our enthusiastic cries, but we looked at each other in silence.

He said crossly, 'I thought you would be pleased. Mrs. Cudden seems fully prepared to welcome you. I believe there may be some light duties involved, with you, Miss Nanette, taking on some of the work of a companion, but you will be living with your own family in the heart of the country, and there has been no hesitation on Mrs. Cudden's part, indeed, she seems to accept this as the only thing to be done.' Then, as we remained silent, he positively shouted at us, his face going red. 'My dear young ladies, pray show some sense. What else is to be done? You cannot live on ten pounds apiece. You talk of work – what training or ability do you have? Families do not take on a governess with no experience. As for you, Miss Leo, you are too young for any employment except of the lowest kind. Are you prepared to get up at four or five in the morning and work till midnight in some stinking sweat-shop, ruining your health and at the mercy of some brutal overseer? For that is what will happen. You know nothing of the world, either of you. Your poor dear mother was a most charming woman, but she was French –'

I demanded in an icy voice, 'And what is wrong with being French?'

But Mr. Prendergast was too distraught to pay attention. I think he was genuinely concerned for us. He said, 'The French are a delightful people, but everyone knows they are volatile, impractical and frivolous. You have been excellently brought up, but you are neither of you trained to fight your way in a world where charm and manners are unimportant. Miss Nanette, you have no choice, and you know it. You now have the chance to live with your own family, you will lack for nothing, you will meet people of your own class, and I am sure that eventually you will both find a gentleman to offer you marriage.' Then, still confronted with our appalled silence, he exclaimed, 'What more can you want? I do not understand you. I do not understand you at all. I thought you would be delighted, and you look as if I were sending you to Newgate.'

He was right, of course. We had no choice. But I could only think of Aunt Elizabeth with her white, doughy face so devoid of warmth, who had been so unloving to a little girl – a tiresome little girl but still so young – who never smiled, who did not care for her own sex, and who lived in a vast, cluttered mansion continually beaten on by a wild and greedy sea. And I thought too of Tom Easey who seemed so kind and could be so sinister, of the strange John Gonomanaway, and of my cousin Virgil, who had mocked and derided me.

There was something cold and frightening about Cudden Hall. Even Aunt Elizabeth's novels – I had read them all now – were about madness and cruelty and death.

And there was always the sea. Sometimes in the old days we drove down to Brighthelmstone or some other little village near London. We would always choose a warm day and, when little, be allowed to paddle in the nice, calm, blue sea, with our bare feet and our petticoats discreetly raised. There would be a little picnic on the sands with lovely things to eat, and Maman would be very gay and help us build a castle. It was cosy and delightful and we would talk of it for weeks afterwards. It bore no resemblance to the savage, grey expanse of water that hurled itself against the dyke, that had swallowed up a city and even now hungered after the small amount that remained. I heard again that rhythmic roar, saw the breakers white on black, it was almost as if the bells of St. Botolph sounded in my ears.

If it's St. Botolph's that you hear, you can pick up your petticoats and run like hell –

My father, in an unusually indiscreet mood, once remarked, 'Elizabeth doesn't like people but she gathers them round her. I myself believe it is a kind of insurance.'

She had gathered Virgil. Now she was proposing to gather us.

I came up to Mr. Prendergast, putting my hand on his. 'Sir,' I said, averting my eyes from Leonie who was showing every sign of being about to say the unpardonable, 'you have been most kind and considerate to us. I don't know what we would have done without you. Of course we are delighted to accept our aunt's invitation. I – I am sure we will be very happy –'

But I could not finish this pretty speech because the tears that I had so far managed to control, were choking me. I had to turn away and Leonie, seeing this, forgot her own distress and rushed to put her arms round me, clutching me so tightly that I could hardly breathe.

Mr. Prendergast must have been greatly embarrassed by this display but no doubt was also relieved. This after all was the kind of female behaviour he expected. He cleared his throat several times then said, 'Well, well, so that is settled. Oh, before I forget, I have a message from you from Mrs. Prendergast. She – we – we would be very pleased if

40

you would spend the next few days with us. We both felt that to continue living in this house would be most depressing for you. We live in a simple fashion,' said Mr. Prendergast with quiet self-confidence, 'but we would do our best to make you comfortable.'

The thought of spending our last precious days in London with the Prendergasts was almost more than I could bear, but the kindness touched me very much, and it was with the tears trickling down my cheeks that I thanked him, saying that we would prefer to stay here till the end, just to remember Papa and Maman. Poor Mr. Prendergast could hardly argue against this, but I could see that he bitterly disapproved. However, beyond a reference to Mrs. Prendergast's excellent home cooking and a suggestion that we would be looked upon as daughters, he said little more and presently departed, after leaving us a small sum of money with which to buy food and the information that he would be returning on the morrow with full details about the sale of our house.

It was after he was gone that I told Leonie about my first visit to Cudden Hall. I daresay I had already told her all about it ten years back, but she probably did not take it in, and she listened now in fascination, laughing helplessly at the account of my disgraceful behaviour in the garden.

She knew me too well not to guess that my light-hearted account was not the whole story, but at least it made her laugh, and we were too young to remain eternally in tears. And after a while, after we had eaten – we both found food most restoring – we discussed this new stage in our life: it was after all an adventure and anything was better than being a governess or working on some treadmill.

I wrote as warmly as I could to Aunt Elizabeth, and three weeks later we drove down to Cudden Hall in Mr. Prendergast's carriage which he kindly lent us. I am sure he was greatly relieved to have us off his hands, for he and his wife were childless and unused to emotional young females, but he was a good man and I remember him with real affection.

For the first hour of the long drive our main topic of conversation was the letter I received from my aunt three days ago.

It expressed no warm welcome. This astonished Leonie more than me: I found it entirely in character. Gathering in no way connotes affection. But it did inform us that for the past ten years, since the death of Uncle Constantine – he died a few weeks after my first visit – she had held a salon during the late summer and autumn months.

'What is a salon?' Leonie asked.

'I believe it must be a kind of house party, composed of famous persons. With Aunt Elizabeth it is bound to be writers and poets, perhaps celebrated ones.'

This intrigued Leonie so much that she forgot her depression. We both began to visualise arriving amidst a galaxy of celebrities, and, such is the power of female vanity, we began to regret our glum black. From this moment it seemed as if our stay was going to be far more interesting than we had dared hope, especially as we gathered that the guests would be staying until the end of October.

'I fear,' concluded my aunt, 'that you will for the time have to share the small room in the east wing. You will doubtless remember it, Nanette, for that was where you slept during your first visit. However, when our guests have gone, different arrangements can be made.'

From what I knew of my aunt, I suspected that once we were in the small room, there we would stay, but Leonie was still brooding on the prospect of meeting the famous, though she did ask me what the room was like.

'Tiny!' I said. 'We shall have to share a bed.'

But this in no way disturbed her, and when she heard that we faced the sea, with the sound of the waves in our ears the whole night through, she was more delighted than ever.

She wanted to know what our aunt's books were like, for she herself did not care for reading, despite Papa's efforts to persuade her.

I found this difficult to answer, for in all truth I did not like them. They were all very horrid, filled with mad nuns and murderous monks: half the characters were invariably insane and the other half in the process of being driven so. The heroine was always screaming or fainting or on the verge of being violated, skeletons fell from the roof and eerie moans and cries echoed around. Everything ended happily, of course, but the road to happiness was a macabre one, and now that I had grown older, I was inclined to laugh rather than tremble. Maman had always made great fun of these romances, but I felt it would be bad for Leonie if I did so, so I said at last that they were very dramatic and filled with passion and tragedy.

Leonie remarked thoughtfully, 'It doesn't sound at all like Aunt Elizabeth.'

This of course was true. For a moment I brooded on this strange lady who was so unloving and wrote so vividly of thwarted love. It was as if she were putting into her books what was lacking in her heart. Perhaps it gave her a feeling of power: I believed that my aunt desired power above everything, and for that reason gathered people around her to make her feel a queen surrounded by her court. However, I said nothing of this to my little sister, not wanting in any way to destroy her happy anticipation, and we discussed a number of trivial things until at last as the dark was falling, we came near to Greymanswick.

To a child everything is large and strange, and I was prepared to find my memories dwarfed and rendered commonplace. Yet the place was still as grim as I remembered it. The sea was rough – was it ever calm? – thudding against the wall, the marshes, grey in the dusk, might have inspired one of my aunt's gothic romances, and Cudden Hall, on top of the hill with the broken church below, was stark and forbidding.

I felt Leonie, her shoulder against mine, shiver.

She whispered, 'Is that it?'

'That is Cudden Hall.'

'It's not very pretty!'

43

'It's very old.'

And I looked away for I could see the lights flickering on the marshes as I had seen them ten years ago. I remembered Tom Easey, with the nets over his door and windows, and the sleasy girls – for Papa had made it plain that there was no Mrs. Easey – who slipped in and out of his bed and saddled him with indiscriminate children. I wondered if the *Holy Margaret* were even now slipping into the stormy sea, to look for a fresh cargo of Hollands gin. This reminded me of Dolly, and I hoped she was still there, though she would certainly be married by now, perhaps the mother of a large family.

Leonie, still whispering as if she feared being overheard, said, 'You told me there's a city under the sea.'

'So they say. With fifty churches. Sometimes people hear the bells.'

Leonie fell silent. I could see in the dim light that her little face was pinched and pale. It had been a long journey, we were cold and hungry and tired, and despite our frivolous conversation, we had not forgotten the grim reason for this visit. Maman and Papa were dead, our old life was ended, and we were going to live with people we did not really know, who perhaps did not even want us.

We came up the drive in silence. I suddenly remembered the little girl who found herself in such desperate straits and, wanting to make Leonie smile, whispered, 'That is the lawn I watered!'

She giggled faintly. Then I saw that in other ways history was repeating itself. The front door of Cudden Hall was wide open, and all the guests were standing there, more, I think, out of curiosity than welcome.

There were five of them, with my aunt in front like a general commanding her army. My first thought was that they did not look very famous. I suppose famous people look much like everyone else, but I had expected something more remarkable, perhaps a long-haired poet in outlandish garments, or a learned gentleman with a

44

Shakespearian beard. But all I saw was a very young man with a petulant expression, a middle-aged one who looked like a lawyer's clerk, a plain girl with an air of disapproval, and what was apparently a married couple, for they stood there arm in arm, behind the others.

We were naturally introduced, and it was a little while before I remembered who was who, but it will be simpler to name them now for they were all to play a part in this story.

With the exception of the young man and the plain girl, they were local people. They were not famous at all. I can see now that this fantasy was of a piece with the mind that composed the romances: my aunt knew no famous people but the fact that they were invited automatically conferred fame upon them. The petulant young man who was about my own age, was called Jack Lescott: he came from London and he did write verse. The verse was abominable but I suppose it made him a poet. The young woman was called Amelia with a surname that began with Mac: she spoke with a strong accent that I learnt was Scottish, and she came from beyond the Border. I could not imagine why my aunt had invited her for she had certainly never written a line, and her only artistic outlet was an interminable sampler that she worked at morning, noon and night. The middle-aged man was called William Pleydell and he edited the local newspaper: he must have been one of my aunt's rare friends for he was sometimes invited to her suite of rooms and I occasionally saw them talking together in a soft, intimate manner. As for the married couple, who were called Lowry, they were here as an act of charity. It seemed that they were spending a weekend away from their home, which was some twenty miles from Cudden Hall, and during their absence their house had been ransacked, with all the valuables taken and the place battered and destroyed.

'It was the Collector again,' Mr. Lowry told me later, and when I asked who the Collector was, he sighed, saying, 'he is the menace of the county. No one knows who he is,

45

but undoubtedly he has a gang with him, who are desperate men. He is, I fear, an educated man, for he only steals things of value, but no one is safe from him and no one has ever seen him though he has been in action for the past six or seven years, and few of us have escaped him.'

'Has he not been to Cudden Hall?'

This conversation, you will understand, took place some days later, but I am not an experienced writer and must set things down as they come to me. Mr. Lowry gave me what I thought was a strange look.

'No,' he said. 'Cudden Hall has so far escaped. Perhaps John-Gon is too handy with his blunderbuss, or perhaps the situation makes it difficult for thieves to come unobserved. But almost every other mansion has been robbed. I have been stripped of almost everything, Miss Nanette, including rare porcelain from the East and silver that came down to me from my great-grandmother. It is priceless stuff and not replaceable. There was one silver decanter – but there is nothing to be done. Only our home is in such a state that we cannot live in it, and Mrs. Cudden has been kind enough to offer us hospitality until we can go back.'

'Why is he called the Collector?'

Mr. Lowry gave me a bitter smile. 'Because, my dear young lady, he collects without pity all our valuables and belongings, and because he has a collector's knowledge of where these things must be. He is a wicked man. I do not believe in killing, even when the law commands it, but the day he is hanged will be a day of rejoicing for all of us.'

At that moment of course I only knew Mr. Lowry as the most pleasant person there: he was plainly a gentleman and he greeted us with great courtesy. Which is more than I can say for the rest of them – they all seemed to me remarkably dull people. At home in the old days our visitors were not perhaps famous, but they were lively and amusing, they were leagues away from this stuffy gathering who were all staring at us in a most ill-bred way.

As we went a little nervously towards what looked like a

46

reception committee, Leonie whispered to me in a voice of dismay, 'Is that our cousin Virgil?'

Her eyes were fixed disconsolately on Jack Lescott. I could not stop myself from smiling. My little sister was, naturally enough, at the age where she was greatly interested in young men. I myself, now that I am more mature, have outgrown this state, but it was only to be expected that such a pretty girl should dream of cavaliers and marriage. I whispered back, 'Certainly not,' and startled myself by the vigour of my reply. It made me stop smiling, for I realised that I was genuinely disappointed not to see my cousin and affronted by the idea that this gawky youth should be mistaken for someone so handsome.

However, at this point my aunt stepped down to meet us, bestowing a chilly kiss on my cheek. Her eyes moved to Leonie. I remembered now that she had never seen her since she was a baby. I said, 'This is my little sister, Aunt Elizabeth,' and prayed she would welcome her with a little warmth, for I could see that the excitement of the arrival had long since passed, and that Leonie, what with exhaustion and the unhappiness of the preceding months, was near to tears.

But she only said, 'I daresay you are both fatigued. We will go into the drawing-room for a glass of wine.' And with this she turned back into the hall, with ourselves and the guests following like sheep.

My aunt had greatly changed. Even allowing for the distorting memory of childhood, I could not ignore that change. She was of course still small and plump, and the pale face with its hard, opaque eyes briefly took me back ten years, but there was a remoteness to her that I did not remember. I had the feeling that for her we had as much volition of our own as pieces on a chessboard. Only the beautiful hair was the same, as thick and glossy as ever and without a trace of grey. It was hard to believe she could ever have loved my Uncle Constantine, but perhaps she had, perhaps it was his death that had closed the door on all emotion.

As I made my curtseys and was introduced to people who at that moment were simply faceless creatures, I wondered again why she had taken us in. My mother she had always cordially disliked, she and my father had simply been civil to each other and as for her own family, apart from Virgil, she never so much as mentioned them. I could only remember her making us one visit in London, and that was a disaster. Maman could not endure this dull, fat creature who never smiled, and the house became a battlefield. As the days went on, my aunt became grimmer and more formidable, radiating disapproval, while Maman grew more and more theatrically French, making dramatic gestures, laughing at everything and adopting an extraordinary foreign accent. When, after an unimaginably ghastly week, she at last left, we fell into a kind of hysteria, Papa opened a bottle of champagne and Maman danced us through the house.

She never visited us again.

Why, I thought as I continued to smile wretchedly at the dull people shaking my hand, are we here? Surely the desire to gather did not go so far. My aunt was burdening herself with two penniless relatives and whatever use she made of us could not really account for it. I did not believe it was duty, I knew it was not love, and it certainly was not money. It was at this moment that I began to see my aunt as a more devious person than I had imagined: there was a great deal here beneath the surface and one day I would discover what it was.

Dinner was largely taken up with poor Mr. Lowry's wrongs, for the unhappy man was still brooding on what he had lost and told us repeatedly of his precious silver and porcelain, so distraught that once or twice the tears came to his eyes. My aunt, as was her custom, said almost nothing but ate vastly, clearing her plate and with each course demanding a second helping. Apart from Mr. Lowry – his wife remained dead silent – it was Mr. William Pleydell who kept the conversation going: what he said was uninteresting except for a reference to local smuggling and the possibility that a couple of escaped Frenchmen might have landed on the coast.

When he said this, I glanced at Leonie. We were both too tired to eat much, and it had been a heavy meal though well-cooked and washed down by French wine. She was already nodding over her food, half asleep between mouthfuls. Her roast lamb lay almost untouched before her, but as Mr. Pleydell uttered these words she swallowed a forkful and demanded, 'Could this be one of the Frenchmen who came over to help the Scottish Prince?'

There was a prolonged silence. Everyone looked astonished except for the Scottish Amelia who, one would have expected, would be interested. But she simply gasped in a very affected manner and closed her eyes, as if this was the most dreadful subject in the world, and it was my aunt who at last spoke in an icy voice.

She said, 'I cannot understand these foolish rumours. There have always been foreigners here as we are so near to Holland, but certainly they have nothing to do with this young man you mentioned. Besides, it is a very vulgar subject and hardly suitable for the dinner table. The Frenchmen William referred to would of course be smugglers: they will certainly be caught and hanged as they deserve. I understand the Preventives are looking out for them. If you would kindly pass me the dish, Mr. Lowry, I would like another helping of vegetables.'

My poor sister blushed scarlet and said nothing more, but I knew her well enough to see that her interest was aroused. If my aunt believed her snubbing remarks would quench it, she did not know Leonie: Nanette was not the only inquisitive one in the family.

After this the conversation, never lively, virtually died, except for occasional remarks on the weather – 'how the English adore their horrid weather,' Maman used to say – and a sudden prophecy from Mr. Lowry that there would be violent storms next month, of the kind that had once sunk Greymanswick beneath the sea.

We did not leave the gentlemen to their wine, as was the London custom. Perhaps my aunt could not face the prospect of being surrounded by women. We continued to sit there through what seemed to me an interminable meal, when suddenly my aunt declared that Mr. Lescott, whom she called Jack, should read us one of his poems.

He had been the most silent of all of us. I do not believe he had so far uttered one word, only in the fashion of thin, very young men, ploughed through an enormous meal, eating with the utmost concentration.

However, he seemed delighted to oblige, and was obviously prepared, for he produced a sheet of paper from his pocket and proceeded to read from it in such a theatrical fashion that I wondered if he had ever been on the boards. It really was the most dreadful stuff, and I could see that Leonie was struggling not to giggle: I had to think that if this was all my aunt could secure for her salon, we ourselves could have done better at home.

I was thankful when he finished. The whole company wore a kind of glazed look. My aunt, with a brief acknowledgment, rose to her feet, saying to me as we filed out, 'You must both be exhausted. I suggest you go to your room and have an early night.'

I resented being treated as a child, but we were thankful to go. I could see that Leonie was almost sleep-walking. I slipped out before her, as Mr. Lowry, who was obviously captivated by her prettiness, expressed concern about the effects of such a long journey, – and found that John Gonomanaway was waiting in the hall, to conduct us upstairs.

We looked at each other and I smiled. 'Have you forgotten me, John-Gon?' I said, for there was no recognition in his eyes. 'Have you no memory of the tiresome little girl who was always where she should not be and who gave you so much trouble?'

'I remember you well enough,' he said. He had aged

beyond the ten years' gap. He was a great deal stouter and there were white streaks in that vast black beard. But the eyes were the same, watchful, hard, and they looked me up and down in a way that brought the colour to my cheeks. 'You have grown into a right young lady,' he said.

I did not like this, though it was perfectly polite. When he came nearer me, I instinctively backed. I think he smiled. It was difficult to tell with all that beard but there was a brief flash of white teeth. 'You were a meddlesome lass,' he said, 'but I think I could deal better with you now. Are you courting, Miss Nanette?'

I answered haughtily that I was not, and the teeth gleamed again.

'If,' he said very softly, 'you wish to meddle again, you can always come to me. I am good at answering questions.' Then in the same quiet manner, 'What do you want to know, young lady? Tell me. There's no one to overhear. My lady is in the drawing room and the servants are abed. Old John is always at your service. Perhaps we could go somewhere quiet –'

I stared at him, a little afraid. The actual words were well enough, but the implication was clear. I suppose I thought myself to be a woman of the world, but I suddenly felt a child again, and seldom have I been more relieved than when Leonie came out of the dining room. She saw at once that something was amiss, but John-Gon without another word beckoned us to follow him up the stairs, opening the door of our room for us and instantly disappearing without so much as a goodnight.

Leonie demanded, 'What was he saying to you? You are quite pale.'

'Oh,' I said, 'I am simply tired to death. For God's sake let us get to bed.'

'Was he rude to you?'

'Of course not. He just reminded me of what a horrid little girl I was.'

We undressed. The room was even smaller than I

51

remembered and very cold. There was a small grate but no one had lit a fire. There was only one little cupboard for our clothes, and the dressing-table was bare except for the mirror. But the bed was warm and inviting with a comforting number of blankets, and we fell into it, reaching out our arms for each other, thankful to be together.

Leonie muttered into the pillow, 'Those aren't famous people!'

'Well, at least there is a poet.'

'Poet! Did you ever hear such stuff?'

'It was terrible,' I agreed, already half asleep.

'I don't think Aunt Elizabeth likes us very much.'

'I don't think Aunt Elizabeth likes anyone.'

'Tomorrow,' said Leonie in a sudden clear voice, 'I am going to look for French prisoners.'

'Go to sleep.'

'Do you think we'll be happy here, Nan? It's very strange.'

'Go to sleep!'

'And there's no sign of our cousin Virgil. I am so disappointed.'

'Oh Leo, will you go to sleep!'

'I haven't even seen Dolly Easey – oh, all right, Nan. Goodnight.'

We both fell asleep almost immediately. We both woke up at the same moment. There was nothing to hear except the incessant drumming of the sea, yet there must have been something: Leonie sat up in bed, and I rubbed my eyes, wondering what had disturbed us.

The room was pitch dark except for the small square of window. We could see the clouds racing across the moon. Leonie whispered, 'There was something – I want to look out. Oh come on, Nan. Let's open the window.'

God knows why I listened to her for it was the middle of the night and intensely cold, but we both crept out of bed in our night-gowns and stole furtively towards the window as if someone were watching us. I opened the latch and the

52

bitter night air streamed in, winding our hair round our faces. We could smell the salt of the sea. We leaned out, our arms round each other's waist.

It was so beautiful and so dramatic that, what with the piercing cold and the sight of it, we gasped. Now that our eyes were becoming accustomed to the dark we could see clearly the wild sea, its white horses galloping over the blackness, the remains of St. Saviour's church below and the marshes and dunes beyond. This was the back of Cudden Hall, and there was a steep path coiling like a snake, like the slipway where Tom's *Holy Margaret* slid on her smuggling way. The roar of the storm beat upon our ears, the booming of the waves was like a bell.

Leonie whispered, 'That must be one of the churches – oh Nan, look!'

There were men coming up the path. They were carrying what seemed to be an enormous crate, and it must have weighed a great deal for the men – there were three of them – paused from time to time as if to regain their breath. We thought that at the bottom of the path we could see a boat, but it was hard to make sure because of the mountainous waves. We watched in fascination, instinctively backing in case the men might look up and see the white of our nightgowns.

The church clock of St. Saviour's sounded three. It was a strange hour to be abroad, and on such a night.

Leonie whispered again, 'What do you think they're doing?'

'I don't know – perhaps they are bringing in supplies.'

'At three in the morning!'

I could not answer. It was plainly an absurd thing to say, and there was something unmistakably furtive about the men who were glancing around them and making as little noise as possible. I said in a gasp, 'I think we should not be watching this. I'm going to close the window.'

For once Leonie did not argue. I think she, too, was growing afraid. She moved back and I leaned out to pull the

53

window strut towards me. As I did so I saw two people by the side of the path engaged in earnest conversation. One was a young man whom I did not know, but the woman was unmistakably Amelia. I would have recognised that thin, shapeless figure anywhere, revealed as her cloak blew back in the wind. I was so astonished that for a second I simply stared. She seemed to be the last person in the world to hold a secret assignation, yet she was plainly on familiar terms with the young man and, even as I looked, laid a familiar hand on his arm. Then I knew I must not watch any longer and I shot back, pulling the window to but not fastening the latch in case the clicking sound aroused attention.

I said nothing about this to Leonie. We both crept back into bed. We were almost frozen with the cold and clung together, warming ourselves on each other: my teeth were positively chattering.

Leonie said, her breath tickling my ear, 'It's going to be very interesting here, Nan. I feel I am going to enjoy myself.'

This awoke me to my sisterly responsibilities. I said as firmly as I could, 'Now look, Leo. I don't know what all this is about, any more than you do, but I don't like the look of it, and I am sure we should not interfere –'

'You're one to talk!'

'I know. We are a couple of meddlers, but don't let us interest ourselves too much in other people's affairs. I think we might possibly interest ourselves into our graves.'

I might have known this was the infallible way of keeping Leonie's curiosity at fever-heat. If I had not been so tired I would have had more sense. But she simply yawned, said, 'Goodnight, Nan,' and rolled over with her back to me. From her deep steady breathing I knew she was instantly asleep.

I could not sleep for a long while. Leonie was perfectly right: I had no business to lecture her for something that was as much my failing as hers. We were after all both Maman's daughters, and Maman was always delighted by drama and filled with an inveterate curiosity. But I sensed the danger and I knew I was right not to like it. God knows what everyone was up to and how much my aunt was involved. It was hard to believe that such a dull person was mixed up in anything illegal, yet it was hardly normal to have men creeping in at three in the morning, my aunt must know about it, and so obviously did Amelia. I could not begin to understand any of it, and, for all I had just delivered such a sensible piece of advice to Leonie, I was filled with a passionate desire to know what it was all about.

My last waking thought was for no known reason of my cousin Virgil: I found myself sleepily wishing he were there, to explain everything to me. Then I too slept, to be wakened in the bright morning light by a bowl of sweet-smelling chocolate set on the table by my bed.

II

I looked up drowsily into the face of Dolly Easey.

My eyes were too blurred to take her in properly, but I recognised her well enough and I called her by name, crying out, 'Oh Dolly, how pleased I am to see you again. Don't say you have forgotten the horrid little girl who got everyone into so much trouble. I am Nanette, and this is my little sister, Leonie, who has been longing to meet you –'

Then, disappointed by the lack of response, I broke off and looked fully at her.

She was of course like ourselves ten years older. She would be twenty-five. She was no longer a young girl. She was still handsome only it seemed to me she was somehow full-blown: the delicate features had coarsened, the complexion was over-bright, and the mouth that had once smiled so sweetly drooped at the corners, as if in disillusionment and discontent. I had the odd impression that she was both angry and frightened, and my own face changed, I no longer knew what to say. Yet even as we looked at each other, something of the old Dolly returned.

She said in that rough country voice I remembered so well, 'Miss Nanette!' and caught my hand in both of hers, then turned to Leonie who, still half asleep, was smiling at her. 'So this is the little sister,' she said, then, 'I vow she's not as naughty as you were –'

'I'm worse,' said Leonie, and at that Dolly laughed, saying, 'It's not possible, young lady, no one could be that bad.'

'How are you, Dolly? Are you married with lots of lovely children?'

56

Her face changed again. I saw suddenly that there was no wedding ring on her finger. She said, 'Who'd wed the likes of me? There's enough of us at home, ain't there? I don't want no brats of my own.' Then she said more brightly, 'How long are you staying here, young ladies?'

I was surprised she did not know. The servants always know everything, and there must have been long chats below stairs about the two girls my lady had invited to live with her. I said, 'We have come to live here. Did you not hear that our parents were both killed? This is now our home. We have left London for good.'

She looked at me in silence for a moment. I saw the wary look in her eyes, and somehow it frightened me more than anything that had happened. She said, 'I'm sorry about your parents. But I don't know as how you could leave London.' There was a wistful note in her voice. 'Oh, it must be a grand city. They say the streets are paved with gold –'

'Dolly –'

'And all the fine ladies and gentlemen with their carriages and lovely clothes – I'll never go there, mind, but I dreams of it, I could work there in service to some noble family, and perhaps I'd see the King –' She broke off, with a sigh that half turned into a laugh. 'You'll be thinking me daft. But we all have our dreams.'

I had to remember the dreadful things Papa had once told me, of the silly country girls who came up to London and were met at the coaching inn by a kind lady who offered them employment and brought about their ruin. I felt rather sadly that Dolly, shrewd as she might be in most things, would succumb at once to such an invitation. But I only said, 'You might not like London as much as you think. I love it because I was born there, but you would find it dirty and noisy and smelly, and you would probably long to be back in Greymanswick.'

She did not answer this. Perhaps it was not worth her while. She knew as well as I did, that she would never leave her home, so her dream of golden streets and beautiful people was all she would ever have. She only said in a sharper voice than I had ever heard from her, 'You don't want to stay here. Greymanswick isn't for the likes of you. Why don't you go home?'

'But –'

'You must have friends or something. You're good-lookers, the pair of you.' The dark eyes fixed on me. 'You've become quite a lady, Miss Nanette.'

I said, trying to make her laugh, 'You should see me when I'm soaked to the skin and my hair is all down.'

But she ignored this. She turned towards the door. 'You could find yourself a beau,' she said, then, 'Why, you can read and write!' She opened the door as she spoke. 'Don't you stay here, young ladies. If I was you, I'd be on the stage tomorrow morning.'

The door shut behind her.

Leonie and I gazed at each other over our chocolate. Leonie – I could see she was completely restored and once more her cheeky, charming self – remarked brightly, 'This is such a welcoming place, Nan, isn't it? We are bound to be happy here. Everybody loves us and tells us to go away.' Then as I began to laugh she added, 'Somehow I don't think we're going. I think instead we'll take a little walk to the village and see what we can find out.'

We did not take that walk. We met our fellow guests at breakfast and found them more boring than ever. Even Jack Lescott disappointed me, for I had hoped he would provide my little sister with some amusement. He was a rather dull boy but at least he was young, and surely he would be instantly attracted by Leonie who is as pretty a girl as he was ever like to meet, almost as beautiful as Maman. Maman of course was ravishing, and Papa used to tell us that when he met her at a ball in Paris he fell so wildly in love with her that he never looked at another girl again. It was the kind of whirlwind romance my aunt wrote about, and I am sure that their marriage, despite the constant debts and occasional flaming quarrels, was entirely happy. I myself do not resemble Maman, indeed, when younger, I sometimes wept because I found myself so dull. Besides, I have too sharp a tongue, and the gentlemen are frightened of ladies with sharp tongues that they do not always control. In my heart I cannot believe I shall become an old maid, but then no female ever does, and unhappily the gentlemen who admire me are seldom of the kind I admire myself and, when they discover that I do not respond, they begin to confide in me, which is always ominous.

'You need someone to manage you,' Maman once said, and I was instantly offended, saying I would not be managed by anyone, I would rather be an old maid, after all.

But Leonie will never be an old maid, and I do not believe with her looks it will matter a ha'penny whether she has money or not. I was sure, therefore, there would be a little flirt between her and Jack Lescott: she would not be very impressed, but when one is fifteen one is not particular and it would provide distraction.

To my amazement he hardly looked at her. I could see that Leonie was a little piqued, and I myself was furious, almost as if I had been personally insulted. Then, when Dolly came in with a fresh jug of chocolate, I understood. She was at least seven years older than Jack, and she was an uneducated country girl, the daughter of Greymanswick's most notorious smuggler, but he was head over heels in love with her, so openly that we all had to notice: indeed, Mr. Pleydell, whom I was beginning to detest, openly sneered and put a hand to his mouth to conceal his amusement.

Dolly treated Jack as if he were a younger brother, but the poor lad could not keep his eyes off her, nor his hands either. When she poured out his chocolate, he had to hold her wrist to direct her, and when later they met in the hallway, he brushed against her, even giving her apron strings a little pull. Then he whispered something in her

59

ear, but she said quite loudly, 'Oh come on now, Sir, I have my work to do,' and patted his hand as if he were an importunate child.

I do not know what my aunt thought of this. She must have observed it, for she observed everything, and poor Jack made not the slightest pretence. When Dolly walked away from him, he stood there with so disappointed a look that I wanted to laugh. Then I felt sorry for him and he must have sensed this for he came up to me, saying, 'Is she not lovely? I think she is the most beautiful girl I have ever met.'

I said as gently as I could, 'She is a little old for you, Mr. Lescott. I think she must be twenty-five or more.'

He exclaimed, 'Oh, but that is unimportant. What has age to do with love? It would not matter to me if she was fifty.' Then, as if this reminded him of my existence, he said, 'You are very distinguished-looking. Has no one ever told you so? You have fine eyes. You must call me Jack. Have you never been in love? You have so composed an air that perhaps you have not. I think we should take a little walk in the garden. I find you a sympathetic listener. I daresay you have been told that before.'

In all this farrago he gave me no chance to utter one word and, before I realised what was happening, I found my arm being taken and myself escorted on to the lawn. Out of the corner of one of my fine eyes I saw Leonie winking at me – I really shall have to speak to her – but then she was annexed by Mr. Lowry who was as usual wandering around in a lost way, presumably brooding on his plundered home.

We strolled across the lawn to the little wall where a long time ago I had been captured by my cousin. It was plain that I was cast for the role of confidante, but as I was vastly curious about these ill-assorted guests I was not displeased: to pass the time I made a polite conversation about the weather which had grown calmer, and remarked on the strange light over the marshes.

It was not cold and we sat down on the wall, gazing out at

the sea. There was no sign of Tom or the *Holy Margaret*, and the only boats I could see down below were moored to the sea wall, with the men crouching beside them, mending their nets. It looked so peaceful that I had to wonder if the events of last night had some perfectly reasonable explanation.

Jack said, 'She is Tom Easey's daughter.'

I looked at him. He was not a bad-looking young man but it was a pity his mouth had so petulant an expression, and he wore a spoilt, weak look that aroused more pity than admiration. I answered that I knew this and told him that I had met her ten years ago, on my first visit to Cudden Hall.

He said a little doubtfully, 'Mrs. Cudden has been very kind to me. Of course you know she is a famous novelist – it is a great honour for me to be invited. I write poetry, of course.'

I said dutifully, 'I remember you recited some last night.'

'Oh,' he said, quite excited, 'did you like it? Oh please tell me you did.'

After this, of course, there was only one answer. I told him I liked it very much indeed, and only wished I had such a talent myself.

'I have never published, you know.'

'Oh well, Mr. Lescott –'

'Jack, if you please. And I shall call you Nanette because we are friends. Does that please you?'

I found this too disarming to resist and assured him I was delighted. I said, 'You are still very young, you know. There is plenty of time. I believe my aunt did not start writing until she was nearly thirty. Have you – have you enough material for a volume? Perhaps you could show it to Mr. Lowry. I am sure he would advise you.'

He said with a contempt that I did not care for, 'Oh, he would never understand. He is an antiquarian, you know. He writes little monographs on local history, so boring I always think. Besides, he is obsessed with that business of his house. I think myself it serves him right. He knows all about the Collector and yet he goes away and does not even leave a servant in charge. I think the Collector is romantic, do you not, Nanette?'

'No,' I said. 'I can see no romance in something that causes so much distress.'

'Ah,' he said triumphantly, 'but then you're a woman –'

'What has that to do with it?'

'Women always see things from a personal angle. Now I am interested in things as they are. I have a very inquiring mind. I am extremely observant.'

I was beginning to think he was extremely conceited, but I said nothing.

He continued, 'I find this place very strange, so much so that I have little time for writing. In fact, I sometimes think the Collector – but I am perhaps being indiscreet. Dolly always tells me I am too inquisitive.' He gave a little laugh. 'Is she not the dearest, most wonderful girl in the whole wide world, Nanette? I truly believe she is fond of me, only she has these strange ideas about class, so old-fashioned these days, I think.'

I did not know how to answer this. Jack Lescott, though weak and a little foolish, was plainly a gentleman and, apart from anything else, it would be unfortunate for a budding young poet to marry a girl who could neither read nor write. However, he did not wait for any comment, only repeated somewhat irrelevantly, 'I really am very observant.' Then he demanded, 'Have you ever heard strange noises in the night?'

I was very taken aback by this but I had no wish to make a confidante of him so I merely said, 'Sir, if you remember, we have only just arrived.'

He said, 'It happened again last night. It was by no means the first time, though I never saw Miss Amelia there before. Can you begin to understand why men should be carrying big crates into Cudden Hall at such an hour? But I daresay you were fatigued by your journey and fast asleep.

62

You had best forget what I've said. I would not wish to land you in any danger.'

It was plain that Jack was as indiscreet as he was inquisitive. His unexpected use of the word 'danger' aroused a faint alarm in me. It seemed to me that this silly young man was taking far too great a risk, for sometimes the observers are observed, and he was so full of himself that this would never enter his head. I still knew nothing of my aunt's household but I was beginning to be sure that it would be unwise to investigate too closely. However, I could think of nothing to say that would not offend him, besides I too was curious, so I remained silent, pulling at a clump of grass beside the wall and placing a blade of it between my lips.

He suddenly shot a question at me, like a prosecuting lawyer. 'Have you ever visited your aunt's rooms?'

'No. How could I? I told you, we've only been here a few hours.'

'She lives in the west wing. That is where she does her writing. She has three rooms. One of them is always kept locked.'

I found nothing strange in this. My aunt was after all not young, and the old tend to have a strong urge for privacy. No doubt there would be family documents perhaps jewellery and money. It seemed quite a normal thing to do. When this silly boy exclaimed, 'We are none of us allowed there, except for Mr. Pleydell and that Miss Amelia,' I tried to interrupt him, but he went on, 'Why does she want to talk to Miss Amelia? She is so dull. Do you not find her dull, Nanette? She has never once invited me, but I am determined to find out what she keeps hidden – what is the matter with you? Surely you are not going. I thought you would be interested.'

For I was now standing up, so cross with him and at the same time so frightened for him that I could not endure his company any longer. I said, 'We have no right to talk like this. It is none of our business –'

At this he jumped up too, glowering at me. Our moment

of friendship was done. He snapped at me, 'I do not require a lecture from you, Miss Nanette. I see you are as dull and conventional as all the rest. I of course am an artist and I have an inquiring mind. I thought you would sympathise. There is after all nothing more interesting than human nature. Why, all this might – might provide me with material for a new poem –'

At this I am afraid I began to laugh, and he flushed scarlet, saying in a choked voice, 'I am sorry to have incommoded you. As you say, I am very young. No doubt you are bored by silly boys. I will not trouble you with my foolish conversation again.'

And he stalked off back to the house, leaving me rather ashamed and causing some surprise to Leonie who had come out to see what I was doing. She looked at Jack's red, angry face as he brushed past her, then coming up to me demanded, 'What has happened now? You seem to be in trouble with all the gentlemen. First it's John-Gon and now poor Jack – what can you have said to him?'

'I'm afraid,' I said, 'our betrothal is off. We shall not be getting married after all. I shall return the ring tomorrow. But I believe it would never have worked for he, as he always tells me, is a young boy, and an old woman like myself would make him look ridiculous.'

'He looks ridiculous enough already,' said Leonie, 'only I had hoped he would make an honest woman of you. What will you do now? Perhaps you could set your sights on Mr. Pleydell.'

Then we both began to laugh, and I thought that my little sister was more entertaining company than all of the others put together. I said, 'I think we might take our little walk. What are all the guests doing?'

'Well,' said Leonie, 'they are playing with pistols.'

'What!'

'Aunt Elizabeth was terribly angry. Jack Lescott – oh, he is such a silly boy – found a cupboard full of them. Did he not mention this to you? It was just before he took you for that little walk.'

'No, he did not.'

'Perhaps he thought it wiser not.'

'If he thought it wiser, it must be dangerous indeed.'

'Anyway, he and Mr. Lowry started taking them all out, and my aunt saw them and shouted at them. I have never seen her so angry.' Her voice soared up in imitation. '"I will not have you touch these things. They are lethal weapons. You could kill someone!" And Mr. Lowry was very upset and dropped one on his foot. I suppose it might have gone off. And Mr. Pleydell said he did not like weapons, he did not know how to use them, he was the world's worst shot. And Aunt Elizabeth went on shouting, telling us to put everything back, and then she stalked up to her rooms. It was quite exciting. Perhaps she is writing about a duel. I wish,' said Leonie wistfully, 'someone would fight a duel over me.'

And she made as if she were saluting with her sword, but I chose to ignore this altogether. This was Maman's heritage. She told us once how a young man was killed, fighting a duel over her, and it was one of the rare occasions when Papa was really angry, so she never mentioned it again.

I only said, 'Surely they weren't loaded.'

'Apparently they were. They were piled in great heaps. Mr. Lowry and Mr. Pleydell are putting them back now. It's like an armoury.'

'I think this is lunatic. Fancy keeping a cupboard full of loaded weapons!'

We looked at each other. Leonie said pensively, 'The more I see of Cudden Hall, the stranger I find it.' Then she gave a little skip of excitement, for after all she was still a child, and squeezed my arm, saying, 'You haven't forgotten last night, have you? Oh come on, Nan, they are all busy with those horrid pistols. We'll go down to the village and call on that wicked Tom Easey. And then –'

A dry, clipped, Scots voice said, 'I think you two young ladies should come inside. I am sure you do not wish to

65

catch a cold on the first day of your arrival.'

It was Amelia. We both swung round. We were very annoyed and I suspect that for a second it showed in our faces. I managed to say quite calmly, 'It is not cold and we are starved for fresh air. We were going to take a little walk.'

'Then I will come with you,' said Amelia. It was as if she had planned to do this in the first place, for she had a shawl round her shoulders and a tartan scarf over her hair. I do not know anything about the Scottish tartans, but this was a bright check of red and green and blue. I thought she was the plainest female I had ever met. Some plain people can be amusing and charming, but she was neither. She was, I suppose, in her late twenties, but she wore the unmistakable look of the old maid: her clothes were what Maman would simply have dubbed as ter-r-rible, her hair was wispy and out of its pins, and her face had a curiously hungry air as if she longed for the men who must mostly avoid her. I still found it hard to believe in her assignation, yet as Jack Lescott had confirmed it was unmistakably Amelia whom I had seen. Then I suddenly knew beyond all doubt that she had been asked to keep an eye on us. My aunt, who was certainly the instigator, did not propose to encourage our little walks any more than she had done for a naughty little eight-year-old who was always exploring. I briefly met Leonie's eye. If Amelia believed us outwitted, she would soon find out her mistake. There would still be little walks and without Miss Amelia at our side.

But this morning we were plainly defeated so I said in a meek voice, 'Perhaps it is a little cold after all. And I am still fatigued from my journey. How is the sampler progressing, Ma'am?'

We walked back to the house. Leonie jabbed her elbow in my side. Her face was bland and innocent. I knew she was already hatching a plot. We saw that our duenna was surprised and disconcerted, but then she did not as yet know the Cudden girls. However, she answered us pleasantly enough, with some tedious account of how she

66

was running short of red silk, and we came into the Hall to be informed by a maidservant that my lady wished to see me in her rooms.

I was excited to receive this invitation for I was longing to see the place where my aunt produced her romances, and of course Jack Lescott, for all I had snubbed him, had aroused my curiosity. I walked up the big staircase, pausing for a second to look at the miniature of Queen Elizabeth who, two hundred years ago, had visited Cudden Hall with her entire entourage. It was Papa who told me about this. It was still referred to with something like horror. The Cudden family was always well-off but to have the Queen with perhaps fifty followers quartered on them must have stretched their resources to the utmost. I could imagine with some queasiness the slaughter in the kitchen of swans and geese and ducks and chickens. The servants must have worked knee-deep in blood. But doubtless the Cudden of the time somehow managed, perhaps after a visit to the Jews and the sale of some family jewellery. I could picture Her Majesty arriving in state while the Cuddens becked and bowed and smiled. Did she never realise the appalling burden she had laid upon their loyalty? I do not suppose it ever struck her and, after she had gone, the miniature was presented to the family in lieu of thanks. I gazed at it now, this lady encrusted in jewels, her red hair piled high and the beautiful alabaster hands folded in front of her. It was a more generous gift than she knew, it was priceless, it would never be sold.

And reflecting on this, I knocked on Aunt Elizabeth's door.

There was no answer. Perhaps she was involved in some mad murder. I knocked again, then a little apprehensively opened the door.

I stepped into what was obviously the living room. There was no one there. My feet made no sound on the deep-piled carpet. It was furnished luxuriously and without taste: like my aunt it was cold and withdrawn. There was a large portrait of my Uncle Constantine over the fireplace, and I wondered again how the two of them fared together, for he like my father was an emotional man with a deep well of love. By the window, tight shut against the sea wind, was a worktable: there was a stack of paper upon it, together with an ink-well and at least a dozen quill pens. I tried to picture my aunt scribbling away at rape and insanity and completely failed: I could never, however much I tried, blend her personality with the violence of her novels.

As there was still no sign of her I moved back to examine the bookcase that flanked one wall. I am always fascinated by books and I thought that here might lie the key to my aunt's strange character. As I did so, still moving without sound I saw that this room led into another: the door was wide and I stared through.

It was my aunt's bedroom. At the far end was yet another door, which perhaps led into the Bluebeard's room that had aroused Jack Lescott's curiosity. This bedroom was furnished as if it belonged to a courtesan: the big four-poster bed was upholstered in pink satin, there were cushions everywhere, heavy silk curtains and beaded lampshades. My bewildered eyes moved to the dressing-table and what I saw there so astonished me that I all but cried out.

My aunt was sitting there, on a satin-covered stool. Her back was towards me and fortunately the mirror into which she was gazing was not an angle to reflect me. John Gonomanaway stood behind her, combing her beautiful hair which lay on her shoulders. He was twining the locks round his fingers, delicately inserting a pin in the resulting curl. That piratical face which somehow radiated emotion through the beard that covered it seemed to express a savage boredom, yet there was an unmistakable intimacy to the pair of them and I knew they had been lovers for a long time. Appalled by the thought that I might be discovered I moved instantly away and almost ran to the outer door. I came out into the corridor and stood there, my heart

68

beating so violently that I was almost choked.

I suppose I was less shocked than many girls would have been. Maman talked freely of such things and from my earliest childhood I knew about ladies and their lovers. I believe my father did not approve of such freedom, but she was always enthralled by anything to do with love, and Leonie and I knew more about our friends' lives than they could ever have imagined. But I was only eighteen, an age when one tends to think that anyone over thirty is incapable of emotion, and my aunt seemed the least likely person in the world to take her butler as a lover: I was more shocked than I cared to admit, and a little revolted besides.

One thing was dreadfully plain: she must never know what I had seen. I stood there for a while until I was calmer, than I knocked again, very loudly indeed. After the third knock the door opened: I was still so nervous that I jumped when John-Gon appeared. However, I managed to tell him that my aunt was expecting me, and thought he would stand aside so that I could enter. But instead he came out on to the landing, so close that he brushed against me.

He said in his burring voice, 'What a hard-hearted lass you are. How about a kiss for old John? It'll not hurt you.'

I might well have been afraid for he was a powerful man, and I knew enough of the world to see that my aunt, if she witnessed this, would never forgive me, though it was in no way my fault. But instead I was furious, and the temper that Maman always said would be my undoing, spilled over. I hissed at him, like any ingenue in a melodrama, and when he moved his great hands to enfold me, delivered a slap on the cheek that nearly sent him backwards in sheer surprise. 'How dare you!' I said, and I think my fury was partly due to the thought that he could make love to my aunt one minute, then immediately after try to kiss me.

He too knew that if my aunt found out, he would be sunk for good and all. He did not say a word, but the rage blazed from him. It was the second time he had been frustrated. The first time hardly mattered, but the slap was something

69

he could not ignore. I knew I had made an enemy for life. But he stood aside in a heavy breathing silence, and my aunt emerged as I came into the room. I was terrified she would notice how I was shaking, but she seemed unaware of it and motioned me to a chair as John shut the door behind him.

She looked me up and down, almost as if I were a stranger. I had discarded my mourning and wore a soft grey gown. It was pretty, for Maman had chosen it – 'we'll make you a little Puritan,' she said – but it was plain for I had cut away the ribbons, thinking them too frivolous in the circumstances. There was nothing that could be disapproved of, even in a poor relation, yet my aunt continued to regard me in what seemed a condemning manner.

She said suddenly, 'Your sister greatly resembles her mother.'

I found my temper surging: it was still turbulent after my encounter. But I clenched my hands and answered quietly enough, 'Yes, Ma'am. I think she is a very pretty girl.'

'She is a very pert one.'

I found this grossly unfair for she had scarcely spoken to Leonie at all. But I only said, 'I am sure she does not mean to be. She is after all young and high-spirited. It is perfectly natural.'

'Charles,' said my aunt, 'was always too soft. You must instruct her, Nanette. I will not tolerate ill-breeding.'

I could hardly contain myself. I wanted to shout, You talk of ill-breeding, who have taken your butler as a lover! I looked at that strange, expressionless slab of a face that seemed incapable of tenderness, much less of inspiring it, and my eyes moved to the soft, beautiful hair that curled over her ears. Then I suddenly remembered. *Who taught you how to make ringlets?* A disgraced little girl staring up at this strange, bearded man who had done up her buttons and was now brushing her wet and tangled hair. I remembered the reply too: *You ask too many questions.* So John-Gon and my aunt had been lovers while Uncle Constantine

70

was still alive –

And this was the lady who despised and disapproved of my pretty French mother – Maman loved my father with all her heart: for all she flirted with any man within reach, I would be willing to swear she was never once unfaithful to him. I almost choked with my anger, yet I knew I must not put it into words. I was living here, I was not simply a guest, I could not quarrel with someone who was supporting me. So I said nothing, only my heightened colour must have betrayed me, for she said more amiably, 'I hope you will both be happy here.' The light eyes moved over me. 'You have, I must admit, a certain distinction. You were a plain, ill-mannered child. I would not believe you would be so changed. Do you have a lover?'

I could hardly believe my ears. I was mortified by my own ingenuousness but I exclaimed, 'Ma'am!' in such vehement protest that a faint smile twitched my aunt's lips.

She said, 'Is that so extraordinary a question? You are young and attractive. What do you propose to do with your life? Surely you do not just wish to marry and have children. I cannot imagine a prospect more boring.'

I said in a stifled voice – I could hardly believe this conversation was taking place – 'It is what most women want.'

She said, 'I do not believe you are "most women" any more than myself. I know that in our age women are there to breed like prize cows, but I would have thought you more ambitious. Are you interested in politics, Nanette?'

'No, Ma'am.'

'But surely you desire power?'

I said as steadily as I could, 'Power, Ma'am? I do not understand you.'

'Oh,' she said impatiently, 'why do you speak like that? You don't look stupid. Power! It is the only thing worth having. It is more valuable than money, though it is true the two are linked. Do you know the woman I admire most in the world? She is long since dead, but I do not believe there has ever been another like her.' And she went on before I

71

could reply, though indeed I could think of nothing to say, being torn between bewilderment and fascination, 'Queen Elizabeth! She visited here once. I only wish I had been there to see. She played with men and with kings and she held this country in the palm of her hand. She never married. Why should she? It would have taken her power from her. And you want a husband and babies – I cannot believe it of you. I cannot!'

I still did not answer, this time because I could not. I was afraid. I gazed at my aunt and saw that even now her countenance had scarcely changed, except for the eyes which were blazing with some inner excitement. I think that I saw dimly that John-Gon was part of the power she lusted for, and that whatever was going on in this strange household was created by her, to satisfy her craving for domination. But I remained silent, and the sight of me sitting there in my meek grey gown, my face no doubt stupid with shock, infuriated her so that she became once more the person I believed I knew.

She said in the flat, harsh voice I detested, 'You obviously do not understand one word of what I've been saying. You realise of course that you are not here to play the fine lady. You are expected to perform certain duties, and I trust you recognise this as reasonable, you are after all living here as one of the family. A domestic young lady such as yourself, with no ambition, should be delighted.'

I remained silent. I saw that this was my punishment for not responding. For the first time I found a certain sardonic humour in the situation, so I simply waited to learn what it was I was expected to do.

She was a little disconcerted by this. I suppose she expected me to exclaim in outrage. She said, 'for one thing, I intend to leave the cleaning of my personal silver in your hands, while your sister can see to the arrangement of flowers throughout the Hall. When we have guests it will be the business of both of you to look after them. Naturally you are a good sempstress –'

72

'No, Ma'am.'

'What!' She was making fun of me. She did it rather badly, with the spite glistening through. 'I would have thought that so ladylike a young lady would sew her samplers all day long. Do you know nothing of dressmaking?'

'No, Ma'am,' I said, and suddenly wanted to laugh, for it was only too true: neither of us had ever put thread in needle. When our clothes became worn Maman simply bought us new ones; she did not of course pay for them but that was no concern of ours.

Aunt Elizabeth must have sensed my amusement. This was something she could not take, for she was totally devoid of humour, and she said quite sulkily, 'What can you do? Can you cook?'

'No, Ma'am!'

'I suppose your sister is the same.'

'Yes, Ma'am.'

'What a useless couple you are. You will certainly never find the husband you seem to be longing for.'

I said as gravely as I could, 'I do play the piano, and I sing a little. I believe I have a reasonable voice.'

Then I immediately wished I had not spoken, for I had seen the grand piano in the drawing-room, and this might provoke interminable evenings with myself performing and the guests all bored to death.

Fortunately my aunt did not seem impressed by this artistic accomplishment. She probably found the prospect of little recitals as alarming as I did: she did not look like someone who loved music. She dismissed my singing and leaned forward, her hands clasped together. She said, 'Eventually I intend that you and your sister take over the running of this house. Such things bore me, besides, I am entirely occupied with my writing. As you seem to know nothing of domestic things, I shall ask Cook to instruct you. This will involve cooking lessons, the planning of meals and so on. The household linen will be entirely your charge and, when you are better instructed, the servants

73

also, the dismissing of them, the engaging of new ones. I cannot endure the slightest dishonesty or disloyalty –'

This was too much for me. I forgot all Maman's warnings. I said, 'I am not likely to steal the silver, Ma'am.'

She was disconcerted by this. She stared at me then said sharply, 'I never suggested you would. I am merely saying that I expect the servants to do precisely what I tell them: if not, they go instanter.' Then she said, 'I do not regard you and your sister as servants.'

I could have said a dozen things to this, and all of them unpardonable. So once more I remained silent, and I was beginning to learn that silence was something my aunt could not endure, for her next words came out awkwardly as if she were embarrassed. She said, 'You will always dine with us, of course. We do not lead the social life you are no doubt accustomed to, but I am well-known in literary circles, and the friends who come here all have artistic leanings. I am sure you will profit by their acquaintance.'

I thought of last night's dreary dinner and looked down.

She rose to her feet. I saw that she wore a very tight corset that made her bosom shoot up from her gown. There was a decanter and glasses on the side-table but she did not offer me a glass of wine. I might not be a servant but I was a poor relation, and probably poor relations should not expect such courtesy. She said, 'I think that is all, Nanette. I am glad we have had this little talk. If there is anything you want, you can always ask John-Gon, and I am sure Amelia will be delighted to help and advise you. She is an old friend of mine and a most intelligent young woman as you have no doubt already perceived. I have every trust in her, and I hope you will have the same. She comes from Edinburgh, you know. Do you know Scotland?'

'No, Ma'am.'

'You do not seem to know very much! You will of course tell Leonie everything I have said to you. I imagine you will both be pleased to have work to do. I myself work my fingers to the bone. I could not visualise a life of idleness.'

74

She moved back in the direction of the table by the window. She remarked, as I rose to my feet and prepared to leave, 'Your cousin Virgil will be arriving shortly. I suppose you do not remember him.'

'I remember him very well, Ma'am.'

'He lives in London. Sometimes I fear he leads a dissolute life, but then I do not approve of young men living in such a big city, it provides too many temptations.' She added, 'He comes up here regularly. I leave all my business affairs in his hands. We have a great deal to discuss.'

I thought Virgil was now old enough to look after himself, and the boy I remembered did not seem to be the type to handle business affairs, but I made no comment. I longed passionately to ask if he was married, but dared not: however, I was so convinced he must be that I could see the children trailing after him.

My aunt picked up a quill from her desk and moved the pile of papers in front of her. She said, 'One of your first duties will be to prepare his rooms. You and your sister can start today. He always has the suite on the first floor. John-Gon or Dolly will show you where it is and tell you what is needed.'

A suite, indeed! So he must be married. I thought indignantly of the little room allotted to Leonie and myself. However, this was no way for a housekeeper to talk, so I assured my aunt I would do my best, and went away to find Leonie.

As I came down the stairs I almost knocked Jack Lescott down. He looked so guilty that I at once knew he was up to his spying. I was prepared, however, to pass him in silence, only he followed me down and, when we were in the hall said to me in a kind of smug whisper, 'I am right as you will see. I have been investigating. That third room is a most curious affair.'

My mind was too full of the conversation with my aunt for me to listen to this silly boy. I said without interest, 'Why is it a curious affair?'

75

'It stretches along the whole side of the house.'

This did arouse a faint curiosity. We were standing there, whispering, which I felt was unseemly, but I could not stop myself from asking, 'How on earth do you know that?'

He gave me such a self-satisfied smile that I could almost have slapped him as I did John-Gon. The Jack Lescotts of this world are intelligent enough to want to know but they have no idea where to stop: they are driven beyond all sense by their curiosity. I knew now that this was no place for such investigations, and the extraordinary things my aunt had said to me only confirmed this. The word 'power' had been thrown at me and I felt that all this spying and prying would give this foolish and unattractive young man a sense of his own importance. Of course I should have warned him, but then he would not have listened: people of his sort never do listen for they are always sure they know better than everyone else.

He said, 'Oh, I am not telling you. I don't trust you. Women are all untrustworthy, they blab to anyone. But I will tell you just one thing, Miss Nanette. I have done some measuring, never mind how. You would not understand anyway. But I now know the length of the room and it's six times the size of any other. Do you not find that odd?' Then he said very quickly, still whispering in a fashion that carried better than a normal tone of voice, 'It's dangerous too. But I am going to arm myself –'

'You are going to what!'

'Do not raise your voice, please. Do you want to ruin me? Of course I am. I'm not a fool. And I have discovered a vast store of weapons, which makes it all even more interesting. I am going to select a pistol and pocket it. No one is going to take me at a disadvantage.'

I remembered what Leonie had told me, and suddenly I was frightened to the point of hysteria, though I would have found it hard to explain why. My voice shivered up. I knew I had no right to lecture him. It was the kind of thing

76

that made Maman cross with me. 'The gentlemen do not like it,' she told me. 'Indeed, they resent it. If you have a fault, mignonne, it is that you like to manage people. You must stop this immediately. It is a most disagreeable trait. There are of course ways of managing men but never by telling them what or what not to do.'

She was perfectly right but I was too distraught to obey: the thought of this idiot boy running around with a pistol in his pocket was too much for me.

I cried out, 'You must do nothing of the kind. I – I forbid it. You are lunatic. You'll probably end by shooting some innocent person.'

He went white with rage, for which I could hardly blame him. He forgot about lowering his voice and shouted back, 'How dare you speak to me like that! You're nobody, you're just a poor relation that Mrs. Cudden has taken in out of charity. If I had my way you'd be back to London tomorrow –'

He broke off, the colour flooding back into his face. He had just seen Leonie who was standing at the top of the kitchen stairs. I, too, was unaware of her presence but realised she must have overheard a great deal of the conversation. He muttered something to himself then without another word made for the drawing-room. We heard him slam the door.

Leonie and I looked at each other. She said thoughtfully, 'I see what you mean about the betrothal. I really don't think you'll suit, Nan, I cannot see any real prospect of future happiness.'

Then we both began to laugh, myself a little hysterically. The other guests, if they heard us, must think us a couple of giggling schoolgirls. I took her arm and led her back into the garden: it was the one safe and private place and I wished to repeat what my aunt had said to me.

As we wandered across the lawn I said, 'How much did you hear of all that?'

'Not very much. Something about a room being six

times the size of the others –'

'Oh no! Was anyone else there?'

'I don't think so. John-Gon came up the stairs to go to my aunt's rooms. Why? Is it so important? I heard you, of course. You were shouting. About his shooting some innocent person. What has he done? He hasn't taken one of those pistols, has he?'

'That is precisely what he is going to do.'

She gazed at me, wide-eyed. She said at last, 'Aunt Elizabeth will be furious.'

I could only hope this was all that would happen. However, I had no wish to alarm her so I changed the subject to tell her about my visit to the west wing. I did not dwell on my aunt's craving for power but I informed her that our cousin Virgil was coming to stay and that we had been appointed the new domestics. I was happy that she found this amusing, and indeed, the thought of us dancing about in pretty aprons, cleaning silver and arranging flowers, was not lacking in humour, especially as Leonie was the least domestic person in the world and quite incapable of putting a rose in a vase right end up.

We were so entertained that we smiled at each other throughout a stuffy luncheon, during which Jack sulked at one end of the table and Amelia, deprived of her walk with us, looked depressed at the other. My aunt as usual made no attempt to conduct the conversation, Mr. Pleydell watched us all in his silent and sneering way, and such talk as there was, was mainly between me and Mr. Lowry. I heard that the Collector had made another foray but not such an interesting one this time: he and his band had been disturbed by a casual visitor and had escaped through the kitchen, taking with them little more than a few ornaments from the drawing-room.

'Did anyone see them?' I asked.

'No,' returned Mr. Lowry, 'They always wear masks, and they ran so fast that the only thing to be seen was their heels.'

78

Then, poor gentleman, he sighed and looked melancholy, still brooding on the house that was still not entirely put in order. But with the dessert he cheered up and told me a good deal of local information about our district, mentioning things that I stored in my memory for future walks.

'Beyond Cuckold's Point,' he said, 'lie the sandy dunes. Do you know Cuckold's Point, Miss Nanette?'

'No. It is a strange name.'

'Oh,' he said, with a little smile at his wife who had certainly never deceived him, 'cuckoldry is nothing new. Perhaps a sailor's wife betrayed him with a handsome Spaniard or something of the kind. It is a tavern, not for nice young ladies such as yourself. It is at the foot of the marshes and beyond it lie the dunes that once held the northernmost point of Greymanswick. They form a lonely and desolate place but what is interesting is that they were once, before the sea washed over them, a forest. You will still find tree-trunks half petrified, and there are caves filled with ferns that somehow survived the great storm of 1323. It is all most wild and beautiful, though not,' he added hastily, 'for young ladies to walk in, even in daylight.'

I am afraid Leonie was bored by this conversation, but I was fascinated. The swallowing up of the city of Greymanswick never failed to excite me, it made me think of that other city that had been destroyed, which Papa said was called Atlantis. I said, perhaps dimly remembering an inquisitive little girl of eight years old, 'I daresay the smugglers make use of these sandy dunes.'

Here Mr. Pleydell suddenly interrupted. I thought he was a most unpleasant man and, though he was the editor of a newspaper, he normally had little to say for himself. He now repeated my word 'smugglers' in a derisive voice, then broke into a loud laugh that turned everyone's head towards him. He said, 'Do you talk of smugglers? My dear Miss Nanette, this is 1744, not the dark ages. We do not have smugglers any more. Oh, I daresay there's the odd lad who brings in something he should not, and of course our

Tom Easey –' here he laughed again. '– is a trifle, shall we say, light-fingered, but the grand smuggling days are done, my dear young lady, never, we hope, to be recalled.'

I detest being called a dear young lady, which does not describe me at all, and I did not believe one word of this, nor from his expression did Mr. Lowry, though he said nothing. I was sure that smuggling was rife as it was ten years ago: Tom Easey was hardly the type to settle down, and the *Holy Margaret* still went out at night. I had to wonder why Mr. Pleydell uttered such foolish lies, and I determined to see these fascinating dunes. Leonie and I would take that little walk at the first opportunity, and what is more, Miss Amelia would not be with us.

After our meal we meekly set to work, going to the rooms that were to be given to our cousin. Dolly, who found this as amusing as we did, provided us with bed linen and brooms and dusters, and watched, giggling a little, from the doorway as we began our duties. I may say that we had a marvellous time. Leonie insisted on wrapping herself around in a large apron and screwed her hair up on top of her head. We started with the bed, having never made one before, and tossed the sheets high in the air as Leonie took one corner and I the other. It was a miracle that the finished bed looked presentable: we gazed at it with quiet pride and Dolly, who had returned to see how we were getting on, roared with laughter at us and insisted on our eating a handful of cakes she had brought up from the kitchen. 'I have never seen the like,' she said and flung herself down on the bed: we shouted at her to get up immediately, and I do truly think that such a performance had never been seen, even on the boards of Drury Lane. I believe any audience would have given us a standing ovation.

Then we had to sweep up the cake crumbs and Dolly brought in a great bunch of roses which I arranged myself. It was a task I enjoyed and Leonie would have made a great mess of it. The room, when we had at last finished, looked, we thought, very fine, and we hoped Dolly would return to

80

compliment us.

'I only hope,' said Leonie severely, 'our cousin appreciates what we have done for him.' She looked at the large double bed with its silken canopy. 'What do you suppose his wife is like?'

'Well,' I said, 'I do not know if he is married or not, but I think he must be to have two rooms at his disposal. We should do the other room now, Leo. Oh, I expect she is beautiful and very rich. She will probably be too proud to speak to us.'

We discussed her in this foolish fashion for a couple of minutes, then went into the second room, which was smaller but still bigger than ours. It was all very handsome and it made me feel a little resentful that we were not allowed anything so good. By the time we had finished we were both exhausted, and the amusement of being maid-servants had long since gone. When the door opened and I saw John-Gon standing there, I had no energy to put on any kind of act: I suspected he was there hoping to report us for not doing our work properly, and I returned his coldly appraising look with one of equal hostility.

He did not say a word, but his eyes roamed over everything, searching out the forgotten speck of dust or water spilt from the vase of flowers. Leonie, knowing nothing of what had happened, greeted him in her usual friendly way, but I was startled by the anger and resentment that radiated from him. I knew he would never forgive me for slapping him, but I had not realised how implacable an enemy he would be: he was always a quiet man and I had never so far seen him show any emotion. I almost believed he would murder me if he had the opportunity. I saw then that he was a savagely proud man and grew dimly aware of how mortifying his life must be, playing the lover to a plain, old woman who would always treat him like a servant except when he was in her bed. What in God's name could have made him accept such a situation? But it was not my fault and he had no right to try to kiss me, so I remained silent,

81

praying he would not see how he was frightening me, and suddenly he turned and left, the door still open behind him.

Leonie said in astonishment, 'He seems so angry with us. What can we have done?'

'Oh,' I answered indifferently, 'he is a moody kind of man, and I daresay he hoped to find us sitting around, doing no work. Let's go to our room. There is nothing more to do here.'

We were glad to sit down on our bed and presently Dolly came in to bring us a glass of wine.

I asked her as she was about to go, 'What do you think of Mr. Jack Lescott, Dolly?'

She looked at me with a mixture of amusement and scorn. She knew of course that I knew. Dolly might be unable to read or write, but there was nothing wrong with her brain. She turned up her eyes and stuck her arms akimbo. Despite the blowsiness she really was most handsome. 'Him!' she said in her burring voice. 'He's just a babe in arms. Trying to bed me down too – why, I'd roll on him and he'd be stifled, poor little bastard.'

'Dolly!' I said, shocked, but Leonie was laughing so I had to laugh too. I said at last, 'He loves you very much, Dolly.'

'He looks on me as his mammy,' she said with a shrug. 'He'd do better with Miss Leonie here, that he would.'

'Thank you very much!' said Leonie.

'Dolly,' I said, 'what do you know of Cuckold's Point?'

She turned her fine eyes on me. They had lashes any grand lady would have given her own eyes for: no wonder poor Jack had drowned in them. She said roughly, 'It's no place for the likes of you.'

'But there are wonderful sand dunes beyond it and Mr. Lowry says there are the remains of a forest. When we have a free afternoon, we are going to take a look at it.'

'You don't do nothing of the kind,' said Dolly fiercely. 'Now, you just listen to me, Miss Nanette. You was always an interfering little child, even when you was so-high, but you're older now, you ought to have more sense. Cuckold's Point is a bad place, so are the dunes. If you want to walk, there's the pretty garden or you can go down to the sea wall, but if I catch you on those dunes, I'll give you a good hiding, so I will. And I mean it!' said Dolly with the utmost ferocity, then, 'Are you listening to me, Miss Nanette?'

'Yes, Ma'am,' I said.

She raised her hand as if to box my ears, then flounced out of the room.

Leonie and I did not look at each other, nor did we say a word, even later on when we were changing for dinner. But it never pays to underrate people or their curiosity: to anyone who knew us it was evident that come death or damnation or another high tide, the two Cudden girls would be making for Cuckold's Point at the earliest opportunity.

III

For the next three days we were so busy that there was no question of going anywhere. My aunt plainly intended to keep us occupied. I found it a little ironic that she worked us half to death yet insisted that we were members of the family who must dine with the guests and talk with them throughout the evening: by ten o'clock we were so sleepy that all we longed for was our bed.

'It'll not go on like this,' Dolly told us. She was genuinely distressed by the work hurled at us. I think it offended her notion of decorum. Dolly, for all she was so independent, believed firmly in the ruling classes, and to her it was not right that Uncle Constantine's nieces should work as servants. Indeed, she took as much off us as she could. The silver left out for us was miraculously clean when we looked at it, the dusting of my cousin's rooms was done before we arrived, and, in the kitchen, Cook, who was the widow of an Aldeburgh seaman, insisted on making the sauces that should have been left to us and, even when she instructed us, provided us with every kind of delicacy, so that we happily nibbled away, secretly suspecting that the guests never had anything so delicious.

We were in any case young and strong, and we still managed to get enough fun out of it to prevent our feeling depressed. I even managed to spend a happy, undomestic afternoon in the library, and once Leonie and I scrambled down the hillside below the Hall, to take a look at St. Saviour's church.

The Hall had escaped by only a few hundred yards. The sea had swept across the church, taking most of it back into

84

the waves: the living part had gone, leaving nothing but the four walls and battered remnants of pews and pulpit, but amidst the thickets of briar and blackthorn the dead had miraculously survived. The stones still stood, only a few of the coffins were revealed, and we could see that Cuddens shouldered Easeys in classless death. This was where Uncle Constantine had chosen to be buried, and his memorial stone stood clean and new and white: I looked at this, then Leonie called me over to see where Dolly's forbear lay.

'Here Thomas Easey inclosed is in Claie,
Which is the meeting place of Flesh until the latter Day.'

The date was fifteen hundred and something, we could not read the last two figures. It was strange to see it and then look down to the sea wall where our Tom Easey was mending his boat.

But mostly we worked, and it was not until the third day that we threw down our brooms and cloths and pans, and decided to take a walk to the sea wall.

We had still not discussed the question of Cuckold's Point and the dunes, but then Leonie and I knew each other too well for discussion to be necessary. When we saw Amelia come out into the hall, plainly prepared to accompany us, we said nothing, simply glanced at each other. We already had our little plans and if this silly young woman with her sampler believed she could outwit us, she would soon learn her mistake. It made no difference if she insisted on coming with us to the sea-wall, and I smiled politely as she joined us, wrapped around in a tartan shawl, looking determined, if a trifle nervous.

'I need a little fresh air,' she told us 'a wee dander will do me good.'

I was by no means sure it would, for I could see that Leonie was on the war-path, but I made no demur, and we set out briskly for our destination, which was barely quarter of a mile away.

It was plain that she was ill at ease. As we walked she

talked interminably in that high Scots voice of hers, her head turning from one to the other. She spoke of Edinburgh, a city we did not know, told us the shawl was her family tartan, the name of which I have now forgotten, and said it was a pity that we had never visited the Highlands.

Then she came to what was evidently in her mind.

'I see,' she said, 'that Master Virgil has not yet arrived. I believe he simply turns up when he chooses, without so much as a word of warning. A little uncivil to your poor aunt, but then young men are so thoughtless, are they not?'

We agreed that they were, and suddenly Leonie demanded, 'Do you have a beau, Miss Amelia?'

From what I had seen that first night, it seemed that she had, though I still found it hard to believe: I had seldom seen someone so devoid of attraction. However, she flushed up, shooting a defiant look at this young girl who was so much prettier than herself. She said coldly that she had had her offers, but really, the gentlemen were so boring and demanding, and she much preferred to be on her own.

'But of course,' said Leonie in the prattling voice that showed she was out for mischief, 'you must be head over heels in love with our cousin.'

This time Amelia went a deep scarlet, and I suddenly realised that this might be true. I began to feel sorry for her, and longed to check my naughty little sister, but could think of no way of doing so.

'So sad that he's married,' said Leonie.

'He is not married,' said Amelia. Her voice was stiff and tight, her face now averted from us.

'Oh?' Leonie turned to smile at me. 'Do you hear that, Nan? We were so certain he must be. After all, he is quite old, he must be at least twenty-five.'

I managed to pinch her arm, but she ignored this, continuing in the same light, artless voice. 'I expect,' she said, 'he's madly in love with you, Miss Amelia, and that is why he is still single. I do hope you're kind to him. I suspect you're a naughty flirt who likes to make the poor fellow miserable.'

All this was utterly ridiculous, and I promised myself to give my sister a fine scold as soon as possible, but by this time poor Amelia was so confused that I imagine all she wanted was to run back to Edinburgh which, as I had learnt, was her home. However, she mumbled something about not being in the least interested in our cousin, and really, she had better things to do with her time than flirt with wild young men: Leonie at once seized on this.

We were almost at the sea wall. There I saw Tom Easey, tinkering away at the *Holy Margaret*. The name was very bright as if he had freshly painted it. It was the first time I had seen him close to since our meeting ten years ago. He had not worn well. He looked much older than I would have expected, and the face that had smiled at me so pleasantly was thin and lined and suspicious: he no longer wore the air of one who was kind to little girls but from his whole attitude seemed on the defensive. I would not have liked to come up unexpectedly behind him: I believe there would have been a knife in his hands. However, though he must have heard our coming, he did not turn round but went on with whatever he was doing: at his side was another man who had lost his arm and had protruding from his jersey a hook which he managed with an extraordinary adroitness, even picking up a coil of rope.

'Is Virgil wild?' Leonie was asking.

'I have no idea,' answered Amelia, wrapping her shawl more tightly round her.

'But you said –'

'Oh,' she cried in a sudden spittle of temper, 'how you do go on about young men. Have you nothing better to think of?'

'No!' said Leonie with her most wicked and entrancing smile.

Amelia's face changed. She was by no means stupid and she knew perfectly well she was being ribbed. She said in a quieter voice, 'I find you a remarkably silly girl.'

87

Leonie simply continued to smile, and then the poor young woman must have realised that if she were to continue accompanying us on our walks, she must remain on good terms with us. She broke into a rather dreadful little laugh, saying, 'But of course you are very young. You will change in good time. Will she not, Miss Nanette? But I must warn you, it is no good setting your sights on Virgil. He has, so they say, a young lady in London, besides, he would simply regard you as a little girl. It is true that he has a bad reputation, and I am afraid they say that none of the village girls are safe from him. It is all very sad and disgraceful, and you would both do well to keep out of his way.'

'He sounds delicious,' sighed Leonie, closing her eyes as if in ecstasy.

At this point I think Amelia felt she could endure no more. Besides, we could hardly get up to mischief by the sea wall. She shivered in a dramatic way, saying pettishly, 'It's too cold for me. I am going back.' Her eyes moved over Leonie's smiling face. 'Surely you have work to do? I understood that –'

'This is our little holiday,' said Leonie. She moved over to join me as I approached Tom Easey and the *Holy Margaret*. 'Goodbye, Miss Amelia. We will meet tonight at dinner.' –

We watched her walking back to Cudden Hall. She moved in a gawky, ungainly fashion, almost like an old woman. From what I remembered of our cousin Virgil, even if he were not so bad as she painted him, she would not be at all his kind.

I said to Leonie, 'You were very cruel. You did not have to be so unkind.'

Leonie only said, 'She did not have to come with us, but,' she added, 'she will not be there when we go to the dunes. I have already made a plan. I'll tell you about it later.'

It struck me that Leonie was growing more like Maman every day. I myself am sometimes sentimental, but Maman was not: she too would have had no pity for so dull and obstructive a female. I loved my little sister with all my heart, but I had to see that first she was growing up fast and secondly that the gentlemen were going to have a rough ride with her. And even as I thought this she bestowed her loveliest smile on Tom Easey who, now that he could no longer pretend to ignore us, was standing there surveying us.

She suddenly broke into song. It was a local ditty I had never heard: I daresay she picked it up from one of the boys who delivered our food. She sang:

> *'The French are comin',*
> *Oh dear, oh dear!*
> *They're all owd women,*
> *So we don't keer!'*

Tom gave a grunt of a laugh. His eyes moved up and down Leonie then, as if he realised she was too young for him, to me. I did not like that look. I had heard a great deal of him in the kitchen, when Dolly was not there, and nothing to his advantage. There was a new woman every few months or so, and sometimes a new baby too. The little cottage must be bursting at its seams. All his women, Cook told me, were whores, but that did not excuse his treatment of them, for it was said that when the drink was in him, he beat them unmercifully, and his children too. There was a tale of one girl who never recovered, but it was hushed up and perhaps it was not true. I could see well enough that this time there would be no invitation to the cottage and, if I went unasked, I would deserve what I got, and I would get a great deal. How he behaved on his smuggling voyages I did not know, but one would need to be tough to survive, and I should imagine the Preventives avoided him as much as they dared. I almost wished we had not come. He would know of course who we were, though I doubt if he would have recognised me at a casual meeting. His eyes now unmistakably undressed me, and to my humiliation I found myself moving back, the colour coming to my cheeks.

Leonie, however, was unafraid, but then Leonie was afraid of no one. She said in a guileless way, 'Of course, you are Tom Easey. I have heard so much of you. Do tell me, Tom, what you think of the Collector. I gather he's on the warpath again. Do you have any idea who he is?'

I could have shaken her for being so foolish. I saw Tom stiffen, and the man with the hook gave us an ugly, suspicious look. Tom said after a pause, 'I don't know nothing of the Collector. Why would I? He's nowt to do with me. I'm only a poor fisherman, I don't mix with the gentry like he does. You don't want to listen to all that silly talk, it only comes from people who've nothing else to do with their time.' Then he broke off, as if he had said too much, and his eyes moved over me again. He said, almost grudgingly, 'You've grown a great deal. But then you was only a baby. It's a long time, Miss Nanette.'

'It's a long time, Tom.'

He said, 'This is Hookey Miller,' and the one-armed man waved his hook at me. It made me shudder a little, it must be a wicked weapon with the force of a man's arm behind it. Tom said to him with a smile that was not a smile at all, 'She was a right little madam, she was. Wanting to know everything, firing off questions like a cannon, couldn't keep her nose out of everyone's business. Why, they say she couldn't be left on her own for five minutes without her wandering off to see what she could see.'

Hookey remarked, 'They say there's women like that.'

'Not with me they aren't,' said Tom a little grimly, then to me again, 'Are you still that inquisitive, Miss?'

'I'm ten years older, Tom.' And, though a second later I was furious with myself for such a betrayal, I could not prevent my eyes moving to the marshes and the dunes beyond. I do not know if he noticed. I imagine those sharp eyes noticed everything. I could only hope that Dolly had not told him of our conversation. It was a mild day, for all Amelia had complained of it, but I felt suddenly very cold and defenceless and small. The scene was a peaceful one, two young women talking to a couple of fishermen mending their boat, but I wished passionately we were back in the Hall and prayed that Leonie would not say anything indiscreet.

When she spoke it was with perfect calm. I do not know if she sensed my fear for her bright little face revealed no emotion. She said cheerfully, 'You have no reason to be afraid of us, Tom. We are the newly-engaged servants. We work from morning to night. We have no time to be inquisitive about anything. But if we ever have a free afternoon we would like to call on you and have fish for our tea, for that fish is what my sister most remembers, for a while she talked of nothing else.'

He laughed at this, though his eyes remained wary. He said, 'You will always be welcome, young ladies,' and it was very plain that we would not be welcome at all: if we were entangled in the nets over his door, he would accord us as little mercy as a gutted herring.

I began to move away, not wishing to provoke him further, and I took Leonie's arm as I did so, in case she proposed to continue the conversation. I said in the social voice I sometimes used at my aunt's dinners, 'How calm the sea is. When we arrived I thought we were in for another storm.'

It was true that there was a strange, oily calm to the sea that I had never before witnessed in Greymanswick, and the air was heavy and still. It was a little disturbing, but I had to think that Tom, certainly planning to set out in the *Holy Margaret* on one of his secret errands, must be delighted, it would make things easier for him.

He said, with another of his grunting laughs, 'Oh, it'll not last. This heralds a right devil of a storm.'

'How do you know?' asked Leonie, ignoring my tugging at her arm.

'How do I know!' This time he laughed in right earnest, as if this were the silliest question he had heard in years:

Hookey Miller joined him. 'Lord love us, Miss, I'm born and bred in Greymanswick and there's nothing I don't know about the sea. That storm'll come, not now, not this week, but it'll be there, and my guess is it'll be like the one four hundred years ago when all the houses dissolved into rubble and there was a million tons of shingle in the haven mouth.' He jerked his head in the direction of St. Saviour's church. 'See what's left of that? It's mostly cemetery as it stands and there'll be graves in the Hall before it's through.'

I thought suddenly of the other Tom Easey who was enclosed in clay and for that moment there was a kind of smudging of time so that the two Toms intermingled and the houses standing four square and solid in our modern time dissolved like those four hundred years back. The thought made me close my eyes: when I opened them again all was as it should be, just two girls standing there, and Tom staring out to sea.

He suddenly spat on the sandy soil, and Hookey Miller who seemed always to imitate him, followed suit. He said derisively, 'You ask me what I knows about the sea!' Then in a curt voice, 'You'd better run along home, little maids. I think there's something going on up there. Perhaps it's because Master Virgil's arrived.'

Leonie exclaimed eagerly, 'Has he really come at last?'

'I seen him earlier on. After one of the girls I've no doubt. The same young devil he always was, they should have burnt his backside for him a long while back. Daresay he's brought trouble with him. It was always his way.'

I thought all this came well from Tom who must have been after the girls from his cradle days, but Leonie and I instinctively turned to stare up in the direction of Cudden Hall. However, we did not have Tom's keen, long sight and we could see nothing except that the garden was moving as if there were a number of people in it. For some reason this chilled me, though there was no reason why the guests should not be outdoors on such a fine day. I said, 'What's happened, Tom? Do you know?'

'Oh,' he said in the fashion that I found excessively irritating, 'I'm just a simple old fisherman, I don't know nothing, nor old Hookey here neither. What could I know? I've my work to do. I don't go interfering in other folks' business –' his eyes slewed sideways to me '– like some as I could mention. You'd best go, Miss Nanette. My lady won't like it if you're away too long.'

And with this he set once more to his caulking, pressing something into the *Holy Margaret's* seams with his long, flat-fingered hands while Hookey passed him the various things he needed.

It was only then that I realised he was drunk. His speech was steady enough and so were his hands but there was a kind of insolence to him, an impudent droop of the lips and a look in the slightly reddened eyes that betrayed him. Tom when sober would not have spoken so boldly to me nor would he have made such comments on Virgil. I knew little of drunkenness for I had never seen either of my parents even faintly the worse for wine, but somehow I knew, and this coupled with the thought of what was going on in the Hall frightened me so much that I said goodbye abruptly and set off, half-running for home.

Leonie did not comment on my agitation, only said a little breathlessly – for I was lugging her after me – 'What do you think has happened?'

'I don't know. Probably nothing. Perhaps Tom just wanted to be rid of us.'

'He was foxed,' said Leonie, to my astonishment.

'You should not use such an unladylike word – yes, I think he was. How do you know?'

'Oh,' she said, 'I observe. Do you think I know nothing of the world?'

I was beginning to think she knew more than I did, but I did not answer.

She said, 'I'm looking forward to seeing Virgil, aren't you?' She imitated Tom's accent most successfully. 'They should have burnt his backside for him a long while back!'

'Leo!'

'Oh don't be so missish.' She broke off, standing still for a moment and compelling me to do likewise. She said, 'Tom will be furious if we go to the dunes.'

'I think he will.'

'And Dolly will be watching us like a hawk – we'll have to be very careful. We must wear dark clothes and duck behind the hillocks. I wonder what goes on there. It's obvious that something does.'

I suppose I should have played the elder sister here, become missish as she called it. But I remained silent, though I knew this was dangerous, this was not just a bad little girl climbing over a wall. I did try to get the right, admonitory words out, but somehow they would not come. I looked crossly at Leonie and she slowly winked one eye.

I said in what I knew was a weak, ill-assured voice, 'Whatever goes on is none of our business. I don't like Tom any more. He makes me afraid – Leo, you must stop that. It is most ill-bred.'

But she only winked again, burst out laughing then caught at my hand: we ran in the direction of Cudden Hall, flew up the hill and arrived with red cheeks, flying hair and panting breath. It was the kind of thing that would have infuriated my aunt, only as we pushed the gate open we saw that no one was capable of so much as noticing our arrival.

There was a strange tableau on the lawn. Everyone was there and everyone was motionless as if playing statues.

I knew my cousin Virgil at once. He had changed greatly of course, he had been fifteen and he was now twenty-five, but I could not have missed that shock of black hair that he wore country-wise without a wig, the fierce dark face and deep-set eyes. There were lines where there had been roundness, he had grown a great deal taller and there was written on his face a disillusion that had not been there before, but I swear that if I had run into him in London I would have instantly recognised him.

He raised his head as we crept nearer, our faces pale, our hands instinctively linking. For that moment he had no idea who we were. But then I think he would not have recognised anyone: I doubt if he even saw us except as two more people out to watch the show.

Jack Lescott lay across his knee as he half-knelt on the grass. It would have been hard to recognise Jack either, for he was dying, the blood spurting out of his chest. The young face was ashen in death, with great indented shadows from nose to mouth: the whites of his eyes were turned up and his breath came in whimpering gasps. Virgil, supporting him on one arm was trying to staunch the blood, but it no longer made any difference whether he staunched it or not, and the next minute the gasping stopped with a clicking sound, and that was the end of Jack Lescott.

Jack, aged eighteen, was dead.

We were too sick and stunned to utter a sound, then Leonie, the tears streaming down her cheeks, flung herself into my arms, her head buried in my shoulder. I held her tightly, the Lowrys stood side by side, their faces appalled, while Mr. Pleydell was pacing up and down, muttering, 'It was not my fault, I could not prevent it.'

My aunt stood in the doorway. John Gonomanaway was at her side. Her face was pale but expressionless. She was not crying. Her head turned as if to take in all our reactions, then her gaze rested briefly on the dead boy. Virgil had laid him back on the grass. Then John-Gon stepped forward.

He said, 'I will have the body taken inside, my lady.' He added, 'The doctor has already been sent for.' Then, his voice calm and heavy as if this were part of his normal duties, 'I will see that wine is sent up to the drawing-room. If you will let me have the young gentleman's London address I will send someone up to town to break the news to his father. Are there any other children, Ma'am?'

'He was the only child,' answered my aunt. Then perhaps even she could stand it no longer, for she turned her back on the scene and went inside the house: after a pause the other guests followed her.

Virgil and John-Gon picked up the body, Virgil supporting the head and shoulders. I had never seen death before. I had not known how it sponged away humanity. This was no longer a being, it was a thing. We were not allowed to see our parents, and for that I am now thankful: it would have been dreadful to have as our last memory broken bodies and blank masks of people who had been so violently alive and whom we had so dearly loved.

As the little cortège passed us, Leonie still against my shoulder and myself feeling oddly as if I were dangling in space, Virgil halted to look at me.

It was the first moment of recognition. His face was ashen white. He might be the young devil Tom called him, but he was not devoid of feelings. We stared at each other in silence. I saw then how very much he had changed. It was not the translation of a boy into a young man, it was not even the disillusion written large on him, it was almost despair. It was strange to see this on so young a face: he was after all only twenty-five. He bestowed on me a bitter smile, saying, 'So this is the grown-up Miss Nanette. You were an ugly brat. I would not describe you as that now, but I can still see in you that impossible little girl.' His eyes moved to Leonie. 'And that, I gather, is the young sister.'

I did not answer any of this. I was dimly aware that John-Gon was trying to urge Virgil on. It did not strike me as shocking that we should be staring at each other over the dead body of Jack Lescott. I only knew that for that space in time Virgil and I were alone in the world, the rest of the company obliterated. For him it was the same. I knew that, and he knew that I knew. Then suddenly everything shifted into place again, and I was staring at an exhausted, distraught young man supporting the sagging shoulders of a dead boy whose sightless eyes turned up their whites to the sky. The horror of it hit me like a hammer, and I suppose I changed colour, for Virgil's voice boomed out at me, 'I suggest you take that glass of wine. You look as if you are going to faint and this is neither time nor place for the vapours.'

Then, as he stepped into the hall, he said over his shoulder, 'Bring the pistol in with you. I would like to have a look at it.'

I obeyed mechanically, without considering that this was a monstrous thing to ask of me. I stooped over the grass which was rusted with blood: the sight brought the vomit up in my throat but I picked up the weapon and came into the house with Leonie following me. She had stopped her weeping but she looked very ill and her eyes were huge in her pale face. I took her hand and we went into the drawing-room where everyone, still huddled in silence, was drinking wine.

Someone handed me a glass. I think it was Mr. Lowry. He did so without a word. I heard that Mr. Pleydell was still muttering, 'It was not my fault. No one could say it was my fault. How could he be so foolish, the wretched boy? He had no sense at all, he was like a child with a toy –'

My aunt, sitting very upright in an armchair, made no comment. She was always a silent woman with no social small-talk whatsoever, but her silence had a strange power, and I could not endure to look at that pale, expressionless face, so incongruously topped by the beautiful hair. I looked instead at Virgil who had by now laid the body down in the small ante-room across the hall, and who came up to me and took the weapon from my hands. There was blood on his breeches and his sleeve, there was even a streak of it across his face. It was as if Jack Lescott had bequeathed his blood in his memory. I was compelled to remember the poor, silly boy who had told me so proudly of his investigations. 'I am going to arm myself,' he had said. And the memory of this was so frightful that for the first time I nearly did faint and, if Virgil had not pushed me into the nearest chair I would have fallen to the floor.

Someone gave me my glass of wine. I saw through my

swimming gaze that Virgil was turning the pistol over and over. He spoke curtly as if he had taken charge, 'Where did this come from?' –

My aunt answered him. Her voice was clipped and matter-of-fact. 'There is a cupboard filled with weapons. It was a hobby of your Uncle Constantine's. I see now that the cupboard should have been locked, but frankly, the matter never crossed my mind.' She spoke as she might have spoken to Cook in the kitchen. 'After all, I was not to know that this would happen. I simply cannot imagine why the unfortunate boy took one of them. I do not know even how he discovered them. It is all quite incomprehensible to me.'

It was the first time I had caught her out in a lie. I knew she was lying. I remembered Leonie telling me how Mr. Lowry and Mr. Pleydell took the weapons out and how Aunt Elizabeth grew so angry, I was seeing more and more clearly that this whole business was by no means as accidental as it seemed to be. But Virgil of course could hardly know that: he must have arrived here only a few hours ago.

He said sharply to my aunt, 'This is your fault. I know it is. I warned you a long time ago. I hold you entirely responsible for the death of this boy.'

We were all shocked by this and turned to stare at him. My aunt for the first time showed some emotion: a faint tinge of colour came into her pale cheeks. She half rose from her chair, exclaiming in a shrill voice, 'How dare you speak to me like that! This is nothing to do with me whatsoever. If anyone is responsible apart from the boy himself, it's William.'

Mr. Pleydell looked outraged, as well he might. He cried out, 'He killed himself. I could not prevent him. Nobody could have prevented him.'

Virgil said, 'This was fired at point-blank range. It went straight into his heart. You were there when it happened – how did it happen? Surely he did not turn the weapon against himself.'

My aunt said abruptly, 'Virgil, this is none of your business. How dare you interrogate my guests –'

'It is surely better than accusing them,' said Virgil: he looked at Mr. Pleydell and waited.

It was at this point that a kind of bedlam broke out. We had all been such a stuffy gathering with at the best a stilted conversation: Leonie and I had found the evenings boring almost beyond endurance. No one talked of anything but the weather or the dull events of the day; there might be a mention of the notorious Collector if he had made one of his forays or perhaps a reference to the Easeys, who provided the village with gossip, but these were rare occasions. Amelia would enlarge on her interminable sampler and lament that she could not match her silks, Mr. Lowry might refer to some piece of antique history, Mr. Pleydell would sneer quietly and my aunt say nothing at all. Now they were all shouting at each other, and I could see that this restored Leonie a little, for she was always entertained by human behaviour, and at home we had been accustomed to emotional outbursts.

Amelia said shrilly, the accent very marked, 'You talk as if you're judge and jury. What right have you to take charge like this? You have only just come. You know nothing about anything. We all know about you, sir, and I can tell you that your own conduct is hardly so irreproachable that you can accuse others –'

And Mr. Lowry, usually so gentle, 'I really do think that we have all had enough – can we not leave the subject until we are calmer? It is all most distressing but abusing each other will hardly help –'

Nobody of course listened to him. His voice was the voice of reason and we were none of us feeling reasonable. But when my aunt snapped out, 'Virgil! Go to your room, Sir,' we were stunned into silence.

He looked at her, with the twitch of an ugly smile. He said, 'Madam, I am no longer fifteen.'

I could see that she most passionately wished that he were. When John-Gon, standing in the doorway, spoke, she smiled a little, as she must have smiled when Virgil was a little boy due for a thrashing.

He said in a rumbling voice, 'You're not to speak to my lady like that. If she says, go to your room, that is where you shall go.'

It is a shocking thing to say, but we were all enjoying ourselves. For that moment we forgot about poor Jack lying in the adjoining room: even Amelia flushed up, her eyes shining, as if she hoped John-Gon would seize Virgil by the collar, and cuff him.

He did come into the room. He was not a coward. But he was a man in his forties and Virgil was twenty-five, he was five foot seven or eight as opposed to six foot three, and he hesitated, his face dark with rage, his breath coming in gasps, his fists opening and closing.

Then Virgil laughed. 'Do you still keep a birch in the cupboard, John?' he said. 'If you give it me, I'll show you how to use it.'

I knew at that moment that Virgil and my aunt hated each other. She looked at him as if she could kill him and he returned the look with a wide, mocking grin. He turned his back on John-Gon who muttering God knows what under that beard, suddenly swung round and left the room. He had made a fool of himself, and certainly from then on Virgil and I were equally his enemies.

Mr. Lowry exclaimed, 'This is all most unseemly. Do I have to remind you that there is a poor murdered boy across the hall?'

'Did you say "murdered", Sir?' asked Virgil. He had set one booted foot on a chair and swayed slightly as he spoke. I saw my aunt's eyes move to that foot, but she did not say anything.

Virgil's remark was greeted with a great silence. We had all come to our senses. Mr. Lowry flushed up – he had the fine, delicate skin that sometimes comes with age – and said wretchedly, 'I do not know. It is what you seem to be implying.'

'I hope,' said Mr. Pleydell, 'you are not calling me a murderer.'

'No, William,' replied Virgil, 'I am simply asking you how it happened.' He turned towards my aunt, who met his gaze stonily. He said, 'I will shortly go to my room, Ma'am. But I would like an answer to my question. It does concern me, you know. I am not pretending that Jack was one of my greatest friends, but he did die in my arms.'

Mr. Pleydell said in a whining voice, 'May I have another glass of wine?'

It was Amelia who poured it out for him. I thought she looked quite disappointed: perhaps she had expected fisticuffs. Mr. Pleydell drank it down in one gulp. He began to speak, a little thickly: the words came out as if he did not quite know what he was saying. 'I saw him on the lawn,' he said. 'He had the pistol in his hand. I believed him to be a little drunk. He was very excited. When I came up to him, he waved the pistol at me, saying something about how clever he was and how nobody could outwit him, they would all see in a little while, they would be very astonished. It was as if he had discovered something, but of course I have no idea what, I daresay it was nothing at all.'

'The young idiot!' said Virgil. He was no longer smiling. He looked as grim as I had ever seen him.

Mr. Pleydell poured himself out some more wine. It was not only Jack who was drunk. He said, 'I nearly left him to it. I thought him a dead bore. I only wish to God I had done so. But he did not want to let me go, he wanted to make me see how wonderful he was, and he came up to me and clutched me by the arm, waving the pistol in my face. I am very much afraid of weapons,' cried Mr. Pleydell hysterically, 'I cannot help it, I was the same as a boy. It was cocked and he told me it was loaded. Not that I know anything about such things, I am the world's worst shot, but I know how accidents happen, I knew someone once who was killed in similar circumstances –'

'You seem oddly fated in your friends,' said Virgil.

101

Mr. Pleydell cried in a shriek, 'How dare you insinuate –'

'I am insinuating nothing,' returned Virgil calmly. He laid the pistol down on the table beside him. It was a pretty thing, embossed with silver, but to me it was like a dangerous snake. He said, 'You still haven't told me what exactly happened.'

Mr. Pleydell said in a despairing voice, 'I suppose it was partly my fault. But when someone waves a loaded weapon at you – I told him not to be such a fool. He just laughed at me and said he didn't know I was such a coward. So I – I caught hold of his wrist and tried to take the thing from him. We struggled –'

'With a loaded pistol!'

'Yes, it was foolish but in an emergency one does not always think –'

'You could simply have walked away,' said Virgil.

Mr. Pleydell snapped at him, 'If I had, he might have killed himself –'

Then he realised what he had said and flushed up: Virgil, staring at him, remained silent.

He went on at last in a choked voice, 'I suppose I must have twisted his wrist round. I don't know. It went off. At first I thought I was wounded, Then he just fell to the ground. That was when you appeared. You must have seen what happened.' Then he said sullenly, 'I suppose you all think it's my fault.'

At this Amelia, much to everyone's surprise and, I think, to my aunt's disapproval, ran to his side, crying out such things as, It was not your fault, You should not blame yourself, You did your best, and so on. Mr. Pleydell suddenly began to weep, which somehow affronted me, for I thought that gentlemen should not cry.

In the midst of all this there was a tap at the door, and my aunt who had throughout remained silent, rose to her feet. We all turned towards her and Mr. Pleydell's sobs ceased. She was, as I was beginning to believe, a dangerous woman, but there was no denying the strength of her personality.

102

She said, 'The doctor must be here. I have to speak to him. You can stop reproaching yourself, William. What is done is done, and it is plainly not your fault. It is a pity that this wretched boy's folly killed him, but it was his own doing.' She looked at Virgil. She said in a voice like the crack of a whip, 'I want that pistol from you.'

'No,' he said.

'What!' She looked as if she could not believe her ears. Her pale face went an ugly red. She said between her teeth, 'Give it me.'

'No.'

'Did you hear what I said –'

'I heard very well,' answered Virgil, 'and my answer remains the same. No.' He smiled at her, and the antagonism and hate between them was like a flame. 'Do I have to keep on reminding you, Ma'am, that I am no longer a boy? I do as I please. I am not your lackey, nor am I a child to be whipped and shut up on bread and water. Though if you wish to try – would you like me to send for John-Gon? He is a little past his prime and guzzling and whoring have sapped his strength, but I have no doubt he will do his best. It would be a pity to knock down a man of his age, but it would not grieve me overmuch. Shall I pull the bell-rope?'

She only said in a stifled voice, 'I want that pistol. Give it me, give it me, give it me!' And she stamped her foot like a child: her face was wild and also honestly bewildered.

He heaved a deep sigh. He said, 'Do I have to repeat the same word over and over again? If you are frightened that I'll shoot myself, you need not worry. I am in any case armed. I would not have ridden from London without such a protection. And,' he added, 'I would not stay here without it either.'

She was defeated. I imagine no one had ever refused her bidding before. She half reached out her hand as if to snatch the pistol from him, then she saw the derisive look on his face and her arm dropped to her side. She plainly did not know what to do. She hesitated, breathing fast, then she swung round and left the room. She crashed the door behind her: at that moment all dignity had gone.

There was a dead silence. The Lowrys looked miserably embarrassed and as for Mr. Pleydell, I could not see his face for he had walked over to the window. Leonie and I glanced at each other then away. It was only Amelia who rushed in. I imagine Amelia always rushed in. I admired her courage but thought her lacking in sense. She came up to Virgil, her face flaming. She cried out shrilly, 'How dare you speak to Mrs. Cudden like that? When I think of all she's done for you –'

'I am thinking of that too,' said Virgil.

This disconcerted her. She paused, chewing at her lower lip. She said sulkily, 'Well, she adopted you, didn't she? She has brought you up as her own son.'

'Yes,' he said. He surveyed her. She was not beautified by temper, her hair was falling down, and her cheeks blotched with colour as if she had a fever. He said again, 'Yes. I've no doubt she would have treated her own son the same. It is no longer important, Miss Amelia, but there was a little boy who behaved as all little boys do, who was thrashed unmercifully and locked up in his room three days out of the seven. John-Gon had a strong arm in those days, and I was very young. I ran away ten times before I was twelve. It was Tom Easey who found me and brought me back. I believe I would have been beaten to death and starved into the bargain, had it not been for my Uncle Constantine. He used to smuggle food up to my room.' He suddenly swung round on me, smiling. 'I think he liked naughty children. He was a kind man. Did you not find him so, Nanette?'

I said, 'I loved him very much.'

He brooded on this for a moment, his eyes moving from me to Amelia. Then he said quietly, 'Little boys grow into big boys, Miss Amelia, only they never lose the traces of their youth. If you beat a child too much, you beat out love and a great deal more. I do not pretend I am what I should

104

be, but I am what my aunt made me. And I grew fast. When I was fourteen I misbehaved myself once again and John was sent for to discipline me as I deserved. By that time I was a little bigger than he was, besides, I did not drink so much and I was not so short of breath. I blacked his eye and broke a tooth. I took the birch from him and snapped it over my knee. He never laid a finger on me again though he'd hang me on the highest tree if ever he had the opportunity. You have my life story, Ma'am. Have you any further lecture for me?'

Amelia was left with nothing to say at all. She looked as if she were about to burst into tears. Virgil said in a drawl, 'Have I so astonished you? I suggest you go and comfort my aunt. I imagine she needs a little consolation and you are obviously devoted to her.'

She muttered, 'You are quite impossible. I think you are a very wicked young man.'

And with this she too left the room, followed by the Lowrys who must have wished most fervently they were back in their own civilised home, even if the Collector had ravaged it. Mr. Pleydell was obviously longing to follow them but did not quite know how to do it and still preserve his dignity. He looked at Leonie and me, then at Virgil who, his head bowed, was examining the pistol again. He mumbled, 'you don't really believe it was my fault, do you?'

Virgil did not raise his head. He answered indifferently, 'Does it matter what I believe? The boy is dead. *Sufficet.*'

It was strange how that one word – I knew now it was Latin – brought things back to me. *I don't like you.* That is what I said. And, *I wouldn't marry you if you were the last boy on earth.* Mr. Pleydell had gone. I did not see his going. Perhaps he was seeking comfort from Amelia. And I knew that I did like him, that I would marry him this minute if he asked me. It was as if I had suddenly been given spectacles: the world was different, the room was different and the black-haired young man so concentrated on his examinations, illuminated for me as if a lantern hung above him. I was so bemused, so unaware of everything else that when he suddenly spoke, I jumped, nearly knocking over the chair behind me. I saw that he was looking at me in some astonishment. He said, 'I suppose you too think I am a very wicked young man.'

I said simply, 'No.'

'No? Why not?'

I answered him from my heart, without considering what I was saying. I said, 'I think you have been most cruelly ill-used. I could gladly kill the people who mistreated you.'

He stared at me. A faint colour came into the pale cheeks. Then he swung round to Leonie who was standing silently behind me. He said, 'I met your sister ten years ago. At that time she wanted to kill me. How is the temper these days, Nanette?'

'It is still there, Virgil.'

'So I perceive.' His voice was mocking, his eyes were not. He said, 'You have a remarkably pretty sister.' Then, as if the words were jerked out of him, 'Why the devil are you both here?'

I could hardly believe he did not know, for all he lived in London and only came home occasionally. My aunt's relationship with him was plainly as bad as it could be, but if she really had not told him, it was a little alarming, even sinister, as if she had plans for us that must be kept from him. However, I said none of this, only told him briefly that our parents had been killed in an accident, leaving us penniless, and our aunt had offered us a home.

He listened to me in an angry dismay. He exclaimed, 'You propose to go on living here?'

'Yes, of course.' Then, angry myself, I said, 'Where else are we to go?'

'Anywhere but here! Anywhere!' Suddenly he seized me by the wrist. 'Girls, Cousins, whatever you wish to be called – leave this confounded place. Go back to London.

106

Go anywhere. I'll try to find you somewhere. But you cannot, you must not, stay here.' He paused, then went on, 'You do not know Cudden Hall. You do not know your aunt. I can only be thankful that you are grown young women, not children, for what your life would be like if you were younger, I cannot bear to imagine. What sort of childhood did you have?'

The last remark, flung out at me, reduced me to silence for a second. Then I said, with truth, 'A very happy one. A very indulged one.' And as I thought of that childhood, the tears came to my eyes, for Papa and Maman were always with me, and it was unbearable to remember the happy days. Certainly we never, never endured the kind of thing that Virgil had recounted: Papa never raised his hand to us, and Maman, though she sometimes flew into a rage and boxed our ears, was immediately overcome with remorse and plied us with sweetmeats and presents to make up for it.

Virgil did not comment on this, nor did he offer us any explanation as to why he, who so detested Cudden Hall, returned regularly to visit it. He only said quietly, 'I would wish you miles away. You were a remarkably interfering, inquisitive little girl, Nanette. I suspect your pretty sister is the same. At least, take care. For God's sake, take care. Keep to your samplers and your piano practising, or whatever it is young ladies do –' He saw that Leonie was smiling. He rounded on her, his voice harsh. 'Do you find that so amusing, Miss Leonie?'

I think that both Leonie and I were thinking of the work we had put into his rooms: he would certainly never picture us as a couple of maidservants, dusting and cleaning and making his bed. But Leonie did not say this, only bestowed on him her most impudent and enchanting smile. No man would ever set Leonie down, for all she was not yet quite sixteen. She said in the voice that was still high, a young girl's voice, 'It is very strange, Cousin, but ever since we have been here, everyone has told us to go away. Nobody has said, How nice to see you, or, We have been looking forward to your arrival, or, You are such charming girls, we hope you will stay with us for ever. Oh no. It is always, Go home, go away, don't do this, don't do that. Suffolk is a very inhospitable county. But I think we shall stay, all the same.' She sighed dramatically, her eyes always fixed on Virgil's face. 'Even Dolly Easey wants us to go.'

At the name his face changed. 'Dolly!' he said. 'She was always kind to me. She was only a child herself, but she would creep up to my room with anything she could find in the kitchen and sometimes she would kneel beside me and comfort me –' Then he said more briskly, 'So you are staying. And no doubt interfering. You should take warning by what has happened today. Be careful, little cousins. I am sure you are brave girls, but this is no place to display your courage.'

I could not stop myself. I said, 'Do you think Jack Lescott was killed deliberately?'

He turned his head away. His voice was flat. He said, 'I have no idea.'

As we left the room we saw that he was again examining the pistol.

We did not repeat the question to each other when we were in our room, but for the first time I locked the door. I do not know why I did so. There could be no personal danger to us: if someone had killed Jack, he would have no reason to murder us. But we were both afraid. I saw the look of relief in Leonie's eye as I turned the key. While I was talking to Virgil I had almost forgotten what had happened, but now as we sat side by side on the bed, we felt sick and cold with the horror of it all.

Only Leonie, who still looked very white, when at last she spoke, did not refer to Jack. She said, 'You've fallen in love with him.'

I said, 'Yes,' for there was no point in denying it, and Leonie and I had never held anything from each other. Then I said rather crossly, 'Is it so obvious?'

She laughed. 'I know you, Nan. I don't suppose anyone else would have noticed, certainly not Virgil, if that is what is worrying you. Nan –'

I looked at her.

'I know he's very handsome, but he seems very bad-tempered, and I wonder if it would be wise – what a dreadful time he has had, poor wretch, I think our Aunt Elizabeth is a monster. Only with such a childhood and this gloomy place – Oh Nan, be careful. Please be careful. I couldn't bear it if anything happened to you.' Then she said with a heavy sigh, 'Everyone seems to wish us back in London, and I am beginning to wish it myself. We'd be away from all these people who don't want us. At the beginning it was amusing, but now Jack is dead, and you have fallen in love.'

I said comfortingly, 'It had to happen one day, besides, you have been in love since you were a little girl.'

And this was true, for Leonie had developed passions for innumerable men, ranging from friends of Papa's to an unknown soldier we met in the Park, who handed her a rose. But this was different, and we both knew it was different, and somehow I did not want to discuss it with her, so we returned to the subject of poor Jack Lescott. It was as if for the first time there was a widening space between us: I had become through no wish of my own, the elder sister, and Leonie was the little girl, on the other side of the fence. But on the subject of Jack we were totally in accord, and she repeated my question, 'Was he killed deliberately?'

I admitted that I did not know. I said, 'I'm afraid it's possible. He was such a silly boy, and he was like us, he was always interfering. And he couldn't hold his tongue.'

'But what is there to find out?'

'I suspect, a great deal. And whatever it is, it's dangerous.' Then I saw that she was brightening up, and I said quickly, 'Leo, Virgil is right. We're just as bad as Jack, and if we are not careful, we might meet the same end. We must be more careful. No, I mean it, and you are not to laugh. Let's forget about those sand dunes. It's not as if they are at all pretty. Just – just sand and hillocks, and it will be wet and cold and we'll probably catch a chill.'

'Or a French prisoner,' said Leonie sweetly.

But we did not mention this again, and that evening we did not go down to dinner. We felt it would be quite unendurable, and the ghost of Jack Lescott would be there with us: it would be impossible to choke the food down. Nobody sent up to inquire how we were, but Dolly noticed our absence and presently appeared with one of Cook's generous trays. I have to admit that despite our distress we swallowed every mouthful.

Dolly hardly spoke to us until just before she left. She looked like a ghost of herself, the beautiful face fallen in, and she had been crying her eyes out. As she laid the tray down on the table, I said wretchedly, 'Oh Dolly, I'm so sorry.'

She looked at me. She did not answer. She had not loved Jack, but I think she felt it was partly her fault that he was dead. Only as she turned to the door, she suddenly swung round on me, her face fierce and angry: for that moment she was almost her old self.

She demanded, 'Have you had trouble with John-Gon?'

I was disconcerted enough to blush, and I saw Leonie look sharply at me. But I only said, 'No. Why should I have? I hardly ever see him.'

'He seems to have taken a real spite at you,' said Dolly, 'so I thought maybe – He's a right bastard, is John, can't keep his hands off anyone, hand up your skirt before you know where you are. I've had plenty of him, I can tell you, and there was Rosie, she was before your time, he got her with a baby and he got my lady to dismiss her too, without a penny. You keep away from him, Miss Nan, and Miss Leonie too. He likes them young. And if you have any more trouble with him, you just tell me, I'll sort him, I promise you that.'

And with that she was out in the corridor, the door

slammed behind her.

'You didn't tell me,' said Leonie.

'There was nothing to tell.'

She did not pursue the matter and, after our dinner, we went to bed, for we were both exhausted. We slept heavily and, if there were any midnight creepings to and fro, we did not hear them. And three days later, despite my premonitions, we set off for the sand dunes.

IV

A great deal happened in those three days, including the arrival of Jack's father from London. We all dreaded his coming and, when he at last arrived, it was even worse than we imagined. The doctor drove up to town to bring him back: no one envied him such a terrible task and he looked very grim when he drove off. But we did not discuss the matter, indeed, the name of Jack Lescott was never mentioned, though we all glanced covertly at that little locked room off the hall, and the empty place at the table was filled by the dead boy's ghost.

Leonie and I spent most of our working day in the kitchen. My aunt expressed the view that it was not seemly for us to clean Virgil's rooms while he was there, but I suspect she did not want him to know how she used us. She told us repeatedly that we must learn to cook, and we did not argue with her for we enjoyed it enormously. I, to my surprise, discovered in myself a positive aptitude for making delicious dishes, though Leonie did not share it, burning everything she could and mixing up the wrong ingredients. We liked Cook very much, especially as she considered we were half starved and started every session with a plate of cakes and sweetmeats. I sometimes think my happiest memories of Cuddem Hall lie in coming in from the cold, blustery weather outside to the warm, sweet-smelling kitchen, with the range burning brightly, and Cook setting out for us her pots and jars and pans so that we could compose a new pudding or make a glorious stew. And as she stirred and beat and shredded – half the time she did our work for us – she spoke of ancient Greymanswick.

112

We heard of the young lady who received into her bed the devil in the form of a crab: he nipped her and fetched blood so that her soul was mortgaged for fourteen years. And there was the tale of the Preventive captured by smugglers: to keep him busy while their shipmates got away, they made him recite the 'Lord's Prayer' backwards. That night, Leonie and I, as we went to bed, could be heard muttering, 'Amen ever and ever for glory the and power the kingdom the is thine.' We shuddered a little to hear of the disinterred corpse in St. Saviour's churchyard that fell to dust when disturbed, with two chalices of coarse metal on his breast, and learnt more prosaically how the local fishermen always prayed to St. Nicholas – '*Nicholas, ora pro nobis,*' – before they set out on their journeys.

And we listened and we ate: it is amazing that we did not fatten like Christmas geese. The sea beat savagely against the dyke and the waves rode high: once we saw a small boat balanced on the peak of a wave and were incredulous that so frail a thing could survive. Dolly said, 'There is no danger until high tide. That is the bad time, that is what swallowed up the old town.' But we could not really believe there was any danger at all, for Cudden Hall stood fair and square and sturdy, and even the village seemed remote from the storm. If occasionally our eyes strayed to the flashing lights in the marshes and the dunes beyond, no one was to know, for we must have seemed busy and innocent, and even Amelia could hardly believe we would go exploring in such weather.

By this time I was on excellent terms with the guests. But I saw very little of Virgil who did not even join us for meals, who seemed to spend long hours closeted with my aunt in the west wing and who, when we brushed against each other, seemed to want to avoid me. I must admit that I gazed after him, longed to talk with him yet did not dare approach him, and sometimes in my own room wept out of passionate frustration. I told myself repeatedly how foolish I was, but it made no difference at all, and in the evenings I

113

put on my prettiest gown, made Leonie brush my hair for me, and prayed that he would be dining with us. Where he went I do not know, but he was hardly ever in the Hall, and certainly showed no signs of wishing to talk to me. The other guests hardly compensated for him, but they were pleasant enough, though I could not pretend to care for Amelia with her interminable sampler – it was, I believe, intended to go on a fire screen – and she too spent a great deal of time with my aunt where I have no doubt she repeated any indiscretions we uttered. But when I saw how desperately she was in love with my cousin, I was sorry for her, for he treated her no better than he did me, and I knew from her avid gaze how much she longed for him. What did surprise me was the friendship that had developed between her and my sister. I regarded this with the utmost suspicion for I could not believe that she and Leonie had anything in common, but they were always together, with Leonie as sweet as honey, admiring the sampler and dangling the pretty coloured silks between her fingers.

I challenged her on this, but she only made faces at me, then burst into a laugh that confirmed my worst thoughts.

I asked her crossly, 'What are you trying to do? You cannot pretend you are interested in that sampler.'

She said with a bright-eyed innocence, 'But it's so pretty, Nan!' at which I threw a pillow at her head: the matter was then dropped.

The Lowrys were always the odd ones out. Their home was still being restored, but he told me he hoped to return at the end of the month. His wife I hardly saw, for she was very delicate, and the death of Jack Lescott distressed her so that she took to her bed, with all meals served in her room. Once I took up her luncheon tray myself and was shocked to see her so white and thin. She did not seem to know who I was. She said faintly, 'I wish we were back home. Even thieves would be better than this.' Later, when I collected the tray, I saw that she had hardly touched a morsel.

114

Her husband, however, seemed to seek me out, and often after our meal I found myself in deep conversation with him. He was a tall, thin man of about fifty, and he published monographs on the county of Suffolk: being an antiquarian he was particularly absorbed in local history. Leonie, who occasionally joined us, found him a dead bore, but I thought him infinitely preferable to Miss Amelia and her bright-coloured silks and even derived a certain comfort from him in this strange household where nothing was as it seemed.

'We are a race of smugglers,' he told me. He seemed to forget that he had once denied this. It was the day before we set out for the sand dunes. He announced this proudly as if he personally were responsible for all the gin and brandy brought in from Holland. And then, seeing how this interested me, he expounded on the subject.

The cargo, he told me, was usually liquor but sometimes coin, and sometimes too treasure from the drowned city that had not yet been salvaged. When I asked what was done with it, he paused: a secretive look crossed his face.

'I don't know,' he said, 'but I would hazard a guess that there is a buyer in Greymanswick. The ordinary people do not have the money.' The smugglers, he said, were originally privateers, plundering enemy ships during the wars with Spain and our present war of the Austrian succession. The men of Greymanswick had always blended piracy and fishing, and Mr. Lowry spoke lyrically of catches of herring, sprats, soles, flounders and other fish I had never heard of, and explained how the fishermen were peacefully employed half the week, spending the other half in more remunerative and dangerous ploys.

After that we talked of other things: witchcraft, still practised here, strange plants that were found nowhere else, and Greymanswick itself, flourishing under the Saxons and oppressed by the Danes. Of this he spoke sadly and with love, quoting from what I would once have considered my cousin's works.

'*Jam seges est ubi Troja fuit*,' he said, then kindly translated it for me as if I were a pupil in school. 'Where there is now a field, Troy was. *Seges* is literally a cornfield, but I think the rendering is accurate enough in this context.'

And I liked the melancholy sound and looked out of the window where Troy, submerged for ever, lay below.

On the second day I began to feel stifled by Cudden Hall, with its heavy hangings, its windows permanently closed, and the large meals presented to us with such heavy regularity. There were no cooking lessons that day for Cook had developed a migraine, and all I could do was either read in the library or join the company in the drawing-room at their endless games of cards. For once the library did not attract me: I was too restless and thinking too of the arrival of Jack's father, which we were all dreading.

When John Gonomanaway suddenly appeared in his strange, silent fashion, to say that my aunt wished to see me, I was quite relieved. Only I wished he did not hate me so much: the hostility that emanated from him was frightening. I could imagine how a little boy, caught out in some childish misdoing, must be terrified. He spoke civilly enough, but the dark eyes glowered at me, and I could see that he would never forgive that slap. I half wanted to ask him if we could not be friends again, but this was plainly absurd, so I followed him silently up the stairs to the west wing where my aunt had spent her usual afternoon concentrating on cobwebs and skeletons and the ghosts of ravished nuns.

She greeted me more amiably than usual. At least there was one thing I could be certain of: John-Gon would never reveal to her his hatred of me. She even offered me a glass of wine, which astonished me, and motioned me to sit down on one of her antique chairs which looked so charming and which were so excessively uncomfortable.

She began without preamble, saying, 'And how do you find your cousin Virgil after this gap of ten long years?'

Naturally I blushed to the roots of my hair. How I

116

despised myself for this feminine weakness. She saw, of course: she would be blind not to have done so. Her eyes, cold and grey as slate, never moved from my face. She did not wait for my answer, which indeed I had only too plainly given her. She said with a little laugh – I have never known anyone laugh with so little amusement – 'No doubt you are attracted by the handsome face. He is admittedly an extremely good-looking young man. But he is not for you, Nanette. I regret to say this of him, but he has a very bad reputation, he is in no way suitable for a young girl.'

It struck me later that my aunt, for all she wrote novels, was very weak in her judgment of human nature. I would not have cared at that moment if Virgil had been a murderer, but even if I had been less in love, I would have been intrigued by that last sentence. However, I remained silent, and my aunt continued.

'I would not wish,' she said, 'to shock you with the details, but his life in London has been a disgrace, and I understand that even here in Greymanswick he makes no effort to restrain himself. Forget about him, Nanette. He would only ruin you and then abandon you.'

I thought privately that my aunt's conversational style had obviously been affected by her novels, and then that I could not imagine a happier fate than being ruined by my cousin, even if he did abandon me afterwards. But I still said nothing, only wondered why she was taking the trouble to tell me all this, and why it was so important to her that I should have nothing more to do with Virgil.

She assumed that she had said all that was necessary. She said, 'I hope you are happy here.'

'Yes, Ma'am, I am. We both are, only we are very distressed by what has happened.'

'Oh,' she said as if it did not matter, 'Jack Lescott – poor, foolish boy. But then he was a meddler. It was his own fault. Meddlers always suffer.'

I found myself flushing again, this time through anger, but there was no decent comment I could make, so I said nothing.

She said suddenly, refilling my glass, 'Do you like pretty things, child?'

'Ma'am? –'

'Jewellery, fine clothes. Perfume. Pretty necklaces to adorn you – you like those, don't you?'

I said weakly – I could not imagine what she was talking about – 'Why yes, Ma'am. I – I suppose we all do. But –'

'One day,' she said, with that smile that was not a smile at all, 'I will make you a little present. But first we must have a talk. You look trustworthy, Nanette. I feel I could depend on you. I cannot believe you would repeat anything I told you in confidence.'

I did not like this, though I would have found it hard to explain why. The unease, together with the heat from the enormous log fire that was burning, made me a little dizzy.

'You are not like Jack Lescott,' she said.

I thought suddenly and for no reason of a little boy who was whipped and starved and shut up in his room. I looked at this kind lady who was offering me presents, and I hated her so much that her face swam before me. Whatever it was she was offering me, it was a great deal more than necklaces and perfume.

She rose to her feet. She was plainly not interested in what I felt: I suspect that was my aunt's worst disadvantage, for she never considered anyone but herself. She said briskly, 'We will talk again. Virgil returns to London at the end of the week so there will be no fear of interruption. You will remember, Nanette, that everything I have said is in the strictest confidence.'

'Yes, Ma'am.'

'Good girl!'

And I knew that if I disobeyed her she would cut my throat without a qualm. I made her my curtsey and she smiled again, a stout little woman with cold eyes and beautiful hair. The relief of being away from her, as I closed the door behind me, was such that for a moment I stood

118

there, taking deep breaths, thankful to be rid of the sight of her. At last I came down the stairs and went over to the drawing-room, looking in.

The people there made me retreat again. The room was softly lit and the fire was inviting, but I could not endure it. I have forgotten what game they always played, it was something for money. The Lowrys sat together – she had at last emerged – and Mr. Pleydell faced them. They were quite absorbed, and the dullness of it choked me. I longed to fling the windows open and blow them all away in the cold sea air. As I backed away – no one had noticed me – I saw that my little sister was seated with Amelia. The great friendship seemed to be progressing, which amazed me, for I could not see what the two of them had in common.

However, I was not interested in cards or samplers. I decided that despite the weather I would walk round the garden. It was a fierce afternoon, with the wind howling like one of my aunt's banshees, the kind of day I loved. In London I sometimes crept out, to have the rain beating against my face and my hair flattened to my head. It made Maman very cross, especially as my hair had to be freshly curled, but it happened again and again so that in the end she had to accept it, would even say, 'There is a howling gale outside, Nan, you had best take a little promenade.'

I was quite cheered at this prospect and ran upstairs for my cloak and a kerchief to tie round my head. I did not see Virgil and Dolly until I came out of my room: the carpet muffled my footsteps and my cloak faded into the late after-noon shadow.

They were talking together, standing very close as if they were conspirators. Dolly looked as if she had been crying again. But there was something else that I noticed. Perhaps it was because I was attuned to it, but I knew instantly that Dolly was helplessly in love with my cousin. It is hard to say why, – perhaps the intent way her eyes were focused on him, perhaps the fluid attitude of her beautiful body which leaned towards him as if it would enfold him. My immedi-

119

ate reaction was one of shock, though I do not know why I should be in any way surprised. They were both young, of, I believe, the same age, they were both handsome, they were constantly in propinquity, and love, though this was something my aunt would scarcely appreciate, is in no way touched by class. My second thought was one of pure horror lest I too had betrayed myself. But despite my feelings I still had to stare, though it would have been easy to shut my door with a slam, apologise then brush past them.

It was by the most fortunate chance that they did not see me. I think they were too absorbed in their conversation. If Virgil had so much as turned his head, he would instantly have seen me standing there. But he was concentrating his attention on Dolly, who was saying in a hoarse, choked voice, 'The old man will be here tomorrow. I suppose he'll take the body back with him. Oh, it's a terrible thing, a terrible thing. He was only a baby.' She half stretched out her hand as she spoke. 'Mr. Virgil. Do you think he was killed deliberate?'

'Yes. I am quite certain. There can be no doubt of it.' His deep voice rolled out the syllables as if for a funeral.

I could hardly hear Dolly's reply because she spoke so low. 'Was it because of –?

Virgil answered in a grim voice, 'I should imagine so. Why did he have to interfere, the young idiot? I suppose he thought he was playing a game, only this is not a game, God knows, and in this household it pays to be blind and deaf if you wish to stay alive.'

Dolly said flatly, 'It might happen again. What is going to become of us all? They're bound to find out one day. Even my dad is becoming afraid.'

He said, 'It will not go on much longer.'

'What do you mean?'

'What I say.' He turned to go down the stairs. His voice suddenly rose. 'Why the devil do you think I'm here? I'm not to be whistled to heel like a little dog. Oh, I've shut my eyes and ears for a long time, even at my uncle's death – she wore black for him, Dolly. Do you remember? She wore black for three whole months. It was a most touching funeral. I daresay the old man was glad to be dead –'

'Mr. Virgil, don't, please!'

'Oh you know as well as I do. Everyone knows, but nobody dares say a word. It must have been quite a jolt for her when the girl's father came down. I daresay John-Gon kept an eye on him. But now this boy is dead, it's got to stop. Once I would have said I'd not have the family name made a byword, but now I do not care. Let us all end on gallow's hill if need be, but end it must and even if I survive, I'll never come here again. I detest this place with all my heart and soul, I'd like to see it laid waste like St. Saviour's church. It withstood the flood, God knows how, but I pray it will not endure the next. The Hall has a kind of curse on it, and this time I have come to settle the score once and for all, and she'll not stop me, however hard she tries. I'll not leave until it's done, and I'll not be stopped by anyone, certainly not that fine lot in the drawing-room –'

He tilted his chin as he spoke, in the direction of the hall.

Dolly said in a whisper, 'What will happen to my dad?'

'Do you really care?' asked Virgil steadily.

'Yes, Mr. Virgil, I do. You wouldn't understand, Sir. He's my flesh and blood. Oh, I know he's a bad man and he's not used me right, but he is my father, and I wouldn't want him to come to any harm. You'll do what you can, sir, won't you?'

Virgil said, 'He'd gut me with his herring knife any day. You know that, Dolly. I can't make any promises. You must see that.'

Dolly said on a sob, 'Oh my God!' and flung her apron up to her eyes. Then she pushed at the nearest door which was that of the Lowrys' bedroom and stepped inside.

I waited until Virgil disappeared round the bend of the staircase. I heard the drawing-room door open and close. Then I followed him down and stepped into the garden.

I had not realised the full force of the storm. It was glorious, whipping my cloak about me, dragging my hair from beneath the kerchief. It almost made me forget the shocking things I had heard as I ran deliberately into it, tilting myself against the breath-taking wind. For a moment I stood in the middle of the lawn, with the rain beating against my face, the gale all but upsetting my balance. The sea was thrashing against the wall, the waves like snow-peaked mountains. There were no lights on the marshes now. The *Holy Margaret* could never take this, she would be broken asunder. There would be no gin and brandy this evening, no men carrying packages into Cudden Hall, though the Collector might be out, all noise drowned in the tumult outside.

As I stood there, I thought of what I had just heard, and the horror of it made me shake and want to cry.

My father always said that Uncle Constantine died of a malignancy, one of those wicked things that grow within the body and that no surgeon can cure. And now it seemed that my aunt had poisoned him. Virgil had implied this all too plain, and Dolly had not attempted to contradict him. It was hard to believe. I knew her as a cold and ruthless woman, capable of ill-using a little boy, and certainly she had been unfaithful, but all that was miles away from murder, murder too of her own husband. I thought of this, and I thought again of Jack Lescott, and I began to shiver uncontrollably: it was not with the cold.

And then I thought of Virgil. *Even if I survive.* That was what he had said. I thought fiercely, You will survive, you must survive. And because all humour had been knocked out of me, I did not find it ridiculous that I should be thinking this, nor that the reason for it was my determination to marry him.

It was as if I were fulfilling Maman's gloomiest prophecies. She once remarked to me, 'You will fall in love, yes, but you will fall in love with the wrong man. And God help him!' she said, which made me laugh: she sounded so serious and so fierce. She fixed her blue eyes on me. 'You are not to laugh. I mean every word of it. Now Leonie is different. Leonie will never take anything too seriously. I can see it. But I am not sorry for you. I despise broken hearts,' cried Maman, who had after all fallen in love with the right man. She added, rapping her brush against the dressing-table, 'I will not have a daughter of mine going into a decline, do you hear?'

I remember, I just grinned at her. It sounded so silly and I was only fourteen at the time. 'I will never fall in love at all,' I told her, at which she turned up her eyes. And it was true that on the whole I remained aloof, while Leonie was flirting almost from the moment of her birth: it amused Papa how even as a baby she preferred the company of men to that of women. It is true that before we left home I had received several offers, but the gentlemen all bored me, and I began to think I would remain unwed all my life.

And now I had no intention of remaining unwed, and perhaps it was indeed God help Virgil, for I was not going into a decline for him either, I was simply going to marry him, even if it was on gallow's hill. I do not know why I remembered that last phrase, but it made me shudder afresh, and suddenly I realised that I could not stand there in my melancholy, getting soaked to the skin. It was as if I had turned into one of my aunt's heroines who always behaved so stupidly, never laughing or enjoying themselves, just spending their lives in a state of gloom and doom. It really was too stormy to take a long walk and Leonie was not there to accompany me, so I had a sudden urge to take a look at the side of the house where Jack Lescott had discovered his mysterious large room.

It was of course the purest folly. No one could pretend I had not been warned. But my mind was still so concentrated on what I had heard that I did not even consider I might be running myself into danger and death. I think it was my wicked curiosity again. I walked on, turning the corner of the Hall: the wind suddenly cannoned into me so that for a second I had to cling to the wall.

123

It was growing dark, but there was still light enough to see by. The rushing clouds concealed most of the moon and there were no stars: in a little while it would be pitch black. I stood there, staring up at the house. I had never examined this angle of Cudden Hall before. It must have been the oldest part, being plain and dark: lamplight came from the window at the far end. My aunt must be still working, for that would be her sitting-room. I moved slowly along, and then I understood why Jack knew that the third room was six times as large as the other two, and why it was more sinister than one would have expected. There were windows the length of the wall, and they were closer together than is usual and barred as well. It gave the place the look of a dungeon, but the barred windows continued, and the length of the wall was certainly much more than that of the rest. I also noticed a ramp leading from the back of the house: this would be where Leonie and I had seen the men in the middle of the night.

I was so fascinated by this that I simply stood there, staring. The deep voice behind me shot me round so fast that what with the gale and my confusion I all but fell.

The voice said, 'And what, may I ask, are you doing here?'

I was afraid, of course, largely through guilt, for it was perfectly true that I had no business to be there at all, but it was strange how that furious voice – and he sounded as angry as I had ever heard him – decided me to break all my resolutions. I had told Leonie that we would not go to the sand dunes. I knew now that we would. I could not endure Virgil's anger, I could not endure my own feelings for him, and somehow I had to know what all this was about. But of course I said none of this. I could not see him clearly in the dusk, only the threatening size of him. I said as coldly and calmly as I could, 'I am merely looking at the house. Is that so wrong of me? I have not yet had much chance to explore it.'

The word 'explore' was a mistake, as I knew the moment

124

it was uttered. But there was nothing to be done about it, and I prepared to walk away with as much dignity as I could muster, only he sprang forward and seized me by the shoulders. He said savagely, 'You're at it again! You little idiot. Will you never learn?' Then more quietly, 'You saw Jack dying, didn't you?'

'Yes.' I was beginning to tremble. I would never forget that scene in the garden, but his words brought it back to me with the utmost clarity. I said almost inaudibly, 'He was murdered, wasn't he?'

At this he released me and drew back. I could no longer see his face but I felt the rage that emanated from him. He said in a gasp, 'Oh yes. He was murdered. Perhaps I murdered him. Has that not struck you?'

At this I recovered myself and spoke in the forthright way that Maman so deplored. ('So unfeminine, Nanette!' she would say.) 'Nonsense!' I said.

He laughed. I think he was a little taken aback. He said, 'So it's nonsense, is it? How can you be so sure? But whether I killed him or not is immaterial. Instead I'll tell you why he died. You will listen carefully, Nanette, because what happened to him could happen to you. He was eighteen. He was an only son. His father comes down tomorrow to collect the body and take it back to London. You must meet him. I cannot believe it will do much for someone so arrogant, but I still think you should be there. For him it must be the end of the world. But I was going to tell you why Jack's world ended, was I not? Who murdered him scarce matters. He died, Cousin, because he was too inquisitive. He had sharp eyes and ears and he discovered that things were happening in Cudden Hall that were not what he expected. I do not know exactly what it was. He must have heard something, or seen people do strange things. And his curiosity was aroused and he decided to find out what was going on. Whatever it was, it proved to be the end of him. He died.'

I whispered, 'Did he really have to die? He was such a

125

harmless boy.'

It was by now almost dark. We stood there in the howling wind and rain, almost touching, invisible to each other. My kerchief had blown away so that my hair tangled over my face.

Virgil continued in the same calm voice, 'No one is harmless when up against harmful people. All inquisitive people are dangerous. Men who are working against the law cannot afford to take chances. They certainly cannot afford to have a silly boy spying after them. Or a silly girl – a silly girl, Nanette. You cannot imagine your sex will save you. It is as easy to break a woman's skull as a man's. Suppose,' he said, reaching out his hand to grip my wrist, ' – how cold you are! – Suppose I am the murderer after all and decide to put a period to your foolish existence. It would be so easy. This is quite a storm, even for Greymanswick – it is high tide the day after tomorrow so prepare for the worst – and I could carry you to the garden wall and simply throw you over. No one would believe I did it. No one has seen us together, – they are all huddled over the fire. Your body would be found below. You would have lost your balance in the gale. Are you prepared to meet your God, Nanette?' His grip tightened. 'I shall of course be very shocked when they tell me the news. I'll even put on a mourning band for you –'

I knew all this was absurd, yet it was not very agreeable to have one's own death discussed so dispassionately. I snatched my wrist from him. I snapped at him, 'Why do you put on this play? I know perfectly well you're not the murderer, and I'm certain you would not murder me.'

Then he burst out laughing. 'I suspect you are not so sure! But never mind, I'll not kill you now. Later. Only now I am being serious and you will please listen. You have got to behave yourself, Nanette, and your pretty little sister who thinks she can win the world with her smile, will behave too. No more excursions, please. No more wandering round the house like Jack Lescott, prying into this,

126

peering into that. If there are things happening that puzzle you, let them be – have you observed any such thing?'

I hesitated, and he pounced on my hesitation. 'So you have. And what have you observed?'

'From what you have just said, it would be absurd of me to tell you.'

There was a momentary silence. Then he said dryly, 'You are perfectly right, of course, but I trust you are equally discreet with everyone else. After all, I am not asking much of you. Just mind your own business, Cousin, do your duty, do the work my aunt sets you, behave prettily to the guests. Only keep that little nose out of what does not concern you. And do not go to the sand dunes, on any account whatsoever.'

I said, 'I gather that Dolly has been talking to you.'

'It must,' he said, 'have been an occasion when you were not eavesdropping.'

This gagged my speaking as if he had laid a hand across my lips, and he laughed again. 'Did you believe yourself not seen? There are pictures on the walls, Nanette, and they have glass frames. I saw you plain, but it did not matter, there was after all nothing to see that could offend anyone, and I did not wish to deprive you of the pleasure of believing yourself unobserved.'

I was almost too mortified to speak, but I managed to stammer, 'I did not mean to listen, only –' Then because I could not be so cruelly set down, I spoke with more energy. 'You said – was my uncle really murdered?'

It was in every way a strange conversation because we were shadows to each other, we could not see each other's faces. He answered very coldly, 'That is something I cannot discuss.'

We stared at each other, faceless, dark creatures standing only a few inches apart. He seemed to me enormous. Then I said, 'I understand you are going back to London soon.'

'Who told you that?'

127

'My aunt, of course. Why, is it such a secret?'

'What else did she say to you?'

The words were rapped out at me, and I hesitated again: he suddenly shouted, 'She did say something – the old bitch! I'll kill her. I'll not have you entangled in her damnable web. Why don't you tell me? It seems to me you talk too much when you should be silent, and are silent when you should speak. What did she say?'

'She said nothing.'

'I don't believe you.' Then his tone changed. 'Nanette. I think we must stop shouting at each other. Will you go home? Back to London?'

'But –'

'I'll give you the money. I'll procure you a carriage. I'll find you somewhere to stay. Only for God's sake, get away from here. I'd like you to go now. Tonight. Will you go? Please say you will.'

I said miserably, 'I can't.'

'Why not?'

Why not, indeed? Because I love you. Because I cannot bear to leave you. Because I must know what all this is about. I only repeated, very low, 'I can't.'

He said bitterly, 'If I could pick you up and throw you into that carriage – You are an impossible girl. You have not changed from that little brat ten years ago. Do you think I have forgot? Even then you were creeping around, your eyes shining, your nose quivering –'

This was too much. I decided I must end this mortifying conversation. I began silently to walk away, only the wind hit me in the middle and I staggered back: this gave my cousin the chance to finish his speech.

'You've not grown up at all,' he said. 'You've not changed. You are still the little brat who decided to water the lawn. I have seldom seen anything that made me laugh so much. Only,' he called after me, for I had regained my balance and was running away, 'this time I am not laughing. Mind your own business, Nanette. For God's sake,

128

mind your own business. There is one dead already, it will make little difference if there are two or three. This is not a Shakespearian drama to litter the stage with corpses. For your sister's sake, if not your own, have a care and stop interfering with what don't concern you. Try to –'

I did not hear the end of it. I was by now running as hard as I could. I slammed the front door behind me and fled up the stairs. There I flung myself on to the bed and sobbed a little, for I loved him so much and we seemed to do nothing but quarrel, it was unendurable.

I did not tell Leonie what had happened. We always confided in each other, but this would make her angry and perhaps afraid. It was true that she was far braver than I, but it all sounded so very ugly and I felt it best to keep it from her. So when she came into the room, looking, as I had to notice, very pretty and somehow rather cream-fed, I simply told her that I had been for a walk in the wind and rain and was exhausted enough to lie down. As she of course knew my love of storms, she accepted this immediately, and set to recurling my hair which was in a shocking mess, wet and tangled and out of its pins.

She remarked as she did this – she was always deft at such things like Maman – 'Amelia is teaching me how to sew a sampler.'

I sat up very straight. 'Leonie,' I said, 'what are you up to?'

'Up to?' she repeated, all innocence and making big eyes at me.

'Yes, Leo. That is what I said. You know perfectly well that you detest all sewing.'

'The silks are such pretty colours,' she said, still innocent as a baby, then suddenly pulled out a handful of skeins from her pocket.

'Where did you get those from?'

'Amelia lent me them to see if I could match them in the village shop. I think,' said Leonie, gazing intently at the lock of hair she was twisting round, 'I might make a pair of

129

cushion covers.'

The thought of my little sister sewing diligently away at cushion covers was too much for me. We both fell into laughter. This was very good for me, for it rid me of the nightmare that was hanging over me. And I did not pursue the matter, only watched with some cynicism the scene in the drawing-room before dinner, where she and Amelia sat together like best friends at school, gazing at the skeins of silk, then at the frame where the half-finished sampler was displayed. It was quite ridiculous and I knew Leonie was up to mischief, but after all Amelia was not a child, and if she let herself be gulled, it was her own fault.

The storm died down before dawn. It was a wild night, with the waves pounding against the wall and the wind shrieking round the house, but in the morning it grew calmer, though the rain was still coming down and there was a high wind.

Dolly said, 'It's the highest tide of the year the day after tomorrow.'

But this did not mean anything to us, and we did not even think of it for at ten o'clock Mr. Lescott, Jack's father, arrived from London.

V

It was the most dreadful morning I can remember, apart from the time of the death of Papa and Maman. I think Mr. Lescott could not have been such an old man, for Jack was only eighteen, but he was exhausted from travelling all night and wild with grief and anger and pain: he looked a hundred, his whole being centred on his loss.

He strode into the hall, followed by the doctor. He made no pretence of greeting any of us. He simply said in a loud, flat voice, 'I wish to see my son's body.'

Even my aunt blenched, though otherwise she showed no emotion. She and John Gonomanaway conducted the poor man into the little room where Jack was lying and there left him. He stayed there for over an hour. When at last he emerged he spoke to John-Gon for a while, and then the coffin that he had transported from London was brought in, and the two of them placed the boy's dead body inside. I think Mr. Lescott wanted to return immediately but what with the long journey and the force of his despair, was physically incapable of doing so. He even joined us for luncheon, eating voraciously yet plainly not knowing what he was doing. His only conversation concerned Jack, and he kept on looking from one to the other of us, saying in a fierce, hysterical voice, 'What happened? I wish to know every detail. Who killed him? Why did anyone want to kill him? You've got to tell me. I must know. Surely you can understand that I must know.'

He never paused for an answer, and you may be sure that none of us could swallow a mouthful: Leonie, who was as soft-hearted as she was mischievous, cried so bitterly that she had to leave the table.

Even my aunt could hardly eat. She sat there, silent as always, her face very pale. She made no attempt to comfort the poor man, only watched him in a kind of desperation. We none of us knew what to do. There are no social gambits for such a situation. He went on eating, for I suppose it was something to do and, when his plate was refilled, he ate the second helping too. We heard over and over again what Jack was like as a child, how well he had done at school, the things he said and the things he did, and the most terrifying thing about it was that I found himself with a strange, dark picture of an unhappy childhood: Mr. Lescott had worshipped his son but he had been a stern father, and the memory of his own over-discipline somehow mingled with his loss, to double its misery.

Then he said suddenly, 'One of you killed him.'

At this moment my cousin Virgil came in. He had not sat down to luncheon. He looked very grim and white, as indeed we must all have done, and at this remark he turned to stare at Mr. Lescott, who continued in a quieter voice.

'I have heard things of this place,' he said, looking from one to the other of us, then fixing his gaze on my aunt. 'Oh, it sounds most charming, celebrated writer, amiable guests, my boy was delighted to come down. I believe it was through your publisher, Ma'am, that he came at all. But I am a cautious man, I made a few inquiries. He would never have come again –' He stopped, made a choking noise, then continued. His eyes were dry. He had not shed one tear. 'There are stories about Cudden Hall, and they are nothing to do with writing. They say this is a smuggling coast and –'

Virgil had sat down at the table next to him, and at this moment made a clumsy gesture, sending his glass of wine over the old man's knees. I think we were all glad to have something active to do, though Virgil was not a clumsy man and I was amazed he should do such a thing: we all leapt to our feet and ran around like hens, mopping up the wine with our serviettes while John-Gon poured out another glass.

132

Only my aunt sat there, her eyes still fixed on Mr. Lescott's face.

He looked at us as if we did not exist. He went on as if there had been no interruption. 'There are things happening here that you would all prefer to have hidden.' He looked down for a second at his wine-stained breeches. I think he did not see them, any more than he was aware of Virgil's hand which had descended on his wrist. 'One of you is a murderer,' he said. 'I know my boy. He was a good boy but he had one grave fault. I tried to chastise it out of him, I wish to God I had succeeded. He was too inquisitive. He was always meddling in things that did not concern him. I have no doubt whatsoever that he found out something that aroused his curiosity and being as he was, he would not wait until he knew the answer. That is why you killed him.' He rose to his feet as he spoke. 'You think me a poor old man so consumed with grief that he notices nothing, but I can assure you, that is by no means the case. My boy inherited his powers of observation from me. The moment I came in here, I smelt evil, as he did, and that was why you killed him.'

We were all deathly silent. Mr. Pleydell, I saw, had grown ashen white.

'I am going now,' said Mr. Lescott. He turned his head to stare at Virgil: he shook his wrist free from the restraining hand. 'Are you trying to prevent my speaking, young man? Why should you do that? Are you Jack's murderer?'

'No, sir,' answered Virgil quietly.

'I only have your word for it. I see no reason to believe any of you. I shall be back. I shall take steps to investigate this midden. My Jack will not be unavenged. I intend to see that his murderer hangs.'

Then, ignoring us, he moved towards the doorway and looked up at John-Gon who was standing there. He said quite calmly, 'Kindly summon my coachman. I would like the coffin carried out to my carriage.' And with this he went into the hall; he said goodbye to none of us only for a second his gaze met my aunt's.

We sat there like statues, except for my aunt who poured herself out some more wine. I could not see Virgil's face, for his head was bowed. I was thankful that Leonie had left the room, I would not have wished her to witness such a scene. Then I heard the heavy footsteps of people carrying out the coffin, and this was too much for me, I began to run out of the room.

It was Mr. Pleydell who stopped me. I was sorry for him, I could not imagine a more hideous plight for any man, but I still could not like him and tried to ignore him.

But he put his hand on my shoulder so that I was compelled to stop. He said in an abrupt, low voice, 'Go back to London. Go back with Mr. Lescott and take your sister with you.'

I cried out indignantly – it really was becoming too much, the way everyone wished us away from Cudden Hall – 'But I have no intention of –' when he laid his hand against my lips. He repeated in the same soft voice, 'Be sensible and go back to London.'

I did not like the feel of that cold, dry hand on my mouth. I pushed it away, saying, 'I think you are out of your mind. You would have me travel with poor Jack's coffin – I am not returning to London, Mr. Pleydell, I am staying here.'

Everybody must have heard me. I made no attempt to lower my voice. But I was aware that Virgil had got up from the table and was coming towards me. This was more than I could take and I shamelessly fled, not pausing until I reached the door of my own room.

Leonie seemed to have recovered, though the marks of tears were still on her cheeks. She was sitting at the dressing table, brushing her hair. She looked at me in the mirror. She said, 'That poor gentleman – I gather he's gone. I heard his carriage.' She swung round on the stool to face me. We both spoke the same words at the same time. 'I must get away from here. For God's sake, let's go for a walk.'

This was something that frequently happened to us. It

was almost as if we were twins. This time we did not even answer each other. We flung on our cloaks and bonnets and made for the door. At that moment we neither of us had any intention of going where we should not: we simply wanted to leave this house, so filled with grief and murder and hate.

We came downstairs with no pretence of secrecy. There was no one about. Now that Mr. Lescott had gone, the guests were no doubt huddled over the drawing-room fire. Only as we stepped out into the cold – the rain had stopped but the wind was still blowing hard – I remarked, 'I half expected Amelia to come running after us.'

Leonie said airily, gazing ahead, 'Oh, she'll be too upset to do that.'

'We are all upset –'

'I don't mean that. You see, she found out before luncheon that she has mislaid all her silks.' She flashed a sudden smile at me. 'We could not imagine what happened to them. We thought that one of the servants might have tidied them away. But when she started sewing, she found only one green skein. She must be looking for them now. I wonder where they can be.'

'Leo!'

'Yes, Nan?'

'Leo,' I said, giving her arm a shake, 'where are they?'

She began to giggle. Sometimes Leonie can be very childish. We were passing the sea wall. We had neither of us mentioned our destination but we were moving, half instinctively, towards Cuckold's Point. 'Well,' she said, 'they are not really very far. She will find them soon enough. They are in the drawer of the escritoire by the drawing-room window. They will come to no harm. By the time she has discovered them and scolded the maid, we will be well out of sight.'

I told her weakly that she was a naughty girl.

'If you want her to come with us, I can always go back to fetch her.'

Then we both laughed and the subject of Amelia was forgotten.

At the end of the sea wall we paused. I noticed that part of it was down: there were great holes in it that a man could put his fist through. This chilled me a little for the sea was still wild and soon it would be high tide again and the waves would make the holes larger. I remembered Dolly's words. But despite everything Greymanswick looked so secure, and Cudden Hall, high on the hill, could surely not be reached, by even the most tempestuous wave. Smoke rose peacefully from the little cottages and the *Holy Margaret* was moored a short distance away. It was simply an ordinary small fishing village, only the memory of that ancient city remained with me: the citizens there must have felt the same until the cruel sea enveloped them.

Then I saw that we were not alone. A solitary figure stood at the bottom of the hill. I recognised him as Mr. Pleydell. Perhaps Mr. Lescott had upset him so much that like us he had to walk away. He had a gun in his hand and was shooting at seagulls, God knows why, for they were doing no harm and could not be eaten. Men seem to enjoy killing for its own sake. We heard the muffled explosions, and Leonie turned to look in the same direction.

'He is a good shot,' she said, and as she spoke a wretched bird came spinning down. Then she said contemptuously, 'How stupid. Has he nothing better to do?'

Some dim memory stirred in my mind, but I only shrugged: if Mr. Pleydell wanted to kill seagulls, it was none of our business. We began to move away from the sea wall, a little hunched up so that he would not see us, though he was so concentrated on his little massacre that I doubt if he would have noticed. The cold, salt air was glorious to us, wrapped warmly in our cloaks. We both turned our gaze on the sand dunes: in this weather they looked dark and sinister like something out of a fairy tale.

Leonie remarked as if it did not matter, 'It is a good day for it. No one would expect us to explore in such weather. They have no idea how hardy we are. They probably think that Londoners have forogtten how to walk.'

I said nothing, only for some reason I suddenly thought of poor Mr. Lescott travelling home with the coffin beside him. He must wish he was in his coffin too. We all have to die, but papa once said that to lose one's child is the worst of all, it seems – I remember his exact words – so unreasonable, so unfair. I could not endure the thought of his despair and a sob came into my throat so that I had to turn my head away.

Leonie said, 'You are still brooding on Jack, aren't you?'

'How can I help it?'

'What you need is a good walk.'

'Oh, Leonie!'

'It wouldn't take very long. It can't be more than a mile. We'll be back well before supper. Everyone will assume we are in our room. And Aunt Elizabeth always works in the afternoon so she won't disturb us.'

There was another volley and another bird plummeted from the sky. Mr. Pleydell would soon be surrounded by corpses. It was more than I could take and it made up my mind for me. I took Leonie's arm in silence, and we began to walk briskly towards Cuckold's Point.

The inn of that name – it was painted boldly on the creaking signboard – must have been built a long time ago. I do not know about such things but I think Queen Elizabeth might have seen it. The timbers were black and rotting with age, the windows broken and plugged with rags: the whole place was unwelcoming and the dunes which ranged behind it were more desolate than I expected. I was still half disposed to turn back, if only to help Amelia find her silks, but as I hesitated, the door of the 'Cuckold's Point' was flung open. There was a great baying of voices and laughter, and Leonie and I dived back to hide behind the little outhouse to the left.

The fishing population of Greymanswick had been sensibly spending a bleak afternoon drinking ale. It was Tom Easey who staggered out first. He was very drunk. We did

137

not like the look of him, and huddled together. He did not resemble the jolly man I remembered from my childhood. He looked indeed like someone who would shoot the Preventives down if he had to, and Hookey Miller, who reeled after him, was no better. If either rogue had known we were watching, I doubt if we would have received much mercy.

Tom stood there, his jacket flapping in the wind. I saw that he had a pistol in his belt. He called out in a thick, rough voice, 'Come on, lads. That's enough of boozing. There's work to be done.'

I saw that I had under-estimated the *Holy Margaret*. Perhaps like us she was small but hardy. This would be good smuggling weather. The Preventives would be snug at home while Tom and his mates sailed for the Dutch coast. Leonie and I, still as mice, watched. It was the first time we had really seen the villagers, apart from the men who delivered food and wine to the kitchen. They looked neither better nor worse than anyone else but they had all plainly swallowed a great deal of drink, they were all set on their purpose and none of them would have been pleased to know he was being observed by the young ladies from the Hall. They rolled after Tom and Hookey Miller, singing and laughing and swearing, and one of them almost brushed against us as he lurched against the wall.

We were both afraid, but though we were silent and deathly still, we were enjoying ourselves enormously. This was an adventure, this was better than sitting around in Cudden Hall. At that moment we almost forgot about Jack and his father. We watched the men going down the hill towards the sea wall. One of them stopped to relieve himself, and Tom Easey called out, 'Hurry up now, you bastard. You can't keep the old bitch waiting.'

Then, as the men disappeared behind the brow of the hill, we jumped up and ran as hard as we could towards the dunes.

Tom and his friends were certainly too preoccupied to look back, but they would not have seen much if they had done so: the weather was in our favour and our dark cloaks made us inconspicuous. Once on the dunes we straightened ourselves to look around us. The wind blew the sand into our eyes and nostrils in a disagreeable way and, now that the excitement was done, we shivered a little with the cold.

It was all so strange that we were struck silent. Mr. Lowry had spoken of the petrified forest that had once stretched to the north of Greymanswick, but we had not fully understood what he meant. Now we saw that where we stood there had been trees and shrubs and flowering things, birds had sung, small creatures had scurried past. Before that wicked day four hundred years ago, the citizens had stared up at a stretch of green: perhaps they had walked here in the summer evenings, courted, played games, perhaps some of them swung on creaking boughs. It was all gone. The sea had swept across it, carrying with it all living things: nothing remained but trunks and fallen branches solidified by centuries of rain and sand into a kind of yellow stone with furrowed patterns on it. Walking was treacherous for the wind had blown the sand into pyramids with the marks of the waves still clear to see, there were tree stumps to trip one up, and dotted everywhere were caves where no doubt Mr. Lowry's ferns grew. It was like something from a dead world, the surface of the moon, but there was still life here for as we stood, staring, something ran across our path and Leonie gave a gasp, gripping my hand so tightly that she hurt me.

"It's a rat!' she whispered.

'Well,' I said with an elder-sisterly bravery that I did not feel, 'it won't hurt us. The poor thing is probably more frightened than we are.'

She said in a bewildered voice, 'Nothing grows here.'

'We are under the sea,' said I, and this in a way was true; I imagine that if we had dug down we would have found the skeletons and fossilised remains of sea-things. But as I spoke the rain began to fall again, which made things more unpleasant than ever: instead of sliding on dry sand we found ourselves sinking into the mud. We looked around for shelter and decided to make our way to the nearest cave. We neither of us cared much for the prospect of going underground, thinking we might be swallowed up in sand, but we could not stay there getting soaked, and we could not climb down the hill until the *Holy Margaret* was well away. The adventure by now was not so amusing, and the wet sand blown against us was horrid, but we doggedly climbed over a series of pyramids and at last came to a cave-opening that was wide enough for us to slip inside.

It was very dark but it was a relief to be out of the wind and rain. Only Leonie, who seemed to have lost her spirit, muttered, 'It must have been so dreadful. To have the sea over everything – The wall does not look very strong. It's only sand and shingle after all.'

I said comfortingly, 'It's withstood a great deal.'

'And I'm so hungry!'

'You ate no lunch. Neither,' I said with a sigh, 'did I.'

'How could we with that poor man there?'

'Oh I know, but – never mind. The rain will stop soon, and even if it doesn't, we'll run back home. We can go down to the kitchen. Cook is bound to have something for us.'

We were whispering. I do not know why. We seemed to be alone in the world. But the cave was ghostly: my aunt would surely have seized upon it as a setting for a scene from her novels. I gazed around me to adapt my vision to the dim light, then saw almost with relief that Mr. Lowry was right: there were green, ferny spikes a little further down. It gave a kind of warmth to this dead, primitive world, and I leaned forward to pick one of the plants, to have the reassurance of its living contact.

I had forgotten the sloping ground. I stooped too far, lost my balance and the next second found myself, together with Leonie who had clutched at me, in a huddle several feet below. Fortunately the soft sand protected us, but we were both a little shaken. I stumbled to my feet, pulling

140

Leonie up after me, when a voice spoke.

'Keep still!'

It was a man's voice with a marked accent. The accent was somehow familiar but we were too terrified to consider it. We froze like frightened rabbits, then blinked as a lantern flashed in our faces.

There was a pause, a muttered, 'Good God!' then Leonie, coming suddenly to her senses, exclaimed in what was almost a shout, 'Oh Nan, it must be our French prisoner!'

We neither of us paused to consider why this should be so. I suppose we were so convinced we would meet this prisoner that we took it for granted. We both began to speak in French. We were not well-educated in the normal sense, but Papa had made sure that we read well, and Maman was determined that our French should be almost as good as our native tongue. 'You are French girls,' she told us repeatedly, and she would not endure the slightest mispronunciation and made cruel fun of any misused word or grammatical error.

We therefore turned a babble of French on this poor young man, forgetting that he might be armed and dangerous. He must have thought us escaped from the nearest Bedlam. When at last we could see we saw a young man, pale and thin, with a great growth of reddish-brown beard upon him. He seemed quite stunned. He could hardly be blamed. He was indeed armed, for we saw his pistol, and there was a knife in his belt, but it was obvious that, whatever we were, we were not dangerous, so he crouched there in a baffled silence as we bombarded him with questions.

He did not at first attempt to answer us. I think we gave him little opportunity. We asked who he was, what was his name, how long he had been here and how he managed. 'You came over of course with the Prince's ship,' Leonie told him, and the poor fellow simply looked at her as if at any moment soldiers would arrive and take him away.

Leonie went on, 'We will look after you. You have no more need to worry. We will bring food to you every day, will we not, Nanette?'

I agreed that we would. My heart sank as the words left my mouth. The dunes were after all some distance away: we had escaped discovery this time, but such folk as Tom Easey and John Gonomanaway would soon become suspicious, besides, there was Virgil who always had his eye on us. I saw long, sleepless nights ahead of us, with our creeping down to the kitchen at three in the morning. But Leonie was too excited to think of something so practical; it was plain that she was overcome by the glory of it all.

It was at this point that the young man at last spoke. My rather uncertain promise about the food produced a momentary silence, then suddenly he rose to his feet, seized each of us by the hand and lugged us out of the cave so that we were once more in the fading daylight.

The rain had stopped. I think he really wanted to have a good look at us. Before he spoke I managed to have a good look at him. Living underground would make him pale, but he did not have the air of one who was starved. It seemed to me for a moment that the face, half concealed by the beard, was somehow familiar: I wondered if perhaps he had crept down to the village and I had seen him there. But I could not place him and decided this must be imagination. He had very bright light-blue eyes, he was not as young as I had at first believed. His voice was thin and rather high.

He spoke in his accented English. He said, 'Who the devil are you, and what are you doing here?'

'Oh,' cried Leonie – I could see she was a little taken aback – 'we both spèak French –'

He simply repeated, always in English, 'Who the devil are you?'

It was difficult to answer him, and Leonie made no attempt to do so. I spoke at last a little hesitantly: I found myself unreasonably irritated by the fact that he was questioning us, for surely after all it was he who was the intruder. I did not answer him directly. I said, 'I think you should tell us your name. I am Nanette Cudden, and this is my sister, Leonie.'

He repeated in a sharp voice, 'Cudden?'

Perhaps he had heard the name from the villagers – He must after all emerge from his cave occasionally. I said, 'Yes. We live up at the Hall. We are Mrs. Cudden's nieces.'

He looked as if this information were the last straw. He briefly closed his eyes, then muttered, 'I do not understand.'

I said, 'You have not told us your name.'

'An – André.'

I noticed the hesitation and the fact that he did not give me his second name. I thought he must be lying to me, but this I could understand well enough: as a Frenchman in England, perhaps really an escaped prisoner, he was in no position to trust us or indeed anyone. He said, again in English – why could he not speak French to us? – 'I don't understand why you are here.'

Leonie, who had been looking him up and down, answered quietly, 'We were just out for a walk.'

'In this weather?'

Then she lost her temper. I could see she was more frightened than angry, and I was frightened too: it was fine to make a romance about French prisoners but not so amusing to be confronted by one so heavily armed, and with no one within call. She cried out, looking exactly like Maman in one of her dramatic rages, 'You have no right to keep on asking us questions and not answering any of ours. We have been most friendly to you. We have offered to bring you food, we might even help you reach the coast and get back to France. But you seem to look on us as enemies. If that is how you feel, we'll leave you to starve all by yourself.'

Then he laughed. As he did so he looked younger and more vulnerable. He reached out his hand to take hers again. 'You have spirit,' he said. 'I like lasses with spirit.

143

You must forgive me, but you must see that in my position I have to be suspicious of everyone. I would very much appreciate your help. I have been living on what I can steal by creeping out at night, it is not very much and sometimes I feel pretty desperate.'

'Well,' said Leonie, restored to her normal good temper, 'you need not worry any more about food, for we will contrive to bring it to you. We'll be here tomorrow night without fail. I don't think we can risk coming out again today, but tomorrow – we'll be there, will we not, Nan?'

I agreed, rather unhappily. I think this was the first moment in my life when I realised that romance and wisdom by no means always went together. This was the kind of thing my aunt would have used in one of her novels, provided André was mad and myself a ravished nun, but this was not a novel, this was real life, and what made it worse was that my little sister was involved. I wished now that I had listened to Virgil – how he would laugh to hear me say this! – and I glanced around me, shuddering, for the dunes in the late September light were sinister. The thought of coming here in the middle of the night made me sick with apprehension, and I wished childishly and shamelessly that I were safe at home.

However, we had committed ourselves, and Leonie was enjoying herself again, only when André thanked her, this time in French she looked at him with a faint surprise.

'I think,' she said, 'you do not have the Paris accent. My mother was French and came from Paris. This almost makes you one of the family, does it not? Where do you come from, André?'

He answered reluctantly. I received the impression that the question angered him, but of course he was on the run and perhaps he still did not quite trust us. He answered roughly that he came from Marseilles, and I saw Leonie's eyes move over him again as if she did not quite believe him.

I was about to say that we must go back before our absence was noticed when suddenly in the far distance I

144

saw someone coming towards us.

It was John-Gon. I recognised the bulky figure and the rolling gait. I had never before thought of him as a sailor, but I knew now from the way he walked that he would be as much at home on a boat as Tom Easey. However, this was no moment for deliberation, and we all shot inside the cave, huddling against the sandy walls.

Leonie whispered to André, 'You must stay here till he's gone. I cannot imagine why he is here. Perhaps he is looking for us. He is my aunt's butler. It would be disastrous if he saw you.'

We remained there in silence. It was unlikely that John-Gon would trouble to investigate any of the caves. He passed within a few yards of us. He was carrying what looked like a big sack. He was whistling a little tune that I did not recognise. When at last he disappeared from view behind the hillocks, André spoke, giving us both a little shove towards the cave's entrance.

He said, 'You are safe now, lassies.'

I did not care much for the appellation, and the words surprised me. 'It's your safety we're concerned about,' I said as we scrambled out, wet and sandy, back on to the dunes.

He did not answer this. He seemed a man of few words, or perhaps we spoke so much that he had little chance to say anything. We said goodbye and told him we would be back tomorrow night. As we said this his teeth suddenly gleamed white: I could not understand why he was so amused. But he shook us by the hand and we walked quickly away. I looked back once. He was standing there, silhouetted against the stormy sky. I longed to tell him not to be so reckless, but I dared not turn back, for it was growing late.

It was only when we reached Cuckold's Point that we turned for a final look at the dunes.

'They are rather horrid,' said Leonie. She had not spoken a word during our journey. Then she said, 'You

145

know, Nan, he must have a friend here.'

'Why do you say that?'

'There were a lot of bottles in the cave. I don't see how he could steal all that wine and not be caught. I don't see either how he could come down to the village unnoticed. People here all know each other, and they are very suspicious.'

Then before I could answer she caught my hand and we ran like mad back to the Hall. We were for once thankful to be inside the house again, and we went immediately to our room, ostensibly to change for dinner but partly to regain control of ourselves.

I said at last, 'I suppose it's some girl. Leo, we will take food tomorrow because we promised, but it will be for the first and last time. I don't like this very much.'

'I don't like him very much,' said Leonie, 'and I think he is a shocking liar. For one thing, he doesn't come from Marseilles.'

'How do you know that?'

Leonie was doing her hair, the pretty curly hair that no rain could spoil. She said, 'Maman used to imitate it. Don't you remember?' Then she laughed, saying softly, '*Douce-meng, doucemeng*! Anyway, I do not think he is French at all. I think he is a Scot.'

Then I knew where I had heard that accent before. I said, quite cross that she should be so much cleverer than me, 'You're right, of course. I should have known. But why should he let us assume he comes from France?'

'We didn't give him much chance to deny it. But,' said Leonie, waving her brush at me, 'I am sure he came over on that boat. Not all the passengers were French, and a great many Scots live in France. He speaks French quite well after all. As a Scot here, with all the rumours about the Prince coming over, he is perhaps in more danger than if he was French. We'll have to help him, Nan, only I am going to get the truth from him, I don't like being lied to.'

All this went to prove that Leonie, though much more perceptive than I am, and perhaps more cynical, was still a

146

romantic at heart. But I was too tired to argue with her, and her words seemed plausible enough. Presently we went down to dinner, which we badly needed, and it was as if nothing had happened, though I thought that once or twice my aunt turned a strange, considering look upon me. Amelia, glancing at my damp hair, said she gathered we had been for one of our little walks. She had found her silks. I do not know if she suspected Leonie or not, but the little friendship was definitely over.

Virgil at the end of the table did not even raise his head to greet us. It was my aunt who really disconcerted me, just as we were about to rise from the table.

VI

It came strangely and horribly for, as if we had not already endured enough, we were greeted with fresh disaster, after the first course was served.

My aunt, though she seldom spoke, had an acute sense of drama. I suppose this was why she waited until we had finished our soup, and were talking together in a reasonably friendly manner. Conversation at Cudden Hall tended to be both dull and dreary, but I think we were undergoing a reaction to all that had happened, and the talk for us was positively lively. The Collector had been busy again and there had been another robbery. This time it was from a church a few miles away: the box had of course been emptied, irreplaceable silver taken, also some Roman glass which had been discovered by a gardener digging up the flower beds outside. It seemed useless stuff to take for it would at once be recognised, but perhaps the Collector was aptly named and kept everything in some private museum so that he could gloat on it at his pleasure.

Mr. Lowry, who was hoping to return to his own home within a few days, lamented bitterly as if this were something personal, and Mr. Pleydell – there was now an open hostility between the two of them – taunted him, telling him that he never went to church, so why should this affect him, an unbeliever.

I thought Mr. Lowry would burst into tears of sheer rage, and I could see that his wife thought so too, for she put a restraining hand on his wrist. For all she seemed so delicate, with her white face and talk of pills and sleeping powders that she poured down herself, I think she was

148

really the stronger of the two. He managed to control himself and contented himself with remarking, as he had done before, that he hoped that the villain would soon be caught and hanged. We then all made an effort to change the subject, Amelia recounting the saga of her silks, and Mrs. Lowry referring to some pretty pots and jars made at a shop in the village.

It was then that my aunt, bored by all this small talk, spoke.

'I think,' she said in her flat voice, 'you should know that Mr. Lescott is dead. He was stopped by a highwayman during the first hour of his journey, and shot through the head. I only heard a little while ago.'

We none of us said a word. Perhaps we were all so numbed by these continuous tragedies that another death seemed almost incidental. But when my aunt added, helping herself lavishly to the next course, 'It is surely a mercy. He cannot have had anything left to live for. Besides,' she said, 'it is in any case none of our business,' we were too shocked to do more than stare: even Mr. Pleydell shot her a nervous glance.

Virgil said quietly, 'I think it is very much our business.'

'And why, pray?' demanded my aunt, irritated as always by the faintest show of opposition.

He looked at her. It was as if the image of a cruelly-used little boy shimmered between them, and I think she saw it too, for she blinked and averted her eyes. I will never know if even at the beginning there was any feeling between them: from the way she treated him it would be hard to believe. But now there was fierce hatred, and in addition from him an almost frightening menace. The little boy had grown into a man, a man who would never forgive.

He did not answer her and she did not repeat her question. She concentrated once more on her food: the only sign of disturbance was that she ate more rapidly than usual and split some of the meat on to the cloth.

It was at the end of the meal when I was about to go up to

our room, feeling I could not bear it any more, that she suddenly addressed me.

'You once told me you played the piano, Nanette,' she said. 'I am sure we would all enjoy hearing you. It would cheer us up. You shall sing us a little song. A French song, perhaps.'

I was horrified and shocked too. Only my aunt could have suggested such a thing at such a moment. I felt myself going scarlet. Not only was it macabre, it was also somehow humiliating. I had forgotten my first talk with her, and believed she had done the same. It was true that I had often played at home, singing duets with Maman in her small, sweet voice, but that was a family gathering round the piano, this would be performing in front of strangers who would probably be bored to death.

I stammered, 'Oh Ma'am, I don't think – I have no music with me,' but she cut across me. If my aunt had decided I must play – God knows why, for I do not believe she knew one note of music from another – I was going to play. And of course my excuse was a nonsense: I was quite capable of accompanying myself without music in front of me.

Leonie was giggling at my confusion, and I could have killed her. I could indeed have killed the lot of them, which was no tribute to my eighteen years. My only consolation was that everyone would suffer more than myself, and in all truth I have never seen more resigned expressions than those worn by my prospective audience. I could only pray that my cousin Virgil would leave us, as he always did after dinner, but no, he followed us in, and out of the corner of my bemused eye I saw him watching me. By now I could hardly see anything clearly, and I dumped myself down at the piano, which Mr. Lowry had opened for me, and ran my hand over the keys.

Then I said triumphantly to my aunt, 'I cannot play this, Ma'am. It is out of tune.'

She only said, 'It sounds all right to me. Come on, child. We are all waiting.'

There was nothing for it but to begin. The piano was not badly out of tune, but it was agonising to sing against notes that were not quite true. However, I began, with a few soft chords. I did not know what to choose but somehow found myself singing an old French song that was a great favourite of Maman's: *Les marches du palais*, the story of the little shoemaker who fell in love with a princess. And as I sang, I regained heart, for I truly love music, and not even the discords could destroy my pleasure. For that brief while I was home again, with Maman, Leonie and darling Papa, who had a voice like a crow, joining in with what he fondly imagined to be a bass obligato. I forgot my audience and, when I came to the last verse:

> '*Nous dormirons ensemble*
> *Jusqu'à la fin du monde,*'

I found myself near tears, and somehow this did not matter. These silly, dull people listening to me were nothing but puppets: it was my dear parents, so long now in their grave, who were alive. The song released for me all the emotion I had struggled to stifle: this household was empty of love, but the love was still there, I had found it in myself. I swung round on my stool to look at them, as they all dutifully clapped: my aunt so cruel, so obsessed with power, poor sad Amelia, longing for what she could never have. Mr. Lowry lamenting his possessions, Mr. Pleydell out to destroy.

Then I saw that Virgil was standing behind me. I looked up at him. The tears were in my eyes, but I did not care. I waited for some derisive comment. My aunt was telling me without conviction that I had a pretty voice, and Mr. Lowry bestowed on me an approving smile, but Virgil surveyed me gravely, then said, 'The rain has stopped, Cousin. Would you care to take a little walk with me before the storm breaks?'

I was so astonished that for a moment I did not reply. I did not know what he meant about the storm, for there was now a kind of lull: it was no longer as wild as it had been on the dunes. Then I suddenly saw the enraged look on my aunt's face. It was so seldom that she showed emotion that I was a little afraid. But somehow this determined me. I thanked my cousin and said I would fetch my cloak, which I at once did. I ignored my aunt's anger. There was after all nothing she could do. It was perfectly natural that cousins should take a little evening promenade together, but I knew she would do anything to stop us, so I was out of the room before she could think of any excuse.

Leonie was not there when we set out. I felt a little disturbed at not asking her to come with us, but of course I could not do so, and she knew that as well as I. It was a kind of rift, but it had to come, for all we had been so inseparable. Virgil and I stepped out into the garden and made for the hill where lay the remains of St. Saviour's church.

He took my arm, and presently his hand clasped mine. It was a strange evening. There was a keen wind blowing, and the sea, for all it was no longer violent, was rolling in a black and oily way. I shivered a little, and Virgil remarked, 'Tomorrow is the highest tide of the year.'

I said, as we began to clamber down the steep hillside, 'Do you really believe there will be another flood?'

'I daresay,' replied Virgil, 'they asked the very same question four hundred years ago. "Do you really think there will be a flood?" And of course everyone said, "No, of course not, even if there is, the dyke will withstand it, have another stoup of mead and don't be so foolish."'

We were now among the gravestones. Virgil said, 'Let us stay here. There is no better place in the world for conversation than a graveyard. The dead cannot interrupt us. Where would you like to sit, Nanette? Take care of the brambles. I think I shall rest myself by the side of Ann Curlin who departed this life after bequeathing to her husband –' He bent his head as he spoke, to read the words. '. . . *one sonne and daughters syx and who deceased ye XVII of Maye in ye yeare of our Lord, 1576.* I wonder how the poor lad survived such a plethora of females, he must have had so many buttons sewn on for him it is a wonder he ever undressed at all. Who is to be your guide and companion?'

I selected a squat, flat stone next to his. It was in a clearing so that we were half hidden by the briars. 'This,' I said, 'is Mr. Francis Yaxley. I think his last wish was to frighten us. The stone says, "As you are now, so once was I, As I am now, so shall you lie."'

Virgil said scornfully, 'Oh, that is used everywhere. Mr. Yaxley was not a very original gentleman. Perhaps there was nothing good to be said about him.'

We sat side by side with the dead between us. My eyes moved again to the sea. I said at last, 'Tom Easey is out tonight.'

'Tom Easey is making use of the brief calm. I doubt he'll be out tomorrow. I think like everyone else he will be hanging on to his cottage, knee-deep in water.'

I said, my voice shaking a little, 'So the bells of St. Botolph will be ringing.'

'Who told you that? Oh, I know. It's our John-Gon, the old devil. That's a child's story, though there are people who swear they have heard them.'

I said, 'You seem so certain the sea will engulf us.'

'That's what all Greymanswick is saying. How am I to know? I am a Londoner these days. I have never stayed more than a few weeks here since I was seventeen.'

I realised that the wind had dropped. There was a curious hush in the air. There was still a moon to light us, but I could not see Virgil's face: his head was bowed as if he were still studying the gravestone. I said, 'What exactly happened four hundred years ago?'

'Oh, the sea rolled in. And the houses fell down. I daresay,' said Virgil, 'there was a roaring and a rushing and a crashing and a screaming, as walls collapsed and ceilings broke, and little people scurried here and there, with the water rising round their ankles, then their knees, then their waists – what could they do? You cannot run when your

153

whole world is falling round you. A night-black sky and waves as high as mountains. The city was totally destroyed.'

'Cudden Hall survived.'

'Did it?' said Virgil.

'And it will survive again. Look at it. It is as strong as a rock.'

He raised his head to stare at me. In the moonlight I could only see the outline of his face. He said urgently, 'Why won't you go back to London? Why, Nanette? Answer me.'

I only said, 'If I had gone with Mr. Lescott, I would be dead.' Then, 'Was he – was he murdered deliberately?'

'Oh yes. Of course. I tried to warn him. He wouldn't listen. People never listen.' Then he cried out, 'You're not listening either. I'm warning you, Nanette. I want you to leave here. I'll look after you. I'll protect you. Well? Why won't you go?'

'I suppose,' I said, 'it is because I'm in love with you.'

If I had wished to silence him, I could not have chosen better words. I did not mean to say them. In our world we are trained not to say such things. Maman would have been furious with me. But I no longer cared. I felt that if the end of the world were coming, I might as well speak my mind. The song had somehow freed me from all the shackles of convention. Soon we might all be under the sea where modesty and feminine decorum no longer mattered. I said again, 'I love you with all my heart.' I added with some asperity, 'I do not know why. You've scarce been civil to me. But I think that does not matter.'

He said in a whisper, 'Oh my God!' then in complete bewilderment, 'No one has ever said such a thing to me in my life. Once you told me you hated me, do you not remember? You said I was a horrid boy and you wouldn't marry me if I were the last man on earth. Would you marry me, Nanette?'

'Oh yes,' I said. 'Of course I would marry you. Are you

asking me? Mr. Yaxley and Mrs. Curlin will be our witnesses.'

He said again, 'Oh my God!' He did not attempt to come nearer me. He only said after a long pause, 'I want to tell you a story.'

I said, 'I would like you to kiss me first.'

He said with a sigh, 'You are a very forward young lady, Nanette. I'm beginning to think too that you're a very dangerous young lady.'

But I could hear the undertone of laughter in his voice, though he still sat there, with the gravestone between us. It was I who at last rose to my feet, moved across and settled down against his knee. I said, 'I suppose I am. I think my mother would never forgive me. I have no right to speak in such a fashion. Only I no longer care. We have too little time – I know. We are brought up not to show our emotions. We let the gentlemen take the initiative, then we are coy and prim, we play little games, we say, No, when we mean, Yes, we shrug and gesture and make silly faces. I can't be like that with you, Virgil. Perhaps tomorrow the sea will flood over us and we shall both be dead.' Then I said in despair, 'I suppose you are disgusted with me,' and began to cry.

He took me in his arms. He did not kiss me, only rubbed his cheek against mine. He held me tightly against his chest. He said again, 'I want to tell you a story.'

I did not care what he told me. I would have listened to whatever he said, I would have done whatever he asked. If he had asked me to come to bed with him, I would have gone. I no longer thought of the sea and what tomorrow would bring. I only knew it was now, I was with Virgil, I loved him, the waves could rise high above us and I no longer cared. I did not think of Leonie or of my aunt or indeed of anything except the warmth of the arms around me.

I felt him sigh. Then he began to speak.

'You know how it was with me,' he said. 'But of course

155

when I first came here, I expected nothing of the kind. I was very young, as young as you when you defied us all. I liked you for that. I wanted to kill you, but I liked you all the same. They told me to keep an eye on you. My God, I'd have needed as many eyes as there are on a peacock's tail. If I so much as turned my head, you were gone. You were like a little mouse, scurrying here and there, and always interfering in other people's business. I longed to wring your scrawny little neck. But I liked you even then, and oh God, how thankful I was you were not staying, you were going back home. It would have been the same for you, if you had remained here. Your sex wouldn't have saved you. I could see it in my aunt's eye. You would have been whipped and starved, anything to break your spirit. You would have suffered as I did. You see, I was like you, Nanette. I too had been indulged, allowed to do as I wished. I never dreamed there was another world where children were treated like animals. From the first moment she decided to break me. It is not difficult to break another human being, and I was very young. Only there is always something – whatever she did, and her devil of an executioner, I still managed, God knows how, to hang on to something of myself. Why are you crying? You must not keep on crying –'

I sobbed, 'I cannot bear it, I cannot!' and at this he at last kissed me so that presently my tears stopped and I lay quiet in his arms.

Then he began speaking again.

'It is all over,' he said. 'It is not worth tears. Only these things leave their mark. I believe that cruelty defiles. If I have been unkind to you, it is a little because the world was unkind to me. It doesn't excuse me, in no way, but it is the way things are. But as I said, it is all over, and perhaps tomorrow it will be all over for a great many more. And there were kind people, you know. There was Dolly. And my uncle. He was so good to me. Sometimes I think that was why he had to die. Only my aunt never gives up. She could not subdue me with beatings, so she tried another method. It was more successful. I cannot tell you all the details, Nanette, but I discovered something of what was going on, and I suppose it amused me, and she saw it amused me, and she contrived to pull me a little into her web. I knew it was wrong, I took care not to involve myself too much, but how entertaining to find a respectable lady behaving in such a way – I should have walked away. I should have told people what I knew. But I did not, I despised and hated her, but I let myself be embroiled until suddenly I discovered how wicked she was, what vile things she was doing.'

He paused. I had no idea what he was talking about, but it did not matter. I was lying in Virgil's arms and we were in a graveyard, with the menacing sea only a few hundred yards away. Tomorrow we might be dead. Why should I worry? I had been in beautiful places in my time: my parents had taken us abroad, we had seen Paris, we had gazed at mountains, we had been escorted round picture galleries, we went to the opera. It was all wonderful and exciting, but now the whole world consisted of two strong arms, we were surrounded by the dead and the church above us was in ruins. I was completely happy, and I listened while the deep voice spoke again.

'It was like a game. Until – until. You had landed yourself in a thieves' kitchen, my girl, and I, whom you propose to marry, am one of the thieves. But now the play is over. She does not see that. It is the kind of thing she refuses to know. She will never have enough, she does not see that there comes a point when one cannot endure any more. She has the power and money she craves for, she plays with our lives, she believes we are all at her beck and call, she will not understand that the day Uncle Constantine died was the beginning of the end, or that Jack's death was virtually her own. Why should she? She believes we are bound by our wrongdoing, fettered by our wickedness. We are like climbers on a mountain. If one of us falls, the others come tumbling after. She is never afraid that we would ruin her, because she thinks that in so doing we would ruin our-selves. She cannot see that one becomes too sickened to care. This is the end for her, whether the sea invades us or not. And it is the end for all the little men she has gathered round her, Tom Easey, John, William – and me.'

He broke off. Then he said, 'You don't understand me, do you?'

'No.'

'I believe you don't really care!'

'No.'

'But you must see why I cannot marry you.' His hand moved to my chin, tilting up my face. 'I am neither thief nor murderer, but I am involved. I daresay the law cannot touch me, but I am no kind of husband for you.' Then he cried out in a rage, 'You don't really care about that either, do you?'

'No.'

But that was not true, I did care, only I was resolved to marry him, whether he wished it or not. And he must have sensed this for he exclaimed, 'I swear you'd marry me at the gallows' foot!'

'It would not,' I said, 'be my choice for a wedding, but yes, if there were no alternative, it would be the gallows' foot.'

'With your groom swinging high above you, for the honeymoon – you talk like a little old woman. So precise, so precise! How is it that you and your sister are so different? But then you were a little old woman at eight, I remember so well. Even when you watered the lawn – '

'Virgil!' It was not a protest. It was alarm, and he recog-nised it.

He said, 'What is it?' I felt the muscles of his arms tighten.

'There is someone coming down the hill.'

'What of it?' He relaxed again. 'We are doing no harm. We could be doing a great deal worse. There are over three hundred capital crimes in our law-book, but there is

158

nothing yet against a man lying in a graveyard, holding a girl in his arms. What harm there is can only exist in the eyes of the beholder. I speak for a just cause, *virginibus puerisque*. A phrase, Nanette, an apt phrase that I tossed off the other night, only this time it was under another name. I write, you see, under a variety of names. You know me as Virgil, but occasionally I become Horace – '

He broke off. His arms fell away from me. We looked up to see John Gonomanaway standing over us.

I was terrified. John-Gon always frightened me. I could not see his expression, only the dark-bearded outline, but I sensed in him an anger, and a triumph too as if he had caught us out. He was not a tall man but he was broad, and standing over us in our half-reclining attitude gave him both height and superiority.

Virgil pushed me to one side without ceremony. He was sprawling on the gravestone of Mrs. Ann Curlin with her one son and six daughters. One of his long legs dangled over the remains of Francis Yaxley. His voice, when he spoke, was amused and enormously alive. 'Spying on us, John?' he said.

John-Gon spoke in his rusty growl. In the darkness he looked like a gorilla. 'My lady wishes you to return to the Hall,' he said.

'Oh,' said Virgil, 'my lady wishes, does she? My lady orders. My lady rules the roost. We are insubordinate, John. We are slaves who have got above ourselves. You can go straight back to my lady and tell her from me to go to the devil.'

'Master Virgil!'

'And don't you call me Master Virgil! Where's your birch-rod, Johnny? You cannot let such disobedience and impertinence pass. You must thrash me till I'm half-unconscious and put me sobbing to bed on bread and water. We cannot have such behaviour in Cudden Hall. What will Miss Nanette think? What naughty children we are, disporting ourselves in cemeteries, still up at the hour of eleven o'clock. Faith, I do not know what the world is coming to.'

'Sir,' began John-Gon. His voice was stiff with rage. I could see his fists clenching and unclenching.

'That's better,' said Virgil, 'only I should prefer to be called "my lord." If my lady is my lady, without being a lady at all, I see no reason why – '

'Will you please come back – Sir!'

'No. Sir!'

'Then, by God – ' And John-Gon reached out his hand for me – I had not so far spoken one word, only huddled there, cold with fright – but before he could touch me, Virgil was on his feet: I saw that he was head and shoulders above John-Gon and near as broad.

He said, his breath whistling between his teeth, 'I've been waiting for this so long, so long – oh Christ, how I have waited!' And his fist shot out, catching John-Gon in the face so that, standing as he was on the hill-slope, he lost his balance and crashed to the ground, falling into the briars. They must have scratched him half to death, but he was up again immediately. For all he was so heavily built, he was light on his feet like a boxer, and he flew at Virgil, hammering at him, kicking upward with his foot, the great hands doubled into enormous fists then suddenly splayed, clawing at his opponent's eyes.

I could only watch. I had never seen such a spectacle. I was sick with fear, yet a little of Virgil's triumph communicated itself to me so that I was shamefully exhilarated. Somewhere in his vast shadow cowered a frightened little boy, beaten and starved yet who still managed to defy, and now the defiance was six foot three with the thwarted anger of God knew how many years behind it. Virgil was paying off an old, old score, and John-Gon had no chance at all: he fought as he knew how to fight, and he fought to maim and kill, but he could do nothing against Virgil's glorious fury and the blows that relentlessly smashed him down.

He fell for the third time. He did not get up. He lay there

spread-eagled on the thorny hillside, his face hidden beneath his arm. When Virgil stooped to haul him up, I saw that he was about to hit him again.

I cried out, 'Oh don't, don't please don't!'

I thought at first that Virgil did not hear me, with the rage boiling within him. But he let John-Gon fall, shoving him with his foot as he did so. Then he rounded on me. His voice soared up to falsetto. 'Oh don't, don't!' he mimicked me. 'I've waited for this for nearly twenty years, and the tender-hearted little lady cries out, don't!' Then he shouted, 'What bloody business is it of yours? You're not married to me yet, Nanette, and if that is how you would talk as a wife, I swear I'd beat you as soundly as I've beaten him.'

I was shaking from head to foot but this nonsense almost restored me, for I knew that Virgil, however enraged, would never lift a hand to me. I managed to rise to my feet, saying in the precise voice that he always made fun of, 'He has had enough. You've half killed him. I – I don't really want to wed you at the gallows' foot.'

Then Virgil began to roar with laughter, and in that half-hysterical barrage of noise John-Gon managed to stagger to his feet. As he stood there, swaying, the moon gleamed bright between the scurrying clouds and I saw that his nose was pouring blood so that his beard was matted with it: both eyes were blacked and one half-closed. I half approached him with my kerchief in my hand, but Virgil shoved me away with such force that I all but fell down.

John Gonomanaway and Virgil surveyed each other. Virgil was still laughing, but silently now. Then John-Gon spat out a tooth and spoke from the bloodied beard.

'You son of a whore,' he said, 'I'll kill you for that. Just you wait, young master, just you wait –'

Then he lurched down the hillside to the path that led to the Hall garden. Virgil called after him, 'Give my lady my regards. I've no doubt she'll tend your wounds for you. Tell her to come herself next time, instead of sending so poor a messenger.'

I said, 'That is childish and cruel.'

He came up to me, his face black and threatening. I refused to budge. I could smell the sweat and blood on him, hear the breath hissing between his teeth. He moved so close that he pressed against me, but I still stood there, my arms rigid at my sides.

'I could never,' he said, 'endure a nagging wife.'

I answered in a trembling voice, 'I could never endure a bullying husband. If you would please to stand a pace away, Virgil, I will cleanse the blood from your lip. It is badly cut – '

'The soldier's wife!' he said, then in a roar that must almost have carried to the Hall, 'Oh God, God, God!' And he clutched me to him, kissing me violently again and again, pulling at my hair to tilt my face back and digging his hands into me with such force that I wore the bruises for days after.

Then as suddenly he released me. It was as if nothing had happened. Holding hands we walked sedately down the hill, a fine, disreputable couple: me with my hair down and my dress disordered, and him cut and bruised, with the blood trickling down from the broken knuckles of his hands. We walked in silence until we came to the gate. Then we stopped to look at each other, our hands parting. We both began to laugh, at first hysterically then in genuine amusement.

'This,' he said, 'is the greatest evening of my life.' Then, 'Were you very frightened?'

'Yes. For you.'

'For me?'

'Of course.'

'I could have taken on a dozen of him. I had to do it, Nanette. Do you understand that?'

'I understand very well. But he'll never forgive you.'

I half expected him, in this moment of triumph, to say something vainglorious like, I can look after myself, but he

162

did not, only answered gravely, 'No. He never will. I have taught him an unpardonable lesson: little boys grow into big boys and the beating is reversed. He will do his best to kill me. I know that. I know too that she will never forgive me, either.'

This chilled me. Our laughter was ended. We crossed the garden into the Hall. We heard the church clock chime. It was midnight. The house seemed deserted. The guests had all gone to bed. We looked into the drawing-room to see empty wine glasses, cards still littered over the table and a pile of bright silk in one corner. There was no sign of John-Gon or of my aunt.

We walked slowly up the stairs. We came to the landing. Virgil's rooms were on the left and mine on the right. An oil lamp glowed on a side table. We looked at each other. We were both stunned with exhaustion, but if he had so much as motioned with his hand, I would have followed him, and he knew it: he looked at me with a kind of desperation, sighed and shook his head.

Then he said suddenly, 'Has John ever insulted you?'

I was too tired to be anything but truthful. I answered, 'He tried to kiss me.'

'Is that all?'

'That is all, Virgil. I – I slapped his face.'

'You did what!' He broke into a half laugh. He said, 'You did not slap mine.'

'No.'

'Did you want to?'

'No.'

He gave me a long look, unsmiling, then began to move away. He said in a voice drugged with fatigue, 'I have told you why I cannot marry. But if ever I did, it would be to you, though God knows why, for you are a little shrew, Nanette, and I vow you'd spend your whole life trying to tame me.'

'I would not.'

'Why not?'

163

'Because I love you. As you are.'

'As I am!' He put up a hand to his battered face, then extended the other hand, bloodied and torn. Then without another word he turned on his heel and was gone.

I heard the door of his room shut behind him.

VII

I slept heavily, with ugly dreams, then woke early and crept out of bed to the window, not wishing to wake Leonie who was sound asleep when I returned and climbed softly in beside her.

I think she was asleep. I was not absolutely sure, but certainly, she did not stir. Whether it was truth or pretence, I was thankful for it, for never had I been more conscious of the three years between us. We had always confided in each other. If some young man at a dance complimented me, flirted with me, signified his wish to see more of me, I would tell Leonie that very night, and we would discuss whether the business was worth continuing. As for her, her flirts were innumerable: even at twelve she received offers of marriage, and flowers and notes and invitations were constantly arriving at our front door: Maman pretended to reproach her but was secretly delighted. This was a daughter after her own heart. Sometimes Leonie let the romance last for a week or so, but mostly she mocked the poor lovelorn, left his passionate letters unanswered, and it was I who put the flowers in a vase for otherwise the poor things would have withered with thirst.

This was different. I could not bring myself to tell her what had happened, and she did not ask: it was only on reflection that this seemed to me a little suspicious, and once or twice it seemed to me that her eyes, Maman's beautiful, sharp eyes, moved reflectively over me. But she only prattled about the coming night, how we would collect food from the kitchen when everyone was asleep, then creep softly out and make our way to the dunes.

It was only when I was dressing that she startled and shocked me. She remarked in a calm, conversational voice, 'You have terrible bruises, Nan. All over your arms and throat and – I think you had best wear a silk scarf. Wait, I'll find one for you.'

I stared at her, the tell-tale blush almost choking me. But she was kneeling by the drawer, searching for the right thing to wear. I could not see her face. It was not what she said, for indeed, the bruises were only too noticeable: Virgil would probably be dismayed by his own handiwork but he had been too distraught to know what he was doing. It was the calm acceptance of her words. I began, for the first time in my life, to see that my little sister was so no more. Perhaps she had never been so. It was I who was keeping my secrets, but I had to wonder how many secrets had been kept from me. The age gap lessens as the years advance, but I had believed the distance between eighteen and fifteen to be vast. I saw now that it was nothing of the kind, and I stared at that bowed head, the slender, childish neck, the little hands that had at last found the right scarf, and waited almost in terror for the questions that might follow.

She asked me nothing. Her face, when she turned it to me, was calm, amiable and smiling: she put the scarf in my hands and remarked, 'There is going to be a terrible storm.'

I looked at her, but she was utterly without self-consciousness: she nodded at the window, and indeed, the storm was already there. The wind was thundering against the Hall, and we could see in the distance mountainous waves crashing at the dyke.

'It's the great flood all over again,' said Leonie, as if delighted by the drama of it. 'No one will dream we would go out in such weather. We will be safe from being followed, even by old John.'

Then she looked straight at me. For a second her eyes rested on my bruised shoulders. She made no comment, though I was steeling myself for it. She smiled, a wide,

166

wicked smile. She said, 'I saw him come in last night. Oh Nan, he looked terrible. He could hardly walk up the stairs.'

'What do you mean?' I said. I stooped down to fasten my shoes.

Leonie said with the utmost satisfaction, 'One eye is completely closed, and the other is yellow and purple. He has lost most of his teeth, he is scratched to pieces, and his cheeks are all cut. As for his hands, I have never seen anything like it. I don't suppose he'll be showing his face round here today. If I looked like that, I'd lock myself in my room.'

I did not raise my head. I said in a choked voice, 'You certainly had a good look at him.'

'I did! I watched him over the banister. I could not believe my eyes.'

'You sound so pleased –'

'Of course I am.'

'Leo!'

'I'm absolutely delighted. He deserves every bit of it, the horrid man. I only hope it happens again. And again – oh stop being so prissy, Nan. You are as pleased as I am. Men who ill-treat children are the lowest creatures imaginable.'

I raised myself. I could not, after all, remain permanently in a stooping position. I tried to look stern, but I could not prevent myself from smiling. She burst out laughing. She said in a coaxing voice, 'It was Virgil who beat him, wasn't it?'

I made a helpless gesture.

'Of course it was. Oh, I'll ask you nothing, but I am so happy about it.'

'You are really being bloodthirsty and horrid.'

Leonie said calmly, 'You are being silly. You just don't mean it. He is a brute and a bully, and when I think of what he made that poor little boy suffer –'

I said before I could stop myself, 'The poor little boy paid it back well enough last night.'

'Ah!' She was triumphant. 'You see. The tender heart isn't so tender after all. Oh, he is a bad man, and it is about time that someone taught him a lesson. I only wish I had been there to see.' Then she said in a prim little voice, 'Shall we go downstairs, Nan, and say good morning to the nice ladies and gentlemen?'

I exclaimed, 'I think you are a bitch.'

'Oh, oh!' said Leonie in a mocking voice, then flung her arms about me and gave me a hug, carefully rearranging the scarf afterwards. Then she said gravely, the childishness gone from her face, 'Are you happy, Nan? No, no, I'm not going to ask anything, anything at all, but I just want to know if you're happy. Please tell me. I want to know so badly.'

I said with a sigh, 'I don't know.'

'Is it – is it as bad as all that?'

'I'm afraid it is.'

We looked at each other. It was for the moment as if she were older than me. She said at last, 'It will be all right, Nan darling. I know. He is a good man, Virgil. He is right for you.' Her mouth curved into a smile. 'I approve. You can tell him that.'

'Oh Leonie,' I said in despair, 'oh Leonie –'

'Well, we'll not talk of it any more, only you'll kiss him nicely from me for giving that beastly old John such a thumping.'

'You really are impossible!'

'And then we'll discuss what we are going to do tonight when we go to the dunes to feed our prisoner.'

We went downstairs arm in arm, and Leonie told me she had already done a little exploring. There was a cold chicken at the far end of the larder, half a cheese and a fish pie. 'There is so much food there,' she said, 'that Cook will probably not notice. Even if she does, she will never believe we've taken it. I've already stolen a bottle of wine. Am I not clever? It's hidden in the wardrobe. What time do you think we should start? It must be really late. Perhaps three in the morning –'

I listened to all this, making assenting noises and the occasional comment. What I did not say was that I had no intention whatsoever of taking Leonie with me. She was more grown-up than I had ever suspected, she had perhaps experienced things of which I knew nothing, but she was still my little sister, she was only fifteen, and this was a dangerous business: on no account was she to be involved, however furious she might be afterwards. It was only too plain to me now that we should never have embarked on such an adventure in the first place. A shameful, cowardly craving filled me to forget about it altogether, never mind the Scottish prisoner or anyone else. But I had promised, I could not break my word nor could I let the poor man starve. I would go this once and take with me as much as I could carry, but it would be the first and last time.

I was trying desperately to pretend to myself that I was not frightened to death, but even as we crossed the hall to go into the dining room, the wind caught at a badly fastened window: there was a great crash of breaking glass that brought Dolly tearing up from the kitchen.

She made a wry grimace of dismay at me. 'My lady will kill me,' she said, adding with a certain satisfaction, 'there'll be worse to come, mark my words. Tonight's the big tide. I told you. Oh, we'll be lucky if any of us sees tomorrow at all.'

'Nonsense, Dolly,' I said. 'The Hall is as firm as a rock.'

'That's what they said last time,' said Dolly, and disappeared into the side room where the window had blown open: we heard the clatter and crunch of glass as she began to sweep it up.

'Why do you look so scared?' asked Leonie, studying my aghast face with surprise. 'You're always saying how much you like storms.' She smiled as she spoke. She seemed to have no apprehensions about the journey. If she had been frightened before, she had now regained all her courage. 'I must say, you'll have your fill tonight. We'll have to hold

169

on to each other in case we're blown away.'

I agreed that we would. I opened the front door for a moment to look out. The force of the wind was such that I had to hang on to it. The sea was spectacular, and a shudder of primitive fear went through me. I remembered Virgil's words. *A roaring and a rushing and a crashing and a screaming . . . A night-black sky and waves as high as mountains –*

And that was how it was, and it was barely nine in the morning. I thought, oh I cannot, I cannot, I am human, I am small, I am weak – how can I face this awfulness alone and in the middle of the night?

I stared up at the wicked devil's sky, then down at the sea. I could hardly believe the height of the waves, curled over with white bespattered undersides, reaching out like a giant's predatory hand, grabbing, curling up, then reaching out again. I stepped back in a panic, and the door slammed behind me as it had done once before to a bad, skinny little girl, caught out in dire catastrophe. Only this time I was on the other side, safe in the hall, with Leonie, looking a little bewildered, at my side, and Amelia making a sudden distraught appearance, having come apparently from my aunt's room.

I wished her good morning, and she looked at me with hate. I could not understand this for, though we had never been great friends, we had always been on reasonable terms. I wondered at first if she was remembering the episode of the silks, but then I realised this was something much more serious, and so did Leonie who, being good-hearted underneath the levity, took a step towards her, as if to ask her what was the matter.

Amelia backed away from us as if we were poison. Her high-pitched voice was normally soft, but now she was screaming. 'Cheated and betrayed!' she cried out, almost spitting in our faces. 'Cheated and betrayed! Oh, you knew about it too. Of course you did. You're a pair of confounded sluts, you are just like her. You are all liars here, you would rob the world, provided you get your own way. To think

170

that we believed you, that we thought you too had the cause at heart. He could have got away. He would be safe – And now we are without a penny, and soon no doubt they'll hang him, and me too. Not that any of you would care –' She turned on me a look of such loathing that it was like a blow in the face. 'I hope you're proud of yourselves, you little Southron whores. I've no doubt you've laughed yourselves sick at the thought of how you've gulled me.' Then she said more quietly but with a savage conviction, 'I hope you rot. I hope the sea devours you. It is the only thing that will make me feel clean again.'

All this to me was a nonsense, for I had not the least idea what she was talking about. To proclaim that she had been cheated and betrayed sounded like something from my aunt's novels, and the man she kept on referring to I did not know. It could not be Mr. Pleydell or Mr. Lowry, and I decided it must be the person I had seen her talking to, that first night. None of it made the least sense, but there was no denying her genuine fury and despair. I struggled to think of something to say that would calm her, then to my relief I saw Virgil standing in the doorway.

Amelia saw him too. She rounded on him immediately, coming right up to him, pressing her body against his. I thought she was going to hit him. If she had ever loved him, that love had turned to hate.

He did not budge, only stared stonily at her. He did not look in much better shape than John Gonomanaway. Last night's bruises had coloured up, and the knuckles of his hands were red and raw. But to me he was still the most handsome man I had ever seen, and I wanted to pluck Amelia from him, in case she should do him a mischief.

But by now she was in tears. She moved back. She whispered, 'you knew!'

'Yes,' he said with a sigh, 'I knew.'

'You deliberately cheated us!'

'No,' he said, 'that is not so, though I do not expect you to believe me. But I did know. You have every right to be

171

angry.'

By now she seemed to have lost heart, the rage dropped from her. She muttered in a low, desperate voice, 'How could you? You have ruined both of us, and for what? – a small store of weapons and a little money. What will happen to us now?' Her voice rose again as she repeated her former curse. 'I pray you are all drowned. The money'll not save you then.'

'The money will save none of us,' said Virgil. Whatever it was he was accused of, he made no attempt to deny it or excuse himself. 'But there is one thing I can promise you, Amelia –'

'Promise! You think I'd believe your promises?'

'I do not give a damn whether you believe me or not,' said Virgil. 'All I am asking you to do is listen. After all, you cannot say I didn't warn you. You have been fools, the pair of you, and if you have also been fooled, you have only yourselves to blame. You live in a romantic dreamland. There is no reality to either of you, and now you are meeting reality and you do not like it. But there's no point in reproaching and rating each other. I can only try to get you out of the mess you've made for yourselves. I cannot of course get all your money back –'

She demanded suddenly, 'What about *him*?'

'Him?' Then he made a contemptuous noise. 'I am not concerned with *him*, as you call him. He is the least of my worries.'

'How dare you!'

'Oh, don't be so silly. Why should I concern myself with a half-Polish ninny who believes he'll sit himself down on the English throne? He'll manage without your handful of pounds Scots. If he comes, he'll come, and I've no doubt there will be plenty of idiots to support him, for all most of them will end on Tower Hill. A few pounds here or there hardly matter when your neck is thrawn and your torn-out guts laid beside you.'

She looked as if she would faint, for which I could not

172

blame her, at least she knew what he was talking about, which was more than could be said for Leonie and myself. She said, turning away from him, 'You have no right to talk like that. But of course you are a Southron, it means nothing to you.'

'No,' said Virgil, 'it means nothing to me, except that I don't like to think of the blood that will run because of it. I have no time for heroes who ascend to heaven on the corpses of their supporters. But if you would kindly let me finish without squawking at me – I'll get some money to you today, and I'll try to get you both away. That is the only promise I can make. I will simply do my best.'

She said in a growling voice, 'You'll no doubt hand us over to the public hangman.'

'That,' said Virgil with a grim smile, 'is a risk you have to take. But the money, such as it is, will be there, and as soon as the weather calms, I'll get you to the coast, the pair of you.'

'I don't believe you,' said Amelia.

He only said in an indifferent voice, 'What choice have you? You can do little but wait and see. You certainly couldn't get to the coast tonight. There'd not be a boat in the world that would take you. What do you propose to do, swim for it?'

She glowered at him, shrugged a shoulder, then pushed him aside and ran into the hallway. We heard her running up the stairs.

Virgil looked at us, and the pair of us at him. There was no expression in his face, though his eyes – mercifully unblacked – rested briefly on me. When Leonie remarked, 'Old John looks much worse than you,' he stared then laughed.

'What savage creatures women are,' he said. 'They say it's largely the gentle sex who attend a public hanging. I know if I had to face an angry mob, I'd rather it were of men than women.'

I ignored all this. I said, 'What is all this about?'

He said in an exhausted voice, 'I told you this was the end, and you have just seen the beginning. I cannot talk of it now. It would help no one if I did so. You'll know soon enough. We'll all know. All I ask of you is to keep out of mischief until tomorrow. After that it will hardly matter.' He turned to Leonie, who was watching him very seriously. 'Will you look after your sister for me?'

Leonie's eyes flickered to mine. She said after a pause, 'Can you not look after her yourself?'

I was beginning to feel as if I had a high fever. They were talking as if I were not there at all. I felt the temper surging up in me as it did when I was a child: I wanted to shout at them and stamp my feet. But Virgil was speaking again, so I remained silent, the colour hot in my cheeks.

He said, 'That is not possible. But I would be happy to feel she was in your hands, Leonie. You have a very pretty face but despite that I think you are a sensible girl.'

At this I did speak, and in the shrill, childish voice of temper. 'I would like to remind you,' I cried out – how sadly one can revert to childhood! – 'that I am still here. I do not find it civil to discuss me in such a way. I am not a parcel to be dumped on someone. I am perfectly capable of looking after myself.'

And then, for I had slept so little and there was the memory of last night, the tears came. I could have killed myself for them but I could not stop. I put my hands to my face and turned my back on them. Neither of them spoke a word. When at last I regained some self-control, I swung round, to see that Leonie was gone and Virgil still standing there, his eyes on me. He looked so sad that my temper vanished. I came up to him and he took me in his arms.

He said quietly, 'I love you, Nanette. You can remember that. I would like to look after you to the end of my days, though you should never have fallen in love with someone like me. But I have to say this for perhaps I will not have the chance again. I don't know how many of us will survive this night. They say it will be the highest tide ever, and already

174

the sea wall is half down. All Greymanswick is fighting to repair it. It should have been done years ago: now I fear it is too late. I am going down myself to help. They need all the hands they can get. If we are still here tomorrow –'

I mumbled into his shoulder, 'We will be here.'

'Are you turned witch now? Perhaps we will. If we are, you will see the end of the play. Only – only I wish most heartily you were away. I don't trust you. I've never trusted you. Nanette! You are not to do anything foolish. Do you hear me?'

I nodded. I could not say anything. I have always been a poor liar. When I was a child my parents always knew when I was lying, for I used to stare fixedly into their eyes, having been told that liars could not do so. Virgil must have sensed something, for I heard the suspicion sharp in his voice. He said fiercely, 'Are you listening?'

'Yes.'

'Oh Christ, I'd like to tie you up and turn the key on you. I swear you'd manage to climb out of the window – I must go. God help us all, it will be something of a night. And tomorrow, if we are still there, will be the third act, the catastrophe, where everything is revealed and overturned. Goodbye, my darling. Be a good girl.'

He kissed me roughly, then pushed me away. At the doorway he turned to say in a gasp, 'Oh for God's sake, you will be a good girl, won't you?'

Then he was gone, leaving me no time to reply, which was perhaps as well. I went over to the window and flung it open, though the force of the wind seemed almost to blow my teeth in. I saw him running down the hill to the sea wall, where a great crowd of people was gathered. It was a dreadful day, the sky now as dark as night. I have seldom felt so terrified. How desperately I longed to be a good girl! There seemed no more wonderful prospect than being locked into my room, with all choice taken from me. Never would there have been a happier prisoner. But my only prison was the promise I had made, and I followed Virgil out, nearly

175

colliding with Mr. Lowry as I did so.

He ignored my apology, saying without preamble, 'Tomorrow we are going home.'

I could not see him very well in the gloom, though Dolly had by now set lamps everywhere. But I had the impression he was not happy, though I would have thought him delighted to leave us: he had never seemed at ease in Cudden Hall. I said a little lamely, 'I am happy for you, Sir. You must be longing to see your own place again.'

I suppose this was not very tactful of me, but then I was in no state of mind to think about what I was saying. He answered me quite crossly. He said, 'My own place, indeed! Stripped bare by that monster. Oh, my friends have done their best, and I understand the place is furnished again, but so much that I treasured is gone, so much –' Then he said suddenly, 'I do not like this place. Do you?'

I did not know how to answer him. I was disconcerted by the question. I could hardly speak the truth. I chose to ignore it, saying, 'It is always best to be home. I think one should not stay indefinitely in other people's houses. I am very sorry the Collector has stolen so many of your things, but I daresay you will in time be able to replenish your home. It will not be quite the same, I know, but I am sure you will make the whole place beautiful again.'

He was looking at me earnestly, almost studying me. He said, 'At least the move enables me to say something I have wanted to say for some time. I would like to feel that my home is also yours. If ever, Miss Nanette, you or your sister are in any trouble, you must come to me. My wife has taken a great fancy to you, as indeed, I have too, and you will always be welcome. I will write down my address.'

I was very touched by this, and took the slip of paper he offered me, to put in my pocket . . . However, before I could thank him, he spoke again.

He demanded, 'How well do you know your aunt?'

I stammered, very much taken aback, 'I – I – well, she is

176

after all my family.'

And this was no answer at all, as he must have realised, but he only went on, 'And William. Mr. Pleydell. Do you know him at all?'

I did not see why I should be interrogated, and I answered a little coldly, 'I see almost nothing of him. But then I only really meet any of you at mealtimes.'

'He is a good shot,' said Mr. Lowry.

I thought at first this was both irrelevant and absurd, then I remembered how Mr. Pleydell had shot the gulls down, one after the other. I remained silent.

Mr. Lowry said in a strangely conversational tone, 'Do you know, Miss Nanette, I do believe he deliberately murdered that poor, silly boy.' Then very loudly he demanded, 'Why? Why?'

He did not wait for an answer. He walked away. I was beginning to feel the Hall was full of wandering ghosts. Only as I came back into the Hall saw with a sudden shock that my aunt was standing there, halfway down the stairs. Whether or not she had heard Mr. Lowry I did not know, but she had sharp ears, the door was open and he had not lowered his voice.

She did not say a word. She looked down at me, a dumpy little woman of uncertain age, with an abominable figure and beautiful hair that gleamed in the lamplight. I think she was smiling. Why or how she could smile on such a fearful day, I could not imagine, but there was a sleek, satisfied, catlike air to her as if somehow she felt part of the appalling elements outside.

I began to feel as if the flood were already upon us. The sea was nowhere near, the tide had not yet even begun to turn, but it was as if the foundations of the house were quivering: I would not have been surprised to see a thin sliver of water crawl its glistening way across the hall.

I could not take it any longer. Virgil would by now be at the sea wall, beaten by wind and rain, fighting with numbed fingers to fortify a barricade that was already crumbling. Leonie had disappeared. I could not endure the thought of meeting Amelia again, or Mr. Pleydell, or hearing Mr. Lowry voice his suspicions. I did not speak to my aunt. I did not even say good morning. I met that cold, smoky gaze, then turned, almost running, to go down the back stairs, where I could perhaps have a cooking lesson, find something to keep me busy, comfort myself in that warm, sweet-smelling kitchen.

Cook, I discovered, was in bed with another headache, brought on, no doubt, by the storm and her own apprehensions. There was no one there but Dolly, sitting at the table and preparing vegetables for our luncheon. I sat myself down silently beside her. I moved a little stack of potatoes and onions and carrots in front of me and took a knife out of the drawer. It was a wonderfully soothing occupation and just what I needed: as the wind thundered outside, rattling the windows and the rain beat like smallshot against the panes, I quietly peeled potatoes, dropping them into the big bowl between us.

Presently Dolly rose to her feet, went over to the oven and returned with a couple of meat pasties. For some reason everyone in Cudden Hall kitchen believed Leonie and me to be permanently famished, though in fact we ate enormously: my aunt was not, God knows, much of a hostess but enjoyed her own food too much to starve us. However, the hot pasty was irresistible, and I took a large bite out of mine, bestowing an appreciative smile on Dolly, who was doing the same.

There were candles burning on the table, and a rosy glow from the oven. I could see Dolly clearly enough. I thought with a shock that she had aged, she did not look well. Usually a soft light improves the looks, as many an ageing beauty has discovered, but all I saw now were the shadows under her eyes, the over-prominent cheekbones and a droop to her mouth as if she were utterly exhausted. She was still beautiful, she would be beautiful till the day she died, but whereas once she had been lively and teasing and cracking jokes, she was now too weary even to smile. I thought remorsefully that it was Virgil, then decided it must be far more than that: Dolly was only twenty-five, and there must be young men by the score, longing to court her.

I said, 'Dolly, when are you going to get married?'

She answered quite waspishly, 'Oh you young girls, you think of nothing but marriage.'

'Oh come on, Dolly,' I said, laughing at her, 'you talk as if you were an old maid of ninety.'

'That's what I feel like and all.' She put down the knife she was using. She looked at me then for a second screwed up her eyes. 'Oh Miss Nanette,' she said, 'I'm so tired of it all. Sometimes I thinks it would be a good thing if the sea swallowed us all up, we're like that town the preacher used to tell us about at Sunday school, we're no good, we'd be better off dead.' She shook off the hand I tried to lay on hers. 'I can't go on like this much longer, and that's the truth. My dad, he's a clever bastard, he thinks he knows everything, but it'll all catch up with him like it always does, and then he'll swing for it, together with Hookey and the whole boiling of them. You ask when I'm getting married! I'll never get married.'

'Nonsense!'

'It's true. I feel it in my bones. Besides, who'd marry me?'

'Dolly, that's an absurd thing to say. You're so pretty that half Greymanswick must be mad for you.'

'I was pretty enough once,' she said, fixing the beautiful eyes on me. 'But I'm nothing much to look at any more, and anyways, it don't matter, the young men don't want a girl with a dad like mine. They look at me, they say, "That's Tom Easey's girl", then they turn away and walk on the other side. I don't say they wouldn't lay me, given half a chance, but marry – that's something different. Nobody wants a pa-in-law swinging at the end of a rope, specially as I might end up beside him.'

179

'Dolly!'

'That's how it is.' She pulled the bowl towards her and started chopping the vegetables again.

'Dolly,' I said, 'what is all this about?' Then seeing that she was going to brush the question off, I banged my knife on the table and positively shouted at her. 'For God's sake,' I cried, 'can't you tell me? Everybody hints at frightful things, and I know it is something bad and against the law, with my aunt at the centre of it, but really, it is unendurable that nobody will come out with the whole story. What has brought it all to a head like this? We are all behaving like lunatics. Even Amelia, who has always seemed quite sensible, started screaming at me and talking what seemed to me complete nonsense.'

'Oh, her!' said Dolly contemptuously. 'She's a right silly bitch, that one. I could have told her long ago, but she's not the kind to talk to the lower orders, and if I'd said one word she'd have run yowling to my lady, and that would have been the end of me.' She bestowed on me a small, ironic smile. 'You'll know soon enough, Miss Nanette. That poor old gentleman that got hisself killed, he wasn't killed soon enough.'

'What do you mean?'

'They slipped up, didn't they? He got in a bit of talking before they knew what he was doing. I suppose they thought that with him being so upset like, he wouldn't bother, but he did bother. They was just a little too late.'

'Do you mean to say –'

'Oh,' she said with a kind of pity, 'you're still got your mammy's milk on your lips. I don't know exactly what he said, mind, but he stopped off at the justice's house, and they say they'll be making inquiries. Then we'll all be in the fire, my lady too, and serve her damn well right.' Then she said suddenly, 'You look out for old John, Miss Nanette.'

The hate and fear in her voice chilled me. I said a little apprehensively, 'I haven't seen him today.'

'He'll be putting stuff on his pretty face,' said Dolly.

'He's in a right mess. I've never seen the like. You keep out of his way. He's ripe for murder. Oh,' she said, almost with a sob, 'I wish Mr. Virgil was back in London.'

'I think he can look after himself, Dolly.'

'That's what they all say. John's handy with a knife. Just like my dad. If there's a knife at your throat, it don't make no difference how strong you are. He'll never forgive Mr. Virgil. Or you neither, Miss Nanette.'

'How do you know all this?'

She gave an abrupt laugh. 'We knows everything in Greymanswick. If Mr. Virgil had the sense he was born with he'd put a bullet through him.' Then she said, 'You go on upstairs now. I can finish this lot. And don't you get into mischief, do you hear? There's too much mischief here already.'

I found myself flushing. I walked quickly out of the kitchen, as panic-stricken a mischief-maker as could be imagined. I tried not to think of the night to come, but every time I looked out of the window I found my heart sinking more and more: the storm was increasing, and I who professed to like storms was terrified by its fury. I tried to think of what Dolly had told me, but could make no real sense of it, and always my mind strayed to the dunes which in such weather must be almost beyond imagination.

I really do not know how I got through the rest of the day, and everybody in the Hall seemed to be in the same nervous state, except for my little sister who was as lively as usual and obviously looking forward to the excursion. We all huddled together like sheep in the drawing-room, except for my aunt who went upstairs as she always did, to do her stint on her novel. We played cards. We hardly talked. I had hoped while I was down in the kitchen to investigate the larder, even perhaps take some of the food, but Dolly's sharp eyes did not leave me, so it would have to wait till the night when everyone would be in bed.

And so we played at some silly game that I hardly understood, and all the time I was wondering how Virgil was getting on at the sea wall, and praying in a confused way that the night would never come, yet that it would come quickly so that the fearfulness might be over. I could hardly swallow a bite of dinner, and I noticed that Amelia, who avoided my eye, simply pushed the food around on her plate: she was pale and drawn and the hysterical spirit seemed to have fizzled out. The Lowrys did not speak at all, and Mr. Pleydell was so restless that even in the middle of the meal he had to get up and pull aside the curtains so as to peer out of the window.

We went to bed early. Leonie asked, once we were in our room, 'What time do you think we should start?'

'About two or three, I think,' I said, and she gave a melo-dramatic shudder, more, I believe, at the prospect of getting up so early than at stepping out into the storm. I did not tell her that I had asked Mrs. Lowry for one of her sleeping powders. I told her I was feeling so nervous that I could not sleep, and she eagerly offered me as many as I wanted, from the little box she carried round in her reticule. Indeed, I have never seen her so animated, for she was a lady much concerned with her health, and I had to listen to an interminable account of the dizziness and cramps that afflicted her, how she had dreadful nightmares and how sometimes her heart, as she was convinced, stopped dead.

'I think perhaps,' she said, 'you should take two.'

We had neither of us ever taken such a thing in our lives, and I was worried enough about the effect of even one: I would not have used that had I dared risk my sister's staying awake. But we were both over-excited, and I knew that without a draught she might well not sleep at all. I hastily assured Mrs. Lowry that one was sufficient, and I slipped it into my pocket, ready for the hot drink that we usually had at night.

Dolly, when I asked her, heated the milk for us, and I came down to collect it. It struck me that the powder might leave some taste and I asked if we could have a little brandy in our drink. This seemed to Dolly a perfectly sensible idea and she laced both cups generously, saying, 'You'll need this. Even my lady asked for some brandy tonight.'

'Dolly,' I said, 'do you really think the sea will climb so high?'

She answered savagely, 'Christ, I hope it does. I hope it drowns us all. Then we wouldn't have to worry any more.' She looked at me, adding more gently, 'You go straight to bed, Miss Nanette. You look real peaked. Don't you listen to me, I'm a right old misery these days. It'll be all right, and I can swim, I'll look after you.'

I must admit that I did not find this particularly comforting, especially in the circumstances, but I said good night to her, and carried the drinks upstairs, my hand shaking so badly that I slopped some milk into the saucer.

Everyone seemed to have gone to bed as early as ourselves. There was not a soul about, though it was barely ten o'clock. The storm was increasing in fury, and now there was thunder and lightning to add to it. It was like the end of the world, but I was almost past fear, I felt numb and exhausted yet strangely excited at what lay before me. Outside the door of our room I paused to put the sleeping powder into one of the cups, stirring it and leaving the spoon there so that I should recognise it. I felt dreadfully guilty as if somehow I was poisoning my darling sister, but I knew that Mrs. Lowry took two of these powders every night, so the effect could hardly be lethal.

Leonie was, as I had expected, still dressed. She was in a wild state of jubilation, dancing about the room, always looking out of the window and exclaiming at the flashes of lightning that suddenly illuminated us.

She said as I handed her the cup of milk, 'I don't see any point in going to bed.'

I said, 'Oh but there is. We'll not be setting out for hours yet, and we'll need all the sleep we can get.'

'I shall not sleep a wink!'

'I daresay not, but at least you can lie down. I'm going to, I assure you.'

'It's not worth undressing.'

I was compelled to agree. I was possessed of a secret terror that Leonie might somehow read my thoughts, as she had done so many times before. I tried to push out of my mind the fact that she was not coming with me, and averted my eyes as she sipped at her milk.

She remarked, 'This tastes rather peculiar.'

The candlelight was too dim for her to see my flush. I said quickly, 'That's the brandy. Dolly seems convinced there will be a second flood and thinks it would be a good thing to get drunk.'

This amused Leonie who, to my enormous relief, finished her milk. She wandered about the room then said with a stifled yawn, 'I suppose you are right, Nan. We might as well lie down. How boring waiting is!'

We both lay on the bed, fully dressed. I had put out my cloak and bonnet, together with a thick woollen muffler, and I had selected my strongest boots, though nothing, I felt, would prevail against such a storm. Leonie also put out her walking clothes, then curled up beside me. She said a little drowsily, 'I hope that young gentleman appreciates what we are doing for him. He did not seem to me very grateful.'

'I think he will be astounded that we turn up at all.'

'I don't suppose he has ever before met such determined females,' said Leonie.

After this we said nothing more. I lay there watching the lightning that regularly turned the room white and was followed by a crash of thunder that almost burst my ears. After a while I grew aware of Leonie's silence, and raised myself to look at her.

She was deeply asleep. There was no pretence about it. Her breathing was calm and steady, her eyes tightly closed. It was after midnight. With luck she would sleep till the morning: I might even be back before she awoke. I decided to wait no longer. I did not think she could possibly be roused, but there was always the risk, and I knew I would not be happy until I had turned the key of the door on her. I did unhappily drop one of the boots, and swung round, appalled, but she did not even stir. Mrs. Lowry's powders were blessedly effective.

I wrapped myself up as much as I could, even tying the muffler round my bonnet before winding it round my neck. When I at last came into the passage and locked the door behind me, I was so overcome with relief that for a moment I could not move and had to lean against the wall.

Then I crept down to the kitchen.

VIII

There is always something strange about a familiar house at night. Cudden Hall at this hour, huge, empty, seemed almost hostile. Every few minutes there was a monstrous flash of lightning that created disturbing shadows, and everything was rattling and banging in the fury of the wind and rain. I walked softly like an intruder, but my furtive footsteps were unnecessary: in such a din an army would have been unheard. But I could not bring myself to move naturally. I was terrified that Virgil might return from his work at the sea wall or that my aunt, who frightened me even more, might decide to come downstairs.

There was no one abroad. I arrived thankfully in the kitchen. There was one lamp left still lit, and this I carried with me to the larder. There was, as Leonie had said, a vast quantity of food. It seemed somehow shameful that this should be for such a small household. However, I helped myself to a cold chicken, a couple of pasties, some cheese and some fruit, all of which I threw into one of the canvas bags that hung on hooks on the wall. I dared not take more for it would have been too heavy to carry, and I would need all my strength to fight against the wind. Mr. André, or whatever he called himself, would have to make do: I could only hope it would not all be blown away on the journey.

As I was about to let myself out by the kitchen door, which would take me round to the side of the house, I heard voices. I was filled with despair and fury at being stopped at this last moment by idiotic people who ought by rights to be sound asleep in bed. I waited. There was no sound of footsteps. I crept cautiously to the side window to see in the

186

distance, illuminated by a sudden flash, Amelia scuttling away, with someone at her side whom I could not make out. It was a young man and I had the impression it was the one she had been talking to on my first night here. I watched as they disappeared into the distance, almost running, Amelia's skirts blown round her like a winding sheet, her arm tightly enlaced in that of her companion.

I could not see where they were going, but it would certainly not be the dunes: no sane person would go to such a place on a night like this, only a foolish young woman bound down by a promise, who ought to know better. I was beginning to think there was a general exodus from Cudden Hall. Amelia had plainly chosen to disregard Virgil's warning: rather than stay in this house she was prepared to risk a journey, though surely not by sea. When I at last bolted the kitchen door – it made a great grinding noise that was drowned in the din outside – and stepped out into the storm, I shuddered at the thought of anyone attempting to ford those mountainous waves.

Yet when I was in the cone of the storm, the power and excitement of it was such that I forgot my fear. It was monumental, it was like nothing I had ever experienced. The wind must have been of gale force, and I had to charge into it head down, for otherwise it would have spun me round like a top. My skirts whirled about me, almost upsetting my balance: it would have been wonderful to wear breeches like a man. I was thankful I had taken the muffler, for otherwise my bonnet would have been snatched from my head. I soon found that running was better than walking, for it gave me more impetus, and precious silly I must have looked, charging ahead like a small, intoxicated bull, weaving this way and that, the bag clutched under one arm while the other grasped my cloak, to keep me from billowing out and sailing into the air.

For a while I could only think that this was a magnificent adventure, and I almost regretted that Leonie was not with me, she would have enjoyed it so much. But she would still

187

be deeply asleep, and the glimpse of the dunes that I had from time to time in the lightning flashes, made me thankful she was safely in bed. Tomorrow we might have our first quarrel – we never quarrelled as sisters are supposed to do – but at least she was out of danger.

I felt like an orphan in the storm, which I suppose I was. As I made my half-running, half-staggering way to Cuckold's Point, I remembered inconsequentially an episode in one of my aunt's books where a ruined maidservant – only the lower orders were allowed to be ruined, the upper classes were ravished, which was not the same thing – was thrown out of the house with her baby in her arms. I have forgotten what happened to her. I daresay they both perished. My aunt had little time for maidservants, ruined or otherwise. I tried to amuse myself by holding the bag as if it were an infant, for by now the glory of it all was fast disappearing. I was growing frightened again, and very cold, for the rain was seeping through my skirts.

Near Cuckold's Point I paused to regain my breath. I stared around me. I had never seen anything like it. It was entirely desolate. The only life came from the clouds of foam and spray that enveloped the monstrous waves, the scurrying clouds that raced across the sky and the blinding white flashes that momentarily turned night into day. In those flashes I could see there was no one now by the sea wall, indeed, with a chill of horror inside me, I suspected there was no wall either. And then to my amazement I saw one human thing: the *Holy Margaret*, tightly moored yet lifted up and dashed down again by the rage of the sea. She would surely be smashed to pieces, but tonight it would not matter: neither Tom Easey nor his fellow smugglers would be abroad: even the Collector would be huddling at home by his fire, and I wished I had had the sense to do so myself.

The village seemed abandoned, dead. Every window was barred. I realised suddenly that Greymanswick always lived, always would live, in the shadow of that first disaster. It had happened four hundred years ago and in its complete destruction had erased all security from people's minds: it could never be forgotten. The citizens simply waited, knowing that one day it would occur again, and now it was happening and they had all barricaded themselves in, waiting for the end.

And I stood there, a silly, sturdy girl, now in such elements as frail as the sea-pinks tossed from side to side by the wind. It was at this point that I did something only Leonie would have appreciated. It was both vulgar and greedy, but I was beginning to shake with panic, and it was the only thing I could think of that would comfort me.

I opened the bag, with some difficulty, took out a pasty and ate it. It seemed a little hard on the young man, no doubt longing passionately for his supper, but I felt that unless I sustained myself I would never get to him at all. It was difficult to eat with the wind rattling through my teeth, and the last piece was whirled out of my hand by a sudden gust, but it made me feel better, there was a little more warmth in me, and I began to walk more cheerfully, on my way to the dunes.

When I arrived at the inn, I saw that Greymanswick was not dead after all. The entire village must be assembled there; they had no doubt barricaded and fortified their homes, now they were fortifying themselves. I could not blame them. I too could have done with a little fortification, and it seemed a shame that my sex prevented me from joining them. A glass of brandy was exactly what I needed. I looked longingly through the windows of the 'Cuckold's Point.' The noise inside was such that it even penetrated the storm. They were plainly all intoxicated. I was not afraid of being seen for I thought that nothing bar a tidal wave would bring them out, but it crossed my mind that Virgil might be there, and at this I gathered up my petticoats and ran like a hare, so that in a few minutes the inn was out of my sight and I out of theirs.

The dunes could never seem inviting, even on a summer's day, and now they were frankly terrifying.

However, I had come so far and nothing was going to stop me. The wind blew the sand up in clouds so that I was half-blinded, and suddenly jerked the muffler off my head so that my poor bonnet, which Maman would deplore for it was at least six months out of fashion, flew up in the air like a bird and vanished. God knows what kind of spectacle I presented, with my hair down and thick with sand, my face red with the cold and my skirts bedraggled with rain, but I plodded on, stumbling over ossified tree-trunks, nearly falling into pits and holes, and in the end half-weeping with despair. I thought the young man would be looking out for me, but there was no sign of anyone, and I had forgotten how like one cave was to another: it seemed as if I had made this terrible journey for nothing.

I called out at the top of my voice, 'Sir! Mr. André! Oh, can you not hear me? I have brought food for you.'

The wind carried my voice away. If there was any answer, I did not hear it. I was now crying in good earnest, mostly from rage and humiliation at my own weakness. There was only silence, – if that is what it could be called, with crashes of thunder like cannon and the howling of the wind. At that moment I simply wanted to lie down and die. I would not have cared if my aunt had suddenly materialised beside me. But just as I was about to hurl myself face downwards on the sand, I saw something that instantly stopped my tears.

It was a wine bottle. It lay outside the opening of one of the caves. I instantly recognised the cave as the one where Leonie and I had sheltered, though of course this was pure imagination: it looked precisely the same as all the others. Clutching my precious bag of food, now lighter by one pasty, I ran towards it and immediately climbed inside, calling out the young man's name and noticing with joy the familiar debris of food and bottles.

There was still no reply. I called out once more, my voice hollow in the enclosed space. I think it was at this moment that I came to my senses: it must be admitted that so far sense had been remarkably lacking. I realised with the flat conviction that accompanies exhaustion – my knees were giving beneath me from pure fatigue – that I had been gulled. I was the elder sister, I had smiled indulgently at Leonie's foolish romanticism, and now I had to see that I was infinitely sillier than she was: my only consolation was that I had at least had enough sense not to bring her with me. I knew now without the least doubt why the young man had seemed so familiar. I had seen him this evening through the kitchen window, I had seen him before through my own. He was almost certainly Amelia's brother, and now he was gone, I would never see him again, I had taken this monstrous journey for absolutely nothing at all. There was not, it was true, any marked resemblance between the two of them, but I could see now that the eyes, the colour of the hair and of course that unmistakable Scots voice should have made everything clear from the very first moment. What he was doing here, what Amelia was doing, I had no idea. She claimed to have been cheated and betrayed and talked of this mysterious 'him'; they were obviously both involved in something dangerous and perhaps illegal. It must indeed be very bad for them to try to escape in such weather, though the storm, if they managed to survive it, might prove as helpful as it was terrifying.

The fact remained that I too had been cheated and betrayed, and I was wild with anger: nothing is more infuriating than making a fool of oneself.

I ate another pasty. Food is always a solace, and I remembered suddenly the bottle of wine in our bedroom wardrobe, which I had forgotten to take with me. The bottles around me were all empty. No doubt the young man had taken the full ones with him. At least I could eat this in peace without the wind tearing at me: the cave muted sound for all I was not so far inside, and only the dull booming and lightning flashes that penetrated the entrance reminded me that all hell was let loose on the dunes.

And somehow in that hell I had to make my way home.

I stumbled to my feet, almost falling down again. I have never felt so utterly exhausted. I had been sustained by the prospect of meeting a grateful young man and thrusting the welcome food into his arms, but now there was nothing but my own humiliation. The very thought of that homeward journey was unbearable. I had been battling against the storm for over an hour, I ached all over as if I had been beaten, and my skirts were so heavy with rain that they weighed me down. However, my teeth were already chattering with cold, and it was plain that I could not stay the rest of the night here. I said aloud to myself, 'You are a silly bitch, go home at once, do you want to die?' and took tottering steps towards the entrance.

Then I became aware with a jolt of terror that someone was blocking the opening to the cave.

For a second I thought I had maligned the young man, he had waited for me after all, he had walked across the dunes to look for me. Then there was a vast flash of lightning that clearly illuminated the face of John Gonomanaway.

We stared at each other in silence. He had always frightened me from that first day when I was a naughty little girl of eight. In that white flash he looked appalling enough to shock the dead back into their tombs. Virgil's handiwork was plain to see, and the passage of a day had not improved it. The flare revealed an eye that was every colour of the rainbow, a swollen nose, a hideously cut lip and the other eye completely closed. He had shaven off some of the beard: there was a mean, cruel face beneath it.

And as I looked and the light faded, the cut lip twitched up into an evil grin.

'I look pretty, don't I, Miss?' he said.

I was cold, so cold I thought I would die. I had never before known that fear is cold as ice. I knew John meant mischief. I knew he had found out where I was going and waited for me. I knew too that I was going to pay for every blow of Virgil's fist, every mark made on that ruined face. There was nothing I could say or do. There was no point in entreating him, it would only delight him the more. Dolly had said he would never forgive me, and he had always hated me since the day I rebuffed and slapped him. He was a man who would never pardon an insult, and I was alone with him, small and exhausted, with not a soul in sight, and the stumps and sand-pits there to trip me up if I tried to run for it.

I had in any case no strength to run. I looked weakly around me for some kind of weapon, but even if I had found one, what could I do with it? There were only empty bottles, and a blow from my feeble hands would either make him laugh or anger him so much that he would instantly kill me. And as I thought this I knew that killing was not the only thing in his mind. John, as Dolly had once said, was a terror with the women. I have no doubt that all the maidservants of Cudden Hall knew this and, if Dolly herself had not suffered, it was because she had spirit and temper and Tom Easey was her father. John would of course kill me, for he would never dare let me go free, but he was going to enjoy himself first, and what a wonderful revenge this would be, on Virgil as well as myself, if he raped the superior young lady who was too fine to give him a kiss.

I did not cry. I did not shed one tear. I refused to afford him such satisfaction and neither would I entreat him for mercy it would give him exquisite pleasure to withold. The one and only thing I could do was to play for time, and this was as foolish as anything else for there was no one to come to my rescue. We were as marooned as if we were on an island in the middle of the sea. But I have always been an optimist, and I think my only virtue in the midst of such folly was that my spirits rose as my hopes dwindled. The exhaustion miraculously dropped from me, and I sat down calmly on the cave floor, surveying John in the light of the lantern that he had placed beside us, and doing this with such serenity that he was disconcerted, having certainly expected me to roll shrieking on the ground.

It must have resembled some scene from a mediaeval play about devils in hell, the two of us there in that dim, reddish light. John was leaning against the side of the cave and I was sitting at his feet, my wet skirts splayed around me, my hair hanging over my face, and a half-chewed pasty in my cold-chapped hands. From time to time the lightning coldly illuminated us, and the cave seemed to shake with the booming of the thunder and the sea.

I said with perfect calm – I felt as if it were a stranger speaking – 'Now that you are here, John, you can resolve my curiosity. There have been so many strange things happening at Cudden Hall, and I am sure you know the answer to all of them.'

It must have seemed unbelievable to him. It seemed unbelievable to me. He had been about to leap on me, take me no doubt as brutally as he could, and then murder me: he must have known that I knew it. And here I was, chewing at my pasty and making polite conversation. When I added, 'There is a cold chicken in that bag if you are hungry,' he broke into an angry, half bewildered laugh, the one multi-coloured eye moving incredulously over me.

He said in a growl, 'You always was a confounded meddler.'

'Oh yes,' I agreed, 'I always was.'

'And you've been meddling again, Miss, haven't you? Well, I'll tell you something, this will be the last time.' He laughed again. It was the ugliest and most mirthless laugh I had ever heard, and at the sound of it my courage began to dwindle so that I nearly fainted. But there was a pause at that moment in the thunder and lightning, and the torch flame was not strong enough to illuminate my face: I think and pray he did not know how near I was to tears and despair.

He went on, 'So you want to know, do you? Why not? We've all the time in the world and nobody to interrupt us. And when I've done with you, you won't be nosey ever again, Miss Hoity Nanette, who's too much a lady to be

194

nice to a working man only fit to set her feet on. You'll not be sticking that long nose of yours into anything no more, and we'll be laying pretty flowers on your sandy grave.' Then he shouted in a great bellow, 'And stop eating when I talk to you. Have you no manners, you stupid little bitch?'

With this he knocked the remnants of the pasty out of my hand: indeed, it made no difference to me for I had not even realised I was nibbling at it, it could have been seaweed for all I cared. Then he must have remembered my former remarks, for he grabbed at the bag and took the chicken out, beginning immediately to gnaw at the leg. It was difficult for him to eat with that damaged mouth, and this, as I could see, aroused his temper again.

I said, my voice high and over-bright, 'But I don't suppose you know the answers anyway.'

'What the hell do you mean?' he said. 'I always knows everything.' He took another great bite out of the chicken, then hurled the bone away. He ate disgustingly, but perhaps that was due to the lack of teeth. He said triumphantly, 'I knows things my lady – my sweet, lovely lady, God damn her – don't know. Ever snooped into that side room of hers, Miss Nosey Parker? I'll lay you haven't. But I have. Oh, there's fine things in there, silver and china and jewels and all that kind of stuff. That old bastard, Lowry, would give his eyes and ears for a glim at it, and maybe he will at that, for the game's up, and the Collector – that's what she calls herself though o'course she don't do none of the work – won't ever be collecting again. By then I'll be far away, they won't get me. She can manage by herself. She's made a monkey of me long enough, cuddling up to me in bed when she's on heat and paying me no salary, rating me in front of the guests, treating me like bloody dirt and turning me into her fancy-boy.'

The picture thus depicted was almost beyond my imagination, the phrases used such as I had never heard, and the idea of John being anyone's fancy-boy brought the hysteria up in my throat, but I was so fascinated by all this

195

that I almost forgot to be afraid. I think my eager attention flattered him. For all he was so wicked he was in some ways a simple man, and for the first time I could understand something of his rage and humiliation: my aunt had made shameless use of him as she made of everyone, she had never begun to regard him as a human being.

He had started again on another portion of the chicken, talking between mouthfuls: he tore at it like a wolf, spitting out the bones and pieces of skin.

'She even made me do for the old gentleman,' he said, wincing as something hit against a broken tooth. He stopped to swear in a fashion he would never normally have done before me, but if one is preparing to rape and murder, such things do not matter, and I was long past caring what he said or how he said it. He said, 'Of course he wasn't no use to her. I can't imagine why she ever married him, except for the money and the Hall. And Christ knows why he married her. I suppose when she was young, she had something. I think she kind of fascinated him. She never had no real use for gentlemen, she said they made her laugh. She preferred poor bastards like me, who she could order around and get to curl her bloody hair. It was, John, do this, and, John, do that, and if you don't do as you're told, I'll get you strung up on the gallows so high no one will even see you, and the birds will peck out your eyes. That's how she used to talk when you wasn't there. You never heard her talk natural, but I did, I did. She swore like a man. You son of a bitch, that's what she called me, you whoring good-for-nothing bastard. I always promised myself I'd get even with her one day, but she didn't know that, she'd never believe I'd dare. She was so sure of me that she didn't even mind me knowing what I know. It was her as made me put that stuff in her old man's drink. They thought he had a – a malig – malig-something, don't know the word – but it weren't that, it was plain arsenic. It was pitiful to see him, pitiful, and sometimes I felt bad about it, but after all, why should I worry, it was her who made me do it. And it was her as made William kill Jack, he was nosey like you, he knew too much. Pity they didn't kill the old father a bit sooner, but there it is, and the old gentleman wasn't much loss, I don't have no conscience about the likes of him. What my lady really wants is power. So she got Tom and Hookey and me to pinch the stuff for her, and now she's rolling in it, she goes and gawps at it, it makes her feel strong and rich and how she's done everybody down. Of course that Amelia – the silliest bitch I ever met. I used to laugh like hell every time I thought of it. All that talk of the Prince and the Jacobites, whatever they are, and my lady taking all the money in so as to put a Stuart on the throne again – I ask you! That brother comes over from France with his silver and guns, and he was hiding here with Amelia, and Tom found out and told my lady. She took the girl in, but they was after the boy so she left him here. She said she was going to get all the rich men in the county toe ever wanted. That brother's the laddie you brought all that food for, you're as bloody silly as the rest of them. He told me you was coming, and I thought I'd give you a little surprise. I gather they've hopped it. It's just as well for them, otherwise Madam would have had them put in jail and topped. I don't suppose they'll get very far.'

There was a pause. I was silent too. I could think of nothing to say, and the terror was convulsing me again.

Then John spoke once more, throwing the remnants of the chicken on to the ground. 'And now,' he said, 'I'm going to deal with you, Miss Meddler. You'll not be too proud to talk to me this time, you're talking whether you like it or not, and presently you won't be talking any more to anyone, I can promise you that. Oh,' he said, as Virgil had said to him, 'I've been looking forward to this. You're going to learn like everybody else that nobody makes a monkey out of me, I pays off my scores, and my lady's going to find that out just like the rest of you. I never forget. It's in my nature. I never forget. As you're going to discover.'

I saw that it was all over. There was nothing more I could do. I would have liked to faint, but the fear worked in me like a potion, I was soon going to be dead and I felt most desperately alive. But I did not speak a word, only shut my eyes. I think that even now I was thanking God that Leonie was not here. This at least was something she would be spared, my pretty little sister who knew more of the world than I, but who must never suffer like this. When John put his great hands round me, knocking me flat to the ground, I did not even resist, only prayed it would be over soon and I would be dead, the pain and humiliation forgotten.

Only as I lay there, the hands tearing savagely at my clothes, I grew aware of an icy chill beneath me that seemed to be spreading through my whole body. And John Gonomanaway, putting one hand flat on the ground to lever himself up, felt it too. I heard him gasp. The fingers digging into me relaxed. There was a pause then he let out a great cry that was almost a scream. He shouted, the panic shrilling in his voice, 'It's come! Jesus bloody Christ, it's come!'

And, raising feebly my terrified head, I realised that I was lying in sea water: I could now see it everywhere, glistening on the ground.

The killer sea was my rescuer. The wall had gone. It was 1327 all over again.

John Gonomanaway was a brave man, afraid of little, but this was something he could not take. He too had been born and bred in Greymanswick, he had heard about the great flood since his childhood, the fear of its returning had always been with him, like everyone else in the village. He forgot about me, his grievances, his revenge. The only thing in his mind was a primitive urge to save his life. He leapt to his feet and the next instant was out of the cave, tearing down the dunes, vanishing out of sight.

I did not come to myself for several minutes. I was so dazed with shock and terror that I hardly realised where I was or what had happened. I was dizzily aware that the crisis was past, but now that one danger was over, I did not take in the full horror of the next. I huddled there, shivering and exhausted, and it was only as I began to realise how cold and ill I felt that I knew I too must make some effort to get away. I staggered out on to the dunes, skidding and slipping in the wet sand. I looked wretchedly around me at the desolation. This was somehow the emptiness that had been Troy, not a field but a vast and lonely plain. The dawn was coming up and the grey light made everything grim and blurred. I felt as if I stood in emptiness, the sands alive with the water that snaked over them and which was already up to my ankles. The frenzy of the storm was done, but it had loosened the sea's boundaries, and somehow this slow, relentless movement of the water was more frightening than if it had swept up in a torrent. I could smell the salt of it, and all around me was pyramid after pyramid of sand, stretching out, as it seemed to my exhausted eyes, for ever. There was no sign of John. He had left me to drown. I do not imagine the thought of me so much as crossed his mind. I stood there in my loneliness, and I knew I had no strength to walk to Cuckold's Point. I could never drag my feet through the mud and water, and I could not even shelter in the cave, for the water was already filling it and it would become my grave.

This was how it had been for the citizens of Greymanswick four hundred years ago. There would be what Virgil had described, – the roaring of the sea, the mountainous waves, the screaming and the panic – but it had ended like this with lost, exhausted, resigned people, alone, marooned, waiting for the inevitable end.

It seemed to me that St. Botolph's bells were ringing and I was so convinced I heard them that I resigned myself to death, and let myself fall on to the sands, the strength and spirit gone from me. I did not notice that the water was no longer rising, only lay there, my face against the sopping mud, where no doubt I would have suffocated or died quickly from sheer exhaustion.

The voice that sounded in my ears was so removed from anything to do with Greymanswick that some of my numbness left me. I half raised my head. It was faint yet clear, the echo of a time long past. *I will not have a daughter of mine going into a decline*, it had said, and now, *I will not have a daughter so weak and foolish as to give up hope and let herself die in horrid, wet sand*.

That was all. The words were not repeated. I thought this must be some delusion of the dying, yet the voice was Maman's voice, the words Maman's words. I spoke her name. I whispered, 'Maman!' Then I sat up and, putting my hands over my face, began to cry.

I heard the sounds in the distance. I did not move. I could not stop crying, and somehow the energy of my outburst restored me a little, put some life back into me. Even when I realised that the noise was that of horse's hooves I remained as I was, and when Virgil jumped down beside me and shouted at me – he told me afterwards I was like someone blind and deaf – I just sat there, looking certainly ridiculous, my legs sticking out in front of me, my appearance bedraggled beyond belief and my hands as tight on my face as if they were fastened there.

He grabbed at my wrists to pull them away, then jerked me to my feet. It was only then that my senses returned. I flung myself at him, nearly overturning the pair of us in the slippery wetness. We stared at each other in silence. He was not in much better shape than myself. He was soaked to the skin, hair flattened to his head, the water trickling down his face, and on his countenance was a mixture of terror, rage and incredulous relief. But to me he was a miracle, the most wonderful sight I had ever seen in my life, and what with this, my physical weakness and the horror of everything that had happened, I chose to play the society miss, and fainted clean away.

He could hardly have been pleased, but at least it saved him from the hysteria bubbling up within me. When I came to, which I believe was in a minute, I was lying across the saddle, and we were galloping in the direction of Cuckold's Point. I did not know of course – and at that moment would hardly have cared – that the tide was receding and the danger over: the water flowing over the dunes was slowly diminishing and sinking into the sand. If John had not panicked, he would have realised that his terror was unfounded, and I by now would be dead.

So far Virgil and I had hardly exchanged a word. I was conscious now but so tired that I could not raise my head from his shoulder, while he, though he must have been longing to reproach me, saw that I was in no state to receive his anger. Indeed, I think I fell asleep, for the next thing I knew was the taste of brandy in my mouth, and I found myself lying on a settle in a room crowded with people, many of them in as bad a state as myself.

There was no fire, for everything was soaked with sea water, but this was the parlour of the 'Cuckold's Point', and it was hot and steaming with the crowd of men, women and children there, with every other room in the inn, in the same state. The floor was swimming, the windows were broken, and it was only Virgil's fierce determination that procured me somewhere to lie, but of drink there was plenty, for this was the hideout of the Greymanswick smugglers, and the cellars were full of brandy and wine and Hollands gin. The casks must all have been floating, but the iron bands stood firm, and there was no salt in the liquor being poured down me.

I sat up and gazed at the people around me. They were all folk I knew by sight. Here was the grocer, the baker, the candlestick maker, and there were the fine ladies and gentlemen from the big houses on the other side. They were linked by disaster for everybody here had been near to death. The young lady from Cudden Hall and the local doxy, the village fishermen and Sir Somebody Something from across the water, we were simply grateful to be alive, and when we met each other's eyes, we bestowed on each other conspiratorial smiles.

201

I still could not speak. The terror I had endured was like a lump in my throat, and somehow, now that it was over, it was worse, for I could look back on it and see the full awfulness of it. Virgil was crouching beside me. He still had not uttered one scolding word, though he could have said in all fairness that whatever I had suffered, I had brought it upon myself by disregarding his warnings. I suppose I must have looked a fright with my white face and wildly disordered hair and dress. He took my hand and pressed it tightly between the two of his. It was at this point that I looked across his shoulder, to see John Gonomanaway in the far corner, huddled there and drinking wine from the bottle. With his marked face and soaked clothes he looked like something out of a nightmare, and indeed to me he was the worst nightmare imaginable, for the mere glimpse of him brought back to me that brief time – it was brief though it seemed to me an eternity – in the cave. As I stared, half fainting with the shock of it, the sickness coming up in my throat, he saw me, with Virgil beside me. I imagine the shock was as bad for him. When Virgil, remarking my aghast expression, leapt to his feet to see what it was, John had gone. He must have dived through the door. If he thought of me at all, he must have believed me dead.

I began to cry again. I have never been one for easy tears, but I was so tired, I had been so afraid, and I felt it was all too much for me.

Virgil said in a tight voice, 'Was that not John? I thought I saw him when we came in, but I was too concerned to think any more about it.'

I shook my head.

'It was, wasn't it?'

'It might have been. I don't know.' For I knew that if I told Virgil what had happened he would be ripe for murder, and I felt that more violence was something I could not take. I never wanted to see John Gonomanaway again as long as I lived, I did not care what happened to him, provided he was far, far away from me.

202

There was a look on Virgil's face such as I had never seen, and it shot the tears back into their sockets. He said very quietly, 'What did he do to you?'

'Nothing.'

He did not contradict me. He only said in the same flat voice, 'I'll kill him.'

Then he walked away from me, pushing his way through the crowd to look out of the broken window. When he came back he looked much as usual and did not refer to John again. He said, 'You have had a very bad time, Nanette, so there is little point in reproaching you, but –' his voice rose, 'You are the stupidest, most obstinate girl I have ever met.'

This restored me a little. This was the old Virgil. I admitted meekly that he was right, and he suddenly grinned at me. We had neither of us so far even smiled, and it was reassuring.

He said, 'You locked your sister in, didn't you? It seems to be the only sensible thing you've done this evening. The crash of the wall falling in woke her up. One side of Cudden Hall is swept away. I heard her banging on the door. Without her I imagine you would still be lying on the dunes. I've never seen anything like it – Did you not realise the tide had turned?'

I said weakly, 'How could I? I was in no state to be reasonable, I was cold and frightened and tired to death. When I felt the cold water on the floor of the cave I just gave up all hope.'

Virgil did not comment on this, but I saw the look on his face: I think he was beginning to insert all that I had left out. But he only said, 'If the tide had continued to come in, you would probably be dead. The dunes are high, but last time that made no difference. There was a forest there but when the water rushed in, it disappeared. You know that the village is gone?'

'Oh my God! The people –'

'They are mostly here. This time we were prepared. It is mostly the dead who have been disturbed.'

203

'What do you mean?'

'You'll see presently. We shall be returning to the Hall, when you are rested, but first I must ride down to the sea wall. I have just caught a glimpse of Tom Easey and Hookey: I suspect they are planning to get away on their boat.'

'No one could sail in such a sea!'

'I fancy the thought of a rope halter is an inducement to sail anywhere. But they are not going. I'm not going to be deprived of their being brought to justice. However, your sister is perfectly well, though –' He paused, then said in a bewildered voice, 'I had to think she was a little drunk.'

'Leonie drunk? No!'

'Oh yes. She talked about a bottle of wine in the cupboard. I did not know you kept wine in your bedroom. She was upset and angry, but very afraid for you. I saw the half empty bottle beside her. I've no doubt it was to keep up her spirits. She was quite bemused when I opened the door, but told me at once where you were and why. I could hardly believe it, even of you. You'll see her presently. The Lowrys have taken her home with them, and invited us too. I don't think either of us wishes to stay at Cudden Hall.' Then he shouted at me so loudly that the people near us turned to stare. 'Nanette! What lunacy got into you? To go out on such a night and on such a damned idiotic errand – do you not know who this young man is?'

'John –' I began, then broke off.

'John?' repeated Virgil smoothly.

I looked at him despairingly. I said, 'Please, Virgil. One day I'll tell you what happened. I promise. But not now. I couldn't bear it. I know I've behaved badly, indeed, I have been so foolish that I can hardly believe it of myself, but I have paid for it. This has been the worst night of my life. Don't scold me any more for it is more than I can take. I imagine we will neither of us ever see John-Gon again, and that is how I would like it to be. If I told you the whole story, what good would it do? You would be terribly angry, you

204

would set out to kill him as you have just said, and it is possible that this time he would kill you.'

None of this was very sensible as I could see from the look on Virgil's face, but I was in no state to think of what I was saying, and I was in tears again so he did not answer me, only put his arm round me and drew me against his shoulder.

I asked him, when I could speak again, what had happened to Amelia and her brother: I told him I had seen them leaving the Hall.

He muttered, 'The son of a whore!' and he was not speaking of Amelia's brother. But he answered me quite amiably. He said, 'They were gulled, like the rest of us. I doubt we'll hear of them again. If they have the least sense left they will be scuttling up north with the money I gave them in their pockets. If ever they reach home – and they are so unimportant that I don't see why they should not – they will gather themselves together for the famous coming and start their folly all over again. Most of what Andrew brought over from France is now in my aunt's pockets, but I daresay they will find means to raise some more. I have no sympathy with them. Anyone who believes my aunt could take the faintest interest in a Scottish Pretender should be put in Bedlam. There is not a drop of sentiment in her except what goes into her preposterous novels. All she wants is power and money. Do you think she took you in out of love or duty?'

'At least we have no money!'

'She wanted you in her web. As she wanted me. I'll wager she offered you some inducement, perhaps rich and beautiful things. Not that you would ever have received them, any more than Amelia who for a time believed her to be the most wonderful lady in the world. But now the reckoning is at hand. She is so used to destroying that I don't think it ever struck her that the murder of a silly old man could bring about her own downfall. It will be the end for her and all her hangers-on. Including Tom and Hookey – I must go.' He put a hand up to my cheek. 'I'll be back. I've decided to marry you after all.'

I said with a faint return of spirit, 'I am most grateful.'

'Well, someone has to keep an eye on you. I want you to wait here for me. I doubt I'll be very long.'

'No!' I said, and jumped to my feet. The hysteria in my voice was such that he was taken aback, staring at me.

He said roughly, 'Of course you will wait here. What is the matter with you? You are sheltered and warm, nobody will harm you.'

He would never have understood the panic-terror bursting within me. I knew it was not reasonable and the 'Cuckold's Point' was filled with people, but I felt that the moment Virgil was gone, John would reappear, and the thought of seeing him again so appalled me that I believed I would die. I clutched at him, my voice shrilling up. I knew I was behaving abominably but I was entirely out of control. I wailed at him, 'I am coming with you. I am not being left here on my own.'

He was not surprisingly furious with me. He too must have been very tired, it had been a shocking evening for him, and when he set out to find me, he probably believed me to be dead. To be confronted with an hysterical young female was the last straw. He shouted at me, 'I tell you, you are not coming. Are you too genteel to stay a while in a tippling house? You would simply be in my way. What I have to do is a man's business.'

I could have said that I had had enough of men's business to last me a lifetime. I continued to grip Virgil's arm. I cried out, 'I tell you, I am not staying here alone. I don't care if you want me or not. If you don't take me I'll run after you.'

'You will have to run pretty hard,' said Virgil.

But he looked at me in angry resignation. He saw that I meant what I said. I could not possibly catch up with a galloping horse, but equally he could not leave me outside, alone in the cold.

I said in a more muted voice, 'Shall we go?'

Then he began to laugh. 'My God!' he said, 'I can never be with you for more than an hour without wanting to wring your neck. Can you imagine what our marriage will be like? Very well. If you have to come, you have to come. You are not wanted. It will be no place for a woman, and you look as if you're sleeping on your feet. But I suppose it's reasonable, – you have been involved in so much of the drama that you might as well see the end of it.' He glanced round the inn parlour as he spoke. Since our arrival more people had come, though it was hard to believe there was room for a mouse. I think Virgil saw how lost and afraid I would be in such a crowd. He elbowed me through the throng, pushing and shoving his way, and at last we were outside.

IX

The day had come. There were rose-coloured clouds in the sky, the faint glimmer of a sun, the rain had ceased. Only the wind still blew over the monumental sea: if Tom and Hookey Miller hoped to brave those mountainous waves, they must indeed be desperate, no small craft could possibly hope to survive.

We stood for a moment to stare. I had not fully realised the extent of the devastation. It was the most terrifying thing I had ever seen and brought back memories to me of last night so that I could not stop myself from shivering. The dunes were always as lonely as the moon: the sea and the storm and the darkness had made them hideous, but now Greymanswick was equally ugly and strange. There was little around us but boulders, scattered planks and bricks, the debris of boats and houses, with great pits here and there as if the sea had scooped up the land with a giant spoon. The village, as Virgil had said, was gone, a smashed tangle of cottages, with not one left standing. Only Cudden Hall and the broken walls of St. Saviour's church still stood on the hill: they looked as if nothing had touched them for we could not from this distance see the battered west wing.

At last we walked towards the horse which was tethered round the side of the inn, placidly eating his breakfast from a bag of oats the landlord had provided. Virgil lifted me up, and he began to ride down to where the sea wall had once been: we had to go slowly, making our way over and round the debris. Virgil's arm was round my waist, and his anger had expended itself for, as we came down the hill, he spoke softly in my ear.

'You always have to know, Nanette, don't you?' he said: it was not a reproach, simply a statement of fact. 'You are still the meddlesome little girl who could not keep out of mischief.'

'I'm sorry,' I said. 'If you wish it, I'll walk away. I'll not stand there to watch.'

'You might as well see the play out,' said Virgil.

There might never have been a dyke. There was a great mess of shingle and seaweed on the beach at the fringe of the outgoing tide, rolling over the rubble. There were three people there, Hookey Miller, Tom Easey and, to my astonishment, Dolly. The *Holy Margaret* at which Tom was working, had somehow survived: it was unbelievable that she had not been battered to pieces like the other boats we had passed on our way. It seemed as if she were about to slide into the sea, but at the sound of our horse's hooves, all three of them swung round.

Virgil dismounted, leaving me still in the saddle, and made instantly for Tom. I saw how Dolly stared at him. She looked cold and old, for all she was only a young girl. There was a shawl bound tightly round her head, and the face beneath its folds seemed exhausted to the point of death, there was no colour in her cheeks and there were dark shadows under the eyes.

She did not look at me. I do not think she was at first aware of my presence. She only looked at Virgil, as if for the last time. I saw the desolate longing in her face. I felt no jealousy, only sorrow and pity. I was ashamed of myself that I had ever resented her loving, and wanted to jump down and take her in my arms to comfort her. But she only looked at him, and he was so intent on his purpose that he did not even notice. I knew instinctively that this was a farewell, this was the end, and I was angry that he did not speak to her: it was like waving goodbye to someone who turned his back and walked away.

Then she turned her sad face upon me. I suddenly remembered the jolly, smiling girl who had made a fuss of me and taken me to a fish breakfast with her father. The one who was transposed upon the other with a century between. She said quietly, 'Well, Miss Nanette? Did you enjoy the storm?'

I did not know what to say. I looked at the shawl and the cloak she was wearing, then at the bundle of clothes that lay at her feet. I said at last, 'Are you going away, Dolly?'

'Yes, Miss Nanette.'

'Won't you be coming back again?'

'No.'

'I shall miss you.'

She shrugged, then turned away, to look once more at Virgil who was now facing Tom.

Tom Easey stared at Virgil. Hookey Miller stood behind him. I think Virgil did not even see Dolly.

He said quietly, 'So you are going fishing, Tom. I think you will have to stay here a little longer. You are wanted. For murder, theft and a great many other things. You have had a long run for your money. I think you must answer a few questions. There are indeed a great many to answer. You had best forget about the *Holy Margaret*. You'll not need her again for a long, long time.'

Tom looked at him. It was hard to believe that this was the kindly man who had made an inquisitive little girl so welcome. I could see now that my aunt had chosen her aides well, for their toughness and their courage, but there was no feeling in her, and she would never have realised that tough allies are well enough in good times but not dependable when things go against them. Tom would have cut her throat without a qualm if it had been necessary, and I was so frightened for Virgil that my mouth was dry and I could not stop my shaking.

'Why, Master Virgil,' said Tom with a great grin, 'are you wanting to come with us now? After such a sea the fish will be leaping high. It will be a good catch.'

'It is another kind of catch that I have in mind,' said Virgil, his hand in his pocket.

210

Tom shook his head. He was still grinning, but his eyes were as hard as the stones flung out by the sea. I saw Hookey edge up closer to him.

'I couldn't miss such a chance, Master Virgil,' said Tom. 'I'm only a poor fisherman. I have my living to earn. Hookey here will bear me out. I couldn't miss such a chance.'

And Hookey repeated, 'He couldn't do that.'

I saw the hook protruding from his sleeve. I had always been sorry for him but I saw now how dangerous he was. I wanted to clutch at Virgil, say, For God's sake, let us go. But I could not, I had insisted on coming with him, I had to watch and wait.

'You have no choice,' said Virgil. Then the words poured out of him. 'It's all over, Tom. You know that. There is nothing left but the hangman's rope. I don't pity you, you never pitied anyone else. I haven't much to say for an old woman who is as evil a devil as yourself, but it was you and Hookey and John that did all the robbing. It was you who broke into people's houses, and it wasn't just the taking, was it? There was the old man who was knocked on the head, and the young girl who was tied up so cruelly in the depths of winter that she died. There were other things too. I'm thinking of a good man who committed the error of marrying a wicked woman. He died, Tom. Maybe you helped, Tom, though I am not sure if you had the wit. But you knew, you all knew. He died very slowly of a poisonous powder, he died in great pain, and there was no need for him to die, except that he suspected what you were all doing and it was not safe to leave him alive. She only cared for power and possessions, and you and Hookey are the same, you and Hookey are the same.'

He looked at them. They said nothing. Only Dolly moved, her hands fluttering, her face working with terror.

Then Virgil said again, 'So you are going fishing. It is quite a sea for a small boat. What are you fishing for? Hollands gin, French brandy or a houseful of porcelain? So you

211

propose to get away, you believe you'll get off scot-free, while my aunt is left, with perhaps William Pleydell in tow, to take the responsibility.' Then he cried out in a passion, 'No, no no! I'll not rest happy until the lot of you are apprehended. Then we can all sleep peaceful at nights, and the air here will smell clean again.'

He suddenly took out a pistol from his pocket. And at this moment Tom shot forward, a long-bladed knife in his hand.

It was Dolly who flung herself between them. She received the knife in her heart. She fell to the ground, the blood staining her breast.

We were all so shocked as to be transfixed. At last Virgil, with a rush, dropped to his knees beside Dolly and took her in his arms. She was dead. She must have died immediately. Virgil passed his hand over her mouth then tried to feel her pulse. His eyes were fixed on her face, he did not so much as glance around him. If Tom had wished to kill him at that moment, he would only have had to raise his arm. But he only stood there, his hands hanging down, his face white with such a look of horror to it as I have never seen. The next instant he ran towards the *Holy Margaret*, gave her a shove that sent her into the sea, and he and Hookey Miller leapt aboard: the boat was instantly riding the waves.

Whether or not it could have been prevented I do not know or care. Virgil made no attempt to stop them. Still holding Dolly he said in a dull voice, 'Let them be. It doesn't matter any more.'

The wind still whipped the waves mountain high. We saw the *Holy Margaret* balanced on top of them, fragile and minute, like a child's toy. There was a howling of wind, a creak of cordage, the hiss and rattle of spray, then the boat and its occupants vanished from view.

No one ever saw the two men again. I do not know if they survived, if they could survive, or if they went to their grave in the sea that had been their living and their life. They were

212

bad men, but if anyone in the world could ride such a storm, it would Tom Easey. I believe sometimes that he might be somewhere in Holland, working at the same trade, the only one he ever knew. As Virgil said, it does not matter any more. I could only stand there, staring at the little group – for a couple of villagers had run towards us – bent over Dolly Easey. I thought of how we had met, and how friendly and lively she had been. I had offered to teach her to read, horrid, superior little creature that I was. The rough country voice rang in my ears. *I'll remind you of that, Miss Nanette, when we meet again.*

We had met for the last time. I stood there, hardly knowing where I was, and watched as the men carried Dolly away. Virgil at last came up to me, not to comfort but to be comforted: his arms went round me and his head lay heavy on my shoulder.

I could have said a great many things. I did not. I did not weep either. They had laid Dolly's body across the horse's back; she would be taken to the church half a mile away, she would lie there, be buried in the churchyard and forgotten. I could have said, she should not have died, but this was the kind of death she would have chosen. I could have said, she loved you and knew there was no hope, no hope at all. I could have said, this was her home, she would be miserable in a foreign land, away from everyone she knew. But I said none of these things, only bent my head towards Virgil's and held him as if he were a child.

I grieved bitterly for this wickedly unnecessary death but it knocked all anger out of me. I no longer thought of John Gonomanaway who was after all more stupid than bad. If I thought of Tom Easy at all, it was with pity that he had killed his own daughter. As for my aunt and all this nonsense about the Collector that I only dimly understood, it was not even worth considering.

At last Virgil raised his head. He moved a little away from me. His face was drawn and pale. He said in his normal voice, 'We'll go. It must be done. Will you come

213

with me?'

This seemed to me a very foolish question. I did not trouble to answer it, only linked my arm through his, and we began to walk back towards Cudden Hall. It was only then that the tears began to trickle down my cheeks, but I did not even pause to wipe them away. It was in complete silence that we came to St. Saviour's hill.

Then I looked and stopped, exclaiming.

The storm had flattened the briar and blackthorn. It had also torn the bodies from their graves. Cuddens and Easeys, high and low, lay in bony pieces everywhere, limbs torn from sockets, skulls rolling down the hillside, a true dance of death.

Virgil surveyed this impassively. He had after all seen it before, and after what had happened this unseemly resurrection in no way touched him. He only said, 'It will cause difficulties on the day of doom. It seems that at the final roll-call a Cudden may be wearing an Easey's left leg.' Then he said abruptly, pushing aside a decapitated skeleton, 'We'll take the side path. My lady is waiting for us and, if my eyes do not mistake me, there is William at her side.'

I could see now, as we approached the Hall, that most of the west wing had been knocked away by the sea. My aunt and Mr. Pleydell stood at the corner, as if they had been investigating, and as we came nearer I saw revealed the whole of that mysterious room, like the side of a doll's house. I understood now why poor Jack Lescott had been killed.

Within the room, which ran the length of the wall, was every kind of valuable: silver, porcelain, pictures, furniture and everywhere great boxes containing God knows what. The Collector had done herself well. There was no attempt at arrangement, and the sea, sweeping through, had finally disordered the disorder. The most frightening thing about this collection was its chaos. I could understand someone stealing beautiful things for the pleasure of possessing them, of gloating over them, feasting on the loveliness, but it was plain that even before the storm, everything had been simply thrown in here, with no attempt at any kind of order, even to preserve the things themselves. Books lay on top of oriental vases, some broken by the weight, Elizabethan chairs were weighed down by piles of pictures and ornaments. Everywhere were stacks of ancient weapons, silver dinner sets, tapestries, carpets, even garments made of velvet and silk. It must have been worth a fortune, yet to the Collector it was worth nothing, except as something to possess. The salt water had ruined a great deal of it, but much of it had been spoilt a long time ago by sheer neglect. It was like the tales one sometimes hears about, of old people found dead of cold and starvation, with thousands of pounds under the mattress. I had the feeling that my aunt would never have touched it, whatever happened: she simply wanted to feel it was there, taken from its rightful owners by her own ingenuity, so that she knew it was hers and could not even be seen by anyone else. It was shocking to see how the silver was blackened, chairs broken and books, some of them incunabula, torn to pieces with pages lying everywhere.

It reminded me of the scattered skeletons in the church-yard: it was as macabre and as useless.

Leonie told me afterwards that everyone had run out at the sound of the crash which seemed as if the whole Hall had fallen, and she, released by Virgil, had joined them. The servants had simply gawped, but Mr. Lowry had been stunned into silence: he had suspected something of what was going on, but nothing like this. He picked up some of his own things. He looked at them, the tears pouring down his cheeks, then let them fall as if he had no further use for them. When at last he spoke it was to my aunt, who was watching him impassively. He said, 'How could you do such a thing?' Then, 'You have ruined beauty.'

My aunt stood there now. She showed no emotion, but Mr. Pleydell at her side was restless and regarded us with dislike and suspicion. I think on reflection he must always have the least predictable of her henchmen. He was for one thing an educated man, and she was accustomed to dealing with such as John Gonomanaway and Tom Easey who would have an uneasy respect for her as the lady of the house. Mr. Pleydell, I imagine, had no respect for anyone, nor any scruples either: he needed the money and perhaps it amused him to pander to what must have seemed to him insanity. I suspect he would have turned King's evidence a long time ago, had it not been made worth his while to stay, and I would not like to depend on him at any trial for he had the look on him of one who would cheerfully betray his own granny. Certainly he was a murderer, he had killed Jack, perhaps Mr. Lescott as well, and sometimes I believe I would have been his next victim. He was a wicked and useless man, but in a way he too had been ruined by my aunt's passion for power, like John and Tom and countless others. They were none of them good people, but she had made use of them and destroyed them as she had destroyed everything, including herself.

She was quite unmoved by the way in which she had been found out, and not even interested in our obvious condemnation. She was neat and dowdy as always, wearing a brown dress with a string of garish imitation beads round her neck. I thought in a dazed kind of way that this was part of the pattern: there was beautiful and valuable jewellery at her feet, but she would not wear it, she had to put on something cheap and ugly.

The plain, plump face was an expressionless as usual: the pebble eyes surveyed me without curiosity. Only the beautiful hair was impeccably curled and waved, as if it were the one thing that satisfied her pride.

Virgil did not even greet her. He simply said, 'Dolly is dead.'

She turned her head slowly towards him. 'Dolly?' she said. 'And who, pray, is Dolly?'

'Dolly, Ma'am, was Tom Easey's daughter. She worked in your household for most of her life. You must have met

216

her a dozen times a day for the past fifteen or sixteen years.'

'I do not remember the servants,' said my aunt. 'I have better things to do with my time. You say she is dead. How did she die?'

'She saved my life, Ma'am. She received the knife thrust intended for me.'

My aunt did not reply to this, only stared. Her mouth went down at the corners. It was plain that she considered this a pity. She said at last, 'I daresay she was not much loss.'

'No,' said Virgil,' she was not much loss. Why should she be? She was only a common girl, she had no breeding and no money. She had nothing to interest you. Only she was young and pretty and, if it had not been for you, she would still be alive. Jack would be alive too, and his father. Also your husband, Ma'am. Have you forgotten your husband?'

Mr. Pleydell moved uneasily, his eyes flickering from one to the other of us. But my aunt replied, 'Yes, I have forgotten him. What is there to remember? He interfered, that is the only thing I remember of him. He wished to stop me doing what I wanted to do. If he died, it was his own fault. He had no business to spy on me. I do not tolerate any kind of interference.' Suddenly she shot her finger out at me. It made me jerk back, it was like having a pistol pointed at me. 'You interfered too, you and your pert little sister. I took you in out of charity, didn't I? And all the thanks I receive is spying and prying. John told me you were on the dunes. He went out to look for you. He said you tried to buy his silence.'

'What!' I could feel Virgil tauten beside me. I was so horrified that I could only stare.

'Oh yes,' she said contemptuously. 'He said he just laughed at you. If it pleases you, I could see he would have obliged if he had dared. But he did not dare, did he? He would never have told me this if he hadn't been so disgustingly drunk. But it showed me how disloyal he was. I will

217

not have disloyal people around me. I've not trusted John for a long time, and the prospect of you two conspiring together against me was the last straw. You'll not see him again, miss. William took care of that, didn't you, William?'

Mr. Pleydell did not answer. I think he did not care for so plain a charge of murder, any more than I cared for the suggestion that I had tried to sell myself to John Gonomanaway. Only at this point Virgil put his arm round my shoulders and I did not mind any more. He would never believe such a story, he had seen the state I was in, and he had seen John's face too, when he was in the 'Cuckold's Point.' But I could understand now what had happened. John had come home. He had nowhere else to go, and it was the only home he had. He was terrified I would tell my aunt what had happened. But it would have made no difference. Perhaps she had guessed the truth, it was the kind of thing she would understand very well, but what he had not understood was that she would regard his pursuit of me as the final disloyalty. John was her lover, much as she might despise him, and the thought that he had so much as touched me would be his death warrant, with the useful Mr. Pleydell as executioner.

I would never know where John was now. I only knew I would never see him again. And as I turned away, sickened and in some strange way ashamed, I saw the brief look of savage triumph flash across Virgil's face: it was John Gonomanaway's requiem.

Virgil was the next target. My aunt rounded on him, her voice rising. She cried out, 'As for you –' It was one of the rare times when I saw her showing emotion. 'You ungrateful boy! You wicked, ungrateful boy!'

The boy was now twenty-five and she had all but beaten the life out of him. But to her he was still the poor little wretch she had adopted and claimed to have loved. He said nothing, only regarded her grimly as she went on, 'When I think what I have taken into my house –'

Virgil, his eyes moving down to the mess of valuables, said, 'Yes indeed,' but this she ignored.

'If I had only known – I suppose it was you, Virgil, who informed on me.'

'It was Mr. Lescott, Ma'am, but he had the advantage of me by merely a few hours.' She tried to speak again, but his voice rose so that it extinguished hers. 'Yes, my lady – is that not what they all call you? – when I discovered what you were doing, I resolved to end it as soon as I had all the necessary information. I knew you murdered my uncle. I loved my uncle, Ma'am. You wouldn't understand that because you have never loved anyone in your life, but he was good to me, and I never forgot his kindness to a wretched brat whom you and John tormented, tormented for the simple reason that it amused you and added to your feeling of power. He used to creep into my room sometimes with food and an ointment for my stripes, but it was not just that. He would put his arms round me and comfort me. I will never forget. And to kill him so cruelly – I saw John putting the powder in his wine.'

'You spy! If I had only known – '

'Yes, my lady. Ill-treated little boys have sharp eyes and ears. They have to, out of self-preservation. Oh, I saw it more than once. You did not beat me then because I was too big, but I saw, and I remembered. I tried to warn him, but what could I say? Your wife is poisoning you? He would probably have thrown me out of the house. He was too good to understand a demon like you. Once or twice I managed to change the glass, but I could not be there all the time, and I had to watch him grow thinner and weaker day by day. When he died, it was the end for you and your parasites. But it took me a long time. I had to be sure. If it interests you, my lady, every time I came up I investigated a little further. Tom is a cunning man, but he thought I was in the village for my own reasons. It never entered his head that I was interested in him, not the pretty girls.'

She said, calm again as if it did not matter, 'Where is

Tom?'

'God knows. On the sea or in it, it doesn't matter, we will never see him again. You'll have to find yourself new allies, Ma'am though perhaps now it hardly matters. And,' said Virgil more quietly, 'perhaps nothing really matters now. St. Saviour's churchyard is awash with bones, a few more are not important. Yet I am of a more vindictive nature than my poor Uncle Constantine. I would like to see you suffer a little of what you have made other people endure.'

She received this as if it were some kind of accolade. She turned to Mr. Pleydell who was biting his lip and looking as if he wished himself miles away. She said in a cold, authoritive voice, 'William. You have your pistol. I want you to kill both of them. Now.'

So must she have spoken of John Gonomanaway. I could see him there, too bemused with drink to realise what was happening, yet terrified. She was smiling as she spoke. It was then that I knew she was mad. I would have thrown myself across Virgil, only he said with perfect calm, 'Don't be silly, Nanette. I cannot have everyone saving my life.' Then he laughed. 'Well, William? It is a good thing you have overcome your fear of firearms.'

But Mr. Pleydell had had enough. He had murdered, God knows how many times, but he was not a hired assassin, and even he must have quailed at the thought of shooting down an innocent young man and woman whose only crime was that they were standing there at this particular time. John Gonomanaway was to be my aunt's last victim. He looked at her and then at us. Then suddenly, without a word, he turned and ran: she clutched at him in a disbelieving fury but he struck her hand down. We saw him disappear down the hill. I do not know if he was picked up by the justice's men. Men like Mr. Pleydell often survive when the innocent are taken: he had edited the local paper for several years and must have known every nook and cranny of the county.

We watched him go in a kind of dreadful fascination.

220

The sweat was trickling down my face but Virgil seemed unmoved, only laughed again. My aunt, however, after that one act of violence, seemed to have forgotten what had happened, indeed, she seemed to have forgotten everything.

She said quite pettishly, 'I wish I knew where everyone was. Virgil, you will find John-Gon for me and tell him I want him. And Dolly shall bring me my lunch. I declare I am positively famished. It really is too bad the way people just disappear. I would like to speak to Amelia too. Don't stand there, Virgil. Don't you hear what I am saying? As for you, miss' – She suddenly rounded on me. 'Why are you not in the kitchen? You are not here to be idle, you know. Go and help Cook immediately. And Virgil, why don't you do as you're told?'

This silenced even Virgil, but my aunt seemed convinced she would be instantly obeyed. She remarked in a conversational tone, 'I must get on with my novel. So difficult the last chapters – but of course you children would not understand, you are not artists.'

She turned to go. We watched her in a stunned silence. Before she went she glanced round her ravished storeroom. She was smiling. She stooped down and picked up a beautiful piece of what looked like Roman glass. Perhaps it came from the church, the Collector's last haul. It must have been priceless. She twirled it round in her fingers, then with a dramatically negligent air lifted it high, and dropped it to the ground.

It broke into fragments. She kicked the pieces away. We saw her turn the corner, making for her own room.

I turned into Virgil's arms. I buried my face in his shoulder. I could not look at anything any longer: it was all in a fog of madness and evil.

He said, his voice shaken and bewildered, 'It is not possible. These things mean nothing to her, yet everything here has been stolen, delivered at night, and carefully stored. There is a fortune in this room. Other people's fortune. She does not even like what she has. If she came in at night to handle it, caress it, admire its beauty – but it could be a sack of meal for all she cares. She just wants to possess, to own, to say, this is mine.' Then, as I raised my head to stare at him, he said, 'I'll tell you something else, Nanette. I believe, I truly believe, she will get off scot-free. They will hang William if they ever find him, they would have hanged John and Tom Easey and all the rest of them, but I do not think anyone will have the nerve to put a rope round my aunt's throat, though she is the instigator, the real murderer. They call her 'my lady'. Everyone here calls her that. That is how they have been brought up to think of her. She is an institution. The Cuddens have lived here for the past five hundred years. There was a John Cudden in 1216, a Constantine Cudden in 1292. I used to read my history when they locked me in my room. There was nothing else to do. The family is as much a part of the county as the sea. They doubtless hate her, they certainly fear her, but they'll never touch her. I am willing to swear that my damnable lady will live out her days in peace and freedom. Can you believe that, Nanette?' Then he repeated as if he simply could not believe it, 'She will get off scot-free.'

I turned to look at Cudden Hall. It was the last time I would see it close. There was not a sign of life. The rooms were empty, the kitchen bare. Once there had been running footsteps, talk, laughter, the smell of good food. Now there was nothing. The servants had all run away when the flood came. They would never come back. My aunt would sit alone in her room, writing the novels that no one would read. But the ghosts would be there, crowding in upon her, with her beautiful hair and her heart as cold and hard as stone. There would be the ghost of John Gonomanaway whom she had shot down like a dog, who had shared her guilt and her bed. There would be the ghost of my uncle Constantine, dying slowly of the poison she fed him, who had been her husband, who had given her the Hall. And the ghost of Dolly, of Jack Lescott, of many others, more perhaps than we knew: they would all be there, and at night when there was no one to light the lamps, no one to prepare a meal, she would sit there alone in her empty room, with their shadows crowding thick upon her, whispering in her ear, making mouths at her, deriding her: if she turned and screamed there would be no one living to hear her.

I saw Cudden Hall as it would become, – the garden a wilderness, the beautiful rooms black and stinking with dust, the windows broken and thick with grime. The villagers might still call my aunt 'my lady', but they were superstitious people, they would know what had happened, they would never again come near a place so cursed with wickedness and murder.

'No,' I said to Virgil, 'she will not get off scot-free.'

We walked down to what had once been the village of Greymanswick: there a carriage was waiting to take us to the Lowrys. 'Leonie will be wild with impatience,' said Virgil. 'I daresay she will slap and kiss you to death. She has been very frightened for you, almost out of her mind.'

The storm was at last done. The wind had died down. The sea was turbulent but only as it often was during the autumn months. We could see now before us like a picture the full devastation. The cliffs had been washed away, the dyke was no longer there. There was no road left leading to the towns on the other side. All pasture as far as we could see had been destroyed and the beach was piled high with shingle and sand. But already people were abroad: they looked like little ants, gathering up what salvage they could find. In a little while we would all start living our normal lives again.

Until the next time.

As we approached the carriage I paused. It was strange to see Tom Easey's cottage, which I remembered so well, nothing but a huddle of stones and bricks and rafters. In the distance was the 'Cuckold's Point', flourishing on disaster, filled with the homeless drinking their misfortunes away. Only this made me think of John, and I suddenly shivered, for a second closing my eyes.

Virgil looked at me. I believe he read my thoughts. But he did not refer to the matter at all, only said quietly, 'I think we should get married as soon as possible, and go a hundred miles away from here. I never wish to see this damnable place again as long as I live. Will you please marry me, Nanette? I know you once said you would not, but we have changed a little, I think we might do quite well together.'

I said, 'I think so too.'

'So you will marry me?'

'I always intended to! Perhaps even when I was eight years old.'

We did not kiss, but the hand holding mine clenched so hard that his fingers bit into my palm. He said, 'I am beginning to see that I never had a chance.'

'None at all. Absolutely none at all. Only – only I would like to come back here.'

'Never! Never on your life!'

'Why not? I was once happy here. It is very beautiful. To me it is like home. We will come back, Virgil, and be happy again and forget everything that has happened. Only – ' I gave a sudden shiver. ' – we will never go back to Cudden Hall. It is like the graveyard. All the skeletons have been disinterred. It would be like living in a tomb.' Then I said, 'I would like to put flowers on Dolly's grave. She would laugh at me and say I was being silly, wasting my money on something so foolish, but I think she would really be pleased to know that we still think of her. I loved her very much. She was a darling girl.'

Virgil made no comment on this, only briefly shaded his eyes with his hand as if the watery autumn sun dazzled them. He said after a pause, 'I don't know if I should tell you this, and you will think it sounds damnably conceited, but – but I honestly believe that Dolly was a little in love with me.'

I looked at him, then began to laugh softly.

He was quite affronted. He said sharply, 'Why are you laughing, for God's sake? You have no right to laugh, it is heartless of you. She is dead, and in a way it is my fault. Do you think I'll ever forget how she died? She saved my life, Nanette. You must remember that.'

Yes, my darling, I remember. Dolly would not mind my laughing. Dolly would laugh too. It would appeal to her sense of humour. You are a dear, silly man, like all men you only see what lies under your nose. Of course Dolly loved you. She loved you with all her heart and soul. She would have died for you, from the very beginning. She did die for you. Do you think I am laughing at her? I am laughing at you, sweetheart, my love, my dear, because you know so little of women, because you think you are telling me something I neither know nor understand –

'I am sorry,' I said.

Then he did kiss me, hugging me over and over again. It caused both interest and amusement to the villagers who were rummaging through the ruins of their ravaged homes. But we did not see them, we were alone in the world.

Virgil, releasing me, suddenly remarked, 'You are marrying bad blood, you know.'

'No,' I said. 'It's surely the other way round. I am the Cudden. The bad blood is mine.'

He said in an argumentative voice, 'Nonsense! It is I who come from your aunt's family. There is nothing for which you can reproach your Uncle Constantine except for his unfortunate choice of wife. I will not have you usurp my inheritance of evil. I am the villain, not you.'

'Then,' I said, smiling at the absurdity of this conversation, 'we are both villains and well-matched. *Arcades ambo!*'

He almost gaped at me. Even the best of gentlemen are amazed when the opposite sex shows the faintest intelligence. He exclaimed, 'Do young ladies speak the Latin now?'

'Do you not remember? You said that to me a long time

225

ago when you were saying goodbye to a horrid little girl. In those days, my dear Virgil, you were a poet, you had written a little book in several volumes, called the *Aeneid*. I was greatly impressed by your cleverness. Until I discovered my mistake.'

He threw back his head and laughed. It was the first genuine, happy laughter I had heard from him this day. 'My God!' he said. 'I had forgotten, indeed. *Arcades ambo*! Villains both. That settles it. It leaves us no choice. We will marry immediately and breed more villains. I love you, Nanette.'

'I love you, Virgil.'

And we climbed into the carriage that would take us to the Lowrys' home, and Leonie.

Keppel, Charlotte.
The villains

CRANSTON PUBLIC LIBRARY
WILLIAM HALL LIBRARY

WITHDRAWN
WILLIAM HALL LIBRARY